Acclaim for

Jody Gehrman

Summer in the Land of Skin

"Poignant and affecting, Gehrman's debut is brimming with vivid characters and lyrical prose. Like all good summers, you don't want it to end."
—Lynn Messina, author of *Fashionistas*

"Gehrman's debut skillfully draws the reader in…. Her characters are confused, believable and utterly human, which is one of the main reasons the book strikes so many lonely, bewildered and true notes."
—*Publishers Weekly*

"Gehrman's writing is crisp, her observations astute, and her story utterly absorbing and affecting."
—*Booklist*

Tart

"I loved this book. *Tart* is exquisitely written and a deliciously witty treat."
—Sarah Mlynowski, author of *Milkrun* and *Bras & Broomsticks*

"Gehrman's enjoyable novel is as sharp and observant as the title suggests."
—*Booklist*

"Jody Gehrman writes with a poet's vigilance and a comic's wit, both steeped in deep affection for her characters. In between laughing breaks, you'll appreciate the keen eye Gehrman trains on life's small, fine, bitter moments. *Tart* is aptly named."
—Kim Green, author of *Paging Aphrodite*

Also from
Jody Gehrman
and Red Dress Ink

Tart
Summer in the Land of Skin

Jody Gehrman

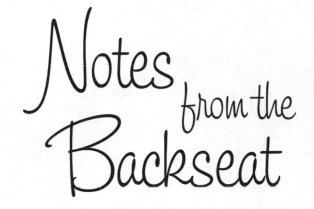

Notes *from the* Backseat

RED DRESS INK™

First edition January 2008

NOTES FROM THE BACKSEAT

A Red Dress Ink novel

ISBN-13: 978-0-373-89548-9
ISBN-10:   0-373-89548-8

© 2008 by Jody Gehrman.

www.RedDressInk.com

Printed in U.S.A.

ACKNOWLEDGMENTS

Thanks to my agent, Dorian Karchmar, and my editor, Margaret Marbury, for their hard work on my behalf. Thanks to their assistants, too, Adam Schear and Adam Wilson, who never failed to get back to me and were always on top of their game. My lovely comrade Terena Scott read endless drafts of Gwen's adventures and continually believed in her, even when I had my doubts. My web designer and good friend, Rosey Larson, is an endless source of encouragement and support. Tommy Zurhellen trained his keen eye on early incarnations and lent his usual priceless feedback to the mix (complete with bad jokes and adorable sketches). Bart Rawlinson offered a steady stream of advice, inspiration and delicious meals to get me through the long haul. Thanks to my family for their continual love and support, especially my mom and dad, who read my rough drafts with an enthusiasm only parents can sustain. As usual, my biggest thanks goes to David Wolf, who put up with more tantrums and freak-outs over this manuscript than any man should ever have to bear.

My best friend, Gwen, talks like an auctioneer when she's excited. Her hands flit about and her mouth moves so rapidly she's already halfway through the story by the time you can say, "Whoa, whoa, whoa. Back up. Start at the beginning." Her mind has a tendency to race ahead, and getting her to explain anything in a simple, chronological sequence is almost impossible. This time, though, she spelled it all out pretty clearly, with only occasional lapses into stream-of-consciousness neuroses peppered with expletives. Who could blame her for those little slips though, when the Creature from Planet Blonde was treating her like the gassy old family dog, making her ride in the backseat for thirteen hours on twisty coastal roads, filling her head with suspicions about Coop, who's probably the only man in the western hemisphere with the body of a rock star but the heart of a—

Oh, wait. I'm doing it now, too, aren't I? Okay, let me back up a little.

I was packing for Paris when I realized I had absolutely nothing to wear. It was one of those dry-mouthed, cold-sweat moments that sometimes hit you when you're leaving the country in less than twenty-four hours with your very French fiancé to meet his upper-crust Parisian parents. We were staying for a month and so far I'd packed my favorite pair of threadbare plaid pajamas, the oversized Mickey Mouse T-shirt I've been wearing since I was twelve, a pair of ancient Levi's with four patches sewn into the butt and my toothbrush. I'm not very schooled in the art of fashion, but even I knew I couldn't very well make a glamorous impression with that wardrobe—at least, not without accessorizing heavily.

There was no question. I had to see Gwen, stat.

A little background: I met Gwen twelve years ago, during our sophomore year at Analy High. I was the new kid, walking around with that dazed, I'm-never-going-to-survive-until-three-o'clock catatonic stare. The minute I stepped foot in the Home Ec room I spotted her and my listless I-don't-care-if-you-talk-to-me-or-not mask slipped away just like that. The morning sunlight through the dirty windows lit her like a starlet waiting for her close-up. She was wearing leopard-print kitten heels and a boxy 1950's pink wool suit. At her throat was a strand of pearls, matching earrings shone from the dark, meticulously arranged sweep of her shoulder-length bob. But here was the touch that rendered her truly surreal—the over-the-top Gwenism that made me wonder if I'd stumbled through a metaphysical portal and come out in 1957: on her head was a pillbox hat. It sat at just the right, casually precise, slightly flirtatious angle, and I could tell by her smirk that she knew the effect was dazzling.

Gwen Matson's reputation at Analy High could be summed up in two words: total freak. Everyone there considered her a tragic example of what could happen if you were just a little too weird to be cool. She was cuter, smarter and better dressed than anyone at that small town school—she was even valedictorian and yearbook editor—but the popular kids treated her like a leper because she insisted on walking around in pillbox hats, patent leather shoes and kid gloves. This was the nineties and Grunge was King. Gwen was the anti-Grunge; she'd sooner set her own hair on fire than don a flannel shirt.

In sharp contrast to Gwen's stubborn eccentricity, I was a die-hard conformist. Gwen's willingness to stand out terrified me, so much so that I was afraid, in those first few seconds, to befriend her. I hesitated there in the doorway of that stuffy Home Ec room, hovering between my just-try-not-to-be-noticed past and the bright pink future of a friendship with Gwen. I guess her allure was more powerful than my fear, because I stepped forward and said in a small, trembling voice, "Hi. My name's Marla." She seized my pale fingers and we shook hands like the wives of ambassadors meeting on the steps of the White House. "Gwen Matson," she said. "Charmed, I'm sure."

As soon as we finished high school we ditched that northern California hippie town and headed off to UCLA together. I studied modern dance—a useless degree, but I couldn't help myself. I'm very impractical. It's one of the few things Gwen and I have in common, though for me it manifests in a rather crippling inability to make a decent living. Gwen's impractical in a different way; she'll pack four mink stoles, three pairs of stilettos, a satin gown and a cigarette holder for a trip to my Colorado hunting cabin in December. She doesn't even smoke. On the career front, though, Gwen's impressively together. She double majored in business and costume design. Now, at twenty-eight, she owns a beautiful little vintage clothing store in Los Feliz and she designs for a handful of little theatre and indie film companies scattered throughout L.A. It's widely understood that Gwen only designs for period pieces, and only when the period is somewhere between 1952 and 1963. Everyone's learned not to even call her unless their show falls between those dates; otherwise, their Juliets always end up looking suspiciously like Jackie O.

Determined to solicit Gwen's professional advice, I left my barely packed suitcase gaping open on my bed and drove east from Santa Monica toward Los Feliz. On the way, I stopped at a Rite Aid and bought a few things I'd need for the trip: Visine, mascara, ear plugs, a French manicure kit (when in Rome...). On my way to the register I passed through the stationary aisle and a small leather-bound book caught my eye. It looked completely out of place there amidst the juvenile primary-colored spiral-bound note-books and plastic neon pencil boxes. It had a soft, buttery cover and the pages felt substantial as I flipped through them. I couldn't find a price tag, but I stuck it in my plastic shopping basket anyway. It was an impulse buy, like the Snickers bar or *Cosmo* you snag just before you reach the checkout—it had the same reckless, slightly sinful flavor, even though I wouldn't normally classify a blank book as indulgent.

When I got to the register, the girl rang up everything else, her long, clawlike fingernails flying over the keys with practiced ease. When she got to the journal, though, she stood snapping her gum, flipping it this way and that with a puzzled look. "Where'd you get this?" She had a thick accent, maybe Puerto Rican.

"Um—stationary aisle," I said.

"This is not a product we carry."

I furrowed my brow. "But...it was there. On the shelf."

"I don't know what this is." She snapped her gum some more, then called out to a short, acne-ridden boy at the next register. "Hey, Tom, you know what this is?"

The boy glanced over his shoulder. "Looks like some kind

of book." He went back to ringing up an endless pile of Huggies for a sad-eyed mother.

All at once I could see they weren't going to sell it to me, and the thought made me feel oddly bereaved—even a little desperate. "You know what? I just realized. That's *my* journal. I bought it at a bookstore down the street." I reached out and yanked it from her, laughing my most convincing vapid laugh.

She looked suspicious, but only shook her head in a way that communicated her thoughts on the subject perfectly ("Why didn't you say so in the first place, bitch?"). She announced my total and handed me my receipt. I escaped with the mysterious book tucked safely inside the white plastic sack, feeling as if I'd gotten away with something.

I'm not religiously inclined, but I do believe in fate and omens and mysterious forces pulsing just under the surface of our painfully normal lives. Looking back on it, I see myself as a messenger that day, a delivery girl, probably one of millions, transporting a necessary object from one place to another. I was like an ant, clutching a crumb in my pincers, following my instincts blindly, all the while working for the good of the colony.

I had no way of knowing that little leather-bound journal would save my friend's life. Well, her love life, at least— which maybe, in the end, is the same thing.

I pushed the glass door open and the bells jangled brightly, drawing Gwen's attention. She was at the counter in a bold black-and-white spiral-print sheath. In one gloved hand she gripped her phone—the retro kind that makes you think immediately of Marlene Dietrich in a feather boa, lounging on satin sheets. Her lips were painted that old-fashioned cherry red that no one under the age of eighty can pull off. Except Gwen, of course.

"So, tomorrow, then?" she was saying into the phone as her eyes followed me around the store. I was browsing, but without much intent. I knew I would have to surrender to her superior taste if I was going to pack a suitcase filled with Paris-worthy ensembles. "Eight o'clock? You think she can get here from San Diego that early?" There was a pause. Gwen played with the rhinestone earring in her hand. She considers pierced ears gauche and always removes her right clip-on before answering the phone, just like the women of film noir. "Okay, great. I guess I'll see you then. Can't wait. Bye."

"Was that Coop?" I asked as she hung up.

She nodded, looking dazed. "Oh my God, Marla. What am I going to do?"

"About what?"

She let out a gusty sigh and adjusted the white scarf at her throat as if she found it suddenly constricting. "We're leaving for our trip tomorrow."

"Oh, right—to Mendocino?"

She nodded, and I noticed then that she'd gone utterly pale. I let go of the wool blazer I'd been examining and went to the counter. "What is it, G? I thought you were really looking forward to that."

"*Was* looking forward to it, yes. Not now."

I folded my arms. "Uh-oh. What month is this?"

She rolled her eyes. "Yes, we've been dating three months, but—"

"Gwen, don't do this. You always do this."

She slapped the counter and her gloved palm made a hollow thudding sound against the glass. "I'm not doing anything! Guess whose retreat got canceled because the swami kicked it?"

"What?" She was losing me, here.

"Oh, God." She yanked at her scarf again, this time more violently. "I'm going to have a panic attack. I can feel it."

"No, you won't. Just breathe. Come on, in and out—you remember. Innn…ooouut. There you go. That's right." I spoke in soft, placating tones like a Lamaze coach. "Here, let's just get that scarf off, okay?" I reached over and untied it with considerable effort; in tugging at it, she'd worked it into a tight little fist of a knot, but I managed to get it off her and a faint wash of pink started to bloom in her cheeks again.

"So, let's just start at the beginning," I said when I was confident she wouldn't hyperventilate. "Whose retreat got canceled?"

"Dannika's," she croaked.

"And who's Dannika?"

"Coop's best friend from college."

"Okay," I said. "So, she's going to Mendocino with you?"

She nodded, her face the picture of misery. "She's driving us. Coop's car is too small."

"And why is this freaking you out? Because she's female?"

She narrowed her eyes at me. "Female, I could handle. In spite of your insinuation, I've come a long way. Coop has no idea of my unstable past. Unfortunately, this particular female friend—his *best friend*," she enunciated the words and raised her voice slightly, imbuing the phrase with ominous significance, "happens to be a statuesque, blond, stunningly beautiful, world-class yoga goddess."

My eyes widened. "Wait a minute. You're not talking about Dannika Winters, are you? *The* Dannika Winters?"

She slapped the counter again and this time the glass rattled, sending a display of sparkly chokers sprawling across the floor. "Yes! I'm talking about *the* Dannika Winters!"

"Oh my God. That is so cool. I've got like four of her DVDs."

Gwen's jaw dropped in indignant shock. "Is this what I need to hear right now?"

I put my hand on hers. "I'm sorry, G, you're right. That was totally insensitive. I mean, no wonder you're freaking out. She's like Uma Thurman, Grace Kelly and Cameron Diaz all wrapped up into one incredibly flexible, probably totally vegan body."

"Marla," she said, her voice a warning.

"But I'm sure she's unbelievably shallow with no real

substance." I saw Gwen's brown eyes regain some of their sparkle when I said this, so I pressed on, ad-libbing bravely. "I bet her poses are done by stunt doubles. When she's supposed to be meditating, she's actually doing her nails."

"You're so right." Gwen's mouth curved into a wicked smile. "I bet she's got the IQ of a hamster."

"Oh, totally. You think anyone who looks that good can conjugate verbs?"

A shadow of doubt passed over her features. "She did go to college, though…"

"So what? Anyone can go to college these days. She's the Vanna White of yoga. She'll be a has-been before her time. Sad, really."

"You're right," she said. "Who cares about stupid old Dannika Winters? She's no threat to me."

I clapped my hands. "Exactly! She's Coop's *friend,* you're his *girlfriend*. Period."

Her face fell. "Wait a minute. What if he's leaving something out? Suppose they're more like…friends with benefits?"

"Right. Because he'd definitely want to be trapped in a car for sixteen hours with his girlfriend and the chick he's doing it with on the side."

She cocked her head. "I guess you're right. That would be pretty masochistic of him."

I reached down and gathered the chokers up, then tried to return them to a display shaped like a woman's throat and shoulders, sculpted in soft, sensual lines out of some sort of pale, opalescent material that made me think of the inner sheen of abalone shells. She took the necklaces from me when she saw my inept attempts to arrange them on the display and, with expert fingers, draped them in provocative shapes across the throat and clavicle, setting off the imitation rubies and sapphires so that they looked like they belonged in Tiffany's.

"I like Coop a lot," I said, looking her in the eye. "More importantly, I think *you* like him a lot. This is no time to pull your classic three-month guy freak-out thing."

She shook her head. "I'm not doing that. I swear."

For as long as I'd known her, Gwen had been living out the same pattern with men, repeating her mistakes over and over like a scratched record. She'd date a guy, get to know him, start to like him, then as soon as they hit the three-month mark, she'd dump him. Like clockwork. And always for the same reason: she was convinced he would, if given the chance, cheat on her. A couple years ago she dumped this incredibly hunky USC sociology professor when she saw the line of perky little coeds loitering outside his office. Another time she gave a Swedish chiropractor the boot because he kept unused toothbrushes in his bathroom for overnight guests. Sometimes, all a guy had to do was glance over her shoulder at an attractive woman walking in the door and Gwen would instantly relegate him to the Tomb of Boyfriends Past.

What it came down to, really, was that Gwen had serious jealousy issues. She knew it, I knew it, every guy she'd ever gone out with knew it. The thought that Coop might end up as another casualty in Gwen's mysterious war against potential infidelity made me ache with sadness. It wasn't just because I'd seen her pull the same old trick so many times it was dizzying. No, it was more than that. If Gwen dumped Coop or drove him away with her compulsive suspicions, it would be more than just annoying this time. It would be tragic. Because I knew, in that weird, bone-deep way that best friends sometimes do, that Gwen and Coop were made for each other.

Just like Gwen and I, Gwen and Coop were opposites on the surface. He was a big guy; that was what you noticed about him first. Next to Gwen's petite, five-foot-two frame, his six-feet-and-then-some looked even more hulking by contrast. He wore old, ratty T-shirts and paint-splattered jeans. His hair was long and usually looked neither washed nor combed. He was a carpenter—a woodworker. He made furniture in his basement that was rough and solid and vaguely bohemian, like him. But the thing I liked best about Coop was the warmth in his rich, hazel eyes. When you looked into his face, you could sense the vast, sun-drenched landscape that lived inside him and all the room he had in there for lost souls. I feared he might be the only man on the planet capable of handling my best friend's fragile, skittish little heart.

"Look at it this way," I said. "Coop and Dannika have been friends since college, right? They've probably known each other—what? Seven, eight years?"

She nodded, frowning.

"If they haven't gotten together in all that time, they must not have chemistry. I mean, otherwise, they'd have at least given it a go, right?"

"Riiight," she said, drawing out the word in a way that implied she wasn't convinced.

"You know how it is. Sometimes you're just not attracted to someone, no matter how hot they are. I bet it's like that with them. They're like brother and sister—absolutely no fizz."

"Or maybe it's more like seven years of foreplay," she grumbled. "By the time they get it on, the simultaneous orgasm will probably blind them."

I laughed. "Stop being neurotic. Do you hear me? Coop is crazy about you."

"How do you know?"

"I just *know*."

She pulled off one of her gloves and fretted with it. "The thing is, if I go on this trip, he's going to see how wiggy-jealous I get. He just will. There's no way around it."

She looked so small and vulnerable, I wanted to put my arms around her. "Gwen, it's not the end of the world if he sees you at your worst. He's probably not going to run screaming just because you're human. Be honest with him. You've got nothing to lose."

"I've got Coop to lose!" she pouted. "Not to mention my pride."

"Yes, I know, but if you can't be yourself with him, there's really nothing there worth saving."

She replaced her clip-on earring and forced a brave smile. "You're right. I'm being stupid. I'll go on this trip, meet his friends, everyone will love me, I'll love them, and we'll all live happily ever after."

"Exactly," I said. "Now, can you please help me find some clothes that don't make me look cheap, dumpy or American? I realized today I can't possibly meet Jean-Paul's parents in my Mickey Mouse T-shirt."

"What?" she gasped. "Confirmed slob seeks flattering attire?"

"Yeah, yeah, yeah," I said. "Whatever. Just, can we get this over with?"

An hour later, Gwen had found me three versatile, elegant, wrinkle-proof outfits that made my thighs look slimmer, my bones more pronounced and my split ends fashionably intentional. She's a genius. I tried to force my credit card on her, but she wouldn't hear of it.

As we were hugging goodbye, I got my brilliant idea.

"Listen," I said. "I've got something for you. Wait here." I ran out to my car, checked the meter, and grabbed the little journal from my plastic Rite Aid bag. Then I dashed back to Gwen's store and pressed it into her hands.

"What's this?" She looked at it and then at me with a quizzical expression.

"Take it with you on your trip. If you start to feel anxious or threatened or even slightly inclined to dump Coop, just write out your thoughts until you calm down, okay?"

She laughed uneasily. "Is this some sort of New Age therapy?"

"It'll give you some perspective, that's all."

"Okay. Well, thanks. It's…really nice."

"It's a going away present."

Her eyes searched mine. "Diaries have never been my style, but I'll give it a try."

"If it doesn't work within the first ten pages," I said, "invest in some Valium."

Thirteen days later, the journal arrived at Jean-Paul's parents' house in Paris, wrapped in plain brown paper. It wasn't alone, though. There were three others: a tiny spiral-bound notebook, a legal pad and a slick journal with whales on the cover that said Mendocino Coast. Every page had been filled with Gwen's old-fashioned, elegantly loopy cursive. As I flipped though them, I saw that sometimes her perfect handwriting gave way to harsh, nearly-illegible scribbles and in places it looked like she'd pressed so hard into the paper that it threatened to tear.

I pretended I wasn't feeling well and urged Jean-Paul and his parents to visit yet another museum without me. It was just as well. If I had to "oooh" and "ahhh" over more

Matisse, I feared I might lose it. After they'd gone, I stuffed all four journals into my bag, went to a café down the street, bought a cappuccino and sat down to read them cover to cover.

7:10 a.m.

Dear Marla,

I decided it's just too daft to fill a book with notes to myself. It's so egocentric—I'd feel like some kind of New Age narcissist—so I'm going to address all my self-absorbed narcissism to you. How's that for passing the buck?

Actually, I probably won't write in this at all. I feel very optimistic about this whole trip, now. The freak-out I went through yesterday is a distant memory. It's early morning, I've had my tea and I'm all packed. The light in Los Feliz is unusually golden and (here's the real miracle) I managed to fit all my clothes for the weekend into the leopard-print luggage set: one large case, one medium, a handbag and a hatbox. Not bad, eh? I'm sure Coop will be impressed that I travel light.

Of course, the shoes had to go in a separate trunk, but so what? I'll just slip that in casually when no one's looking.

All in all, I'm the picture of the elegant, poised traveler.

Hope your journey to Paris goes well today. So exciting! I can't wait for you to come home so we can swap stories.

Kiss, kiss,
Gwen

8:45 a.m.

Shit! Oh my God, oh my God, oh my God!

Okay, I know, breathe. If I hyperventilate back here they won't even notice. I'll be a blue-faced corpse and they'll have no idea until we hit the first pit stop. Marla, I don't want to die alone, in the backseat, wedged uncomfortably between a surfboard and a trunk full of my best shoes!

Then again, at least my white go-go boots will be with me in my last hours.

They suck. Totally, utterly.

Coop and Dannika that is, not the go-go boots.

Why did I ever think I could seriously be with Coop? If

he's in league with this Satan in Organic Cotton, I want nothing to do with him.

Oh, there they go laughing. *Ha ha ha ha ha.* The world is so deliciously funny when you're a big, gorgeous guy riding shotgun with your delectable supermodel hippie chick behind the wheel. Never mind the lump of a girlfriend pouting in the backseat. She's just there to keep the surfboards from flying away.

Marla, what am I going to do? I'm being held hostage by a couple of excessively beautiful bohemians with no appreciation whatsoever for fine luggage, vintage travel wear or—in short—me.

Right. I know what you would say. *Just back up, slow down, start from the beginning.*

I'll try. Thank God I never get carsick. I have a feeling putting pen to paper at the moment is the only thing between me and double homicide.

So, back to the beginning. Let's see…where did I leave off?

As I mentioned, early this morning my outlook was bright and my outfit was impeccable. I was wearing my low-belted chemise suit in autumn green, my leopard-print car coat, and my signature leopard-print kitten heels. I'd tied a green scarf over my hair and at the last minute I added those huge, Jackie O sunglasses you love. No point in modesty here, I looked positively elegant. I surveyed myself in the mirror and was convinced that no matter how glamorous

Coop's best friend might be, I'd give her a run for her money.

Dannika was driving up from San Diego, and since I live farther south than Coop, she was picking me up first. I heard her car pull up, but by the time I got to the window, she was already out of view. I waited for the doorbell, took a deep breath, turned the knob and pulled.

There she was. All the air left my lungs and I stood in the doorway dumbstruck. I know you have her yoga tapes and she's enough of a D-list celebrity, what with her new show and all, to warrant casual recognition from most people, but seeing her in person is a different experience entirely.

She's stunning. There's no other word for it.

I wish I could say her teeth are showing signs of decay or her boobs need propping up—that the way she looks onscreen is all make-up, lighting and flattering camera angles—but the truth is, in person she's five million times more beautiful than she is on TV. Is that just slit-your-wrists depressing or what? Her hair is so shiny-blond, so long and healthy and shampoo-commercial-bouncy, it hardly seems real. I swear the Los Feliz light was caressing every strand, spilling sparkles into the air around her until her whole head was surrounded by a lemon-hued halo. Her skin was dewy-fresh, lightly tanned and radiant. Her eyes were a deep ocean color—Malibu on a good day. She was at least five foot eight and her body was so fit and toned, it's hard to imagine any inch of her succumbing to sag or cellulite.

She was wearing a tank top—one of those sporty little REI numbers with spaghetti straps and a built-in bra—and loose-fitting, wide-legged yoga pants that hung just low enough on her slender hips to reveal an inch of brown belly and a pierced navel. Flip-flops on her feet, sunglasses propped in her hair, a few fleamarket silver bracelets on her arm, a string of jade beads around her neck and a tiny diamond stud in her nose; those were the accessories that set off her features with the irritating minimalism of an all-natural hippie bombshell.

Her fashion choices are diametrically opposed to my own. She's Zen simplicity, I'm Catholic excess. She's flip-flops, I'm kitten heels. She's hemp and organic cotton, I'm wool gabardine and cashmere. She's green tea lip balm, I'm candy-apple-red lipstick.

I wish I could feel disdain for her aesthetic, but let's face it: the look works for her. And then some.

The moment I laid eyes on her, I could feel the ugly tide of envy and insecurity poisoning my blood. She just stood there, beaming at me. She took a step toward me and before I knew what was happening, she had me wrapped up in a hug that smelled of some heady essential-oil mixture—maybe jasmine cut with ylang-ylang. When she pulled away, I could see her lips moving, but I couldn't quite make out the words. I was in shock, I guess. Somehow I managed to mumble a generic response that I hoped would match her greeting in some vaguely logical way. She went back to beaming at me, so I guess I succeeded.

When she saw my luggage, her big, radiant, white-toothed smile died on her lips.

"You taking…all this?"

I nodded. "It is a wedding, right? I couldn't very well go to a wedding without a hat or two." I patted my hatbox affectionately.

"Well, it's a…casual wedding," she said, looking worried. "Are you sure you'll need this many suitcases? Phil and Joni are pretty low-key. They live in the woods."

"I brought casual, too. I like to be prepared for every circumstance."

"Yeah," she said, still eyeing my cases uneasily. "Right. Well, let's just drag it all out to the car and see what we can do."

You know how I've always wanted a convertible—obviously an enormous, gas-guzzling beast from the late '50s? Of course, the fact that I can't drive and have no desire to learn puts a slight damper on this yearning, but occasionally I peruse eBay's classic car pages anyway, just for fun. Well, when I saw Dannika's car, my heart, already dangerously close to failure, dropped two stories and bounced hard in the pit of my stomach. It was the most beautiful vehicle you could possibly imagine: a '57 Mercury convertible, fire-engine red, totally cherry. Propped up in the backseat with its fins in the air was a slightly battered lemon-yellow surfboard. The whole tableau was achingly California, right down to the chrome hubcaps glittering in the sun like precious gems.

I should have been excited. Here I was, about to ride shotgun in the car of my dreams. In a matter of minutes we'd be heading up the coast to spend the weekend in a rugged seaside village, where I'd bond with my new beau and his incredibly hip, glamorous friends. Dannika's car should have filled me with hope. I should have been thinking about how great my leopard-print car coat and oversized glasses were going to look peeking out of that Mercury with the top down.

But that's not what was running through my brain. The single, white-hot, stomach-churning thought that was tearing through my consciousness was this: if you like the same car, you like the same guy.

Period.

Dannika had popped the trunk by now and was wrestling with my suitcases. Her shoulders were pure, sculpted muscle and they rippled as she heaved the largest case into the cavernous trunk. I could see no problem; the boot on that Mercury was so enormous, we could have fit five times as much luggage. All she'd brought besides the surfboard, as far as I could tell, was an old, weather-beaten backpack and a wet suit. Seeing all that room, I was tempted to run inside for my mink, since I know it can get chilly in Mendocino. But I could tell by the way Dannika was huffing that she wouldn't appreciate an additional item added to the cargo.

"Wow," she said, loading the medium suitcase. "What have you got in here? Cement?"

"Mostly toiletries."

That's when I remembered the trunk of shoes I'd left in the hallway.

"Oh, just one more thing," I said, handing her the hat box. "I'll be right back." I was tempted to ask if she could get it, but I didn't want to admit she was in better shape than me and I didn't want her smile, which was already getting tight around the edges, to go completely rigid. I wished she'd picked Coop up first so he could load everything and smooth the tension with his warm, contagious laughter. Somehow, he'd find a way to spin it so he was the butt of the joke, not me.

I came back out with my trunk and, let me tell you, getting it to the sidewalk was no easy task. Guess I never realized just how heavy shoes can be. To my horror, I was starting to sweat by the time I finally made it back to the car.

When Dannika saw me standing there proudly with my trunk of shoes (which was, by the way, hardly any bigger than the mini-fridge we had in college, so what was the big deal?) she folded her arms across her chest and raised an eyebrow.

As you can imagine, that look filled me with a fresh surge of resentment. First, the cocked eyebrow is my signature look. No one can pull it off like me, as I'm sure you'll agree.

But beyond that, she was using it out of context, which is never acceptable. The raised eyebrow is a form of punctuation and to use it without due cause renders it as offensive and sloppy as a random comma or semicolon dropped into the middle of a perfectly good sentence. To think that my innocent little trunk of shoes caused a raised eyebrow was, simply put, insulting. Not to mention stupid.

"Everything okay?" I asked coolly.

She slammed the trunk shut with more force than was absolutely required and jutted her chin at my final piece of luggage. "Why don't you just shove that in the backseat?"

"Oh, there's room in the trunk, isn't there?"

"Coop needs some space, too."

I nodded. "Yeah, but he won't bring much. You know boys—just a couple T-shirts and a toothbrush, I bet."

"Unlike some people," she said under her breath. "Anyway, it's fine, just throw it in the backseat."

I did, but not without tweaking a muscle between my shoulder blades as I tried to display how effortlessly I could haul it up off the sidewalk and into the convertible without even bothering to open the door. I don't recommend it. The pain was unbearable and even now I can feel a dull, throbbing ache near my spine. Of course, my pride had more power than my chiropractic issues, so I slapped a smile on and settled into the passenger seat, reaching instinctively for my seat belt. There was nothing there.

"Oh, no seat belts in this baby," she said, throwing the

Mercury into gear and lurching away from the curb roughly. "Sorry 'bout that. I never wear them, anyway. Just feels too restrictive, you know what I mean?"

Marla, I don't know if I've ever mentioned this, so please don't think I'm weird, but I *love* seat belts. Death by highway is one of my more potent fears and the feel of that strap creating a band of resistance across my chest is, to me, delicious and comforting. I mean, statistically, the 405 is about a thousand times more likely to get us than cancer or terrorists or psycho killers. Most people are in denial about this, but for me it's all too real. Every time I ride in a car, I feel my mortality pressing in on me like sticky, oppressive heat. I suppose that's why I've never learned to drive; if I didn't plow into a semi out of sheer terror, I'd surely contract a terminal stress-related disease within weeks.

Dannika apparently doesn't share my road phobias. She tore through Los Feliz and over to Silver Lake like a New York cabbie on speed. Her hands rarely landed on the wheel. She was perpetually adjusting the radio, playing with her bracelets, swigging water, toying with her hair as it whipped about like a bright gold streamer. I gripped the armrest with one hand and pressed my feet into the floorboards to keep from flying through the windshield.

The only thing that saved us from a four-car pileup was that everyone—men, women, babies—stopped what they were doing as she drove past and stared at her golden beauty. It kept other cars from ramming into her and it cleared pedestrians from her path. As she tore up onto the sidewalk in front of Coop's, steering with her knees while she applied her lip balm, I started to see what people mean by the phrase *a charmed life.*

"Hey!" Coop came bounding toward us, down the steps of his craftsman bungalow and over to the Mercury, a big smile taking up the better part of his face. "If it isn't my favorite girls!"

Dannika screamed and bolted from the car as soon as she heard his voice. She leapt into his arms as if they were long-lost lovers separated for decades by war and famine. I felt this molten lump of something taking shape in my chest—jealousy, I guess, or rage or psychosis—whatever it was, I could feel it congealing and sizzling inside me, like doughnut batter dropped into a vat of boiling grease. I let myself out of the passenger's side, hoping that by the time I walked calmly around the car the hug would be over, but when I got there Dannika was still clinging to him, her blond hair shining more brilliantly than ever in the sunlight, her slender tan arms clasped around his neck fiercely.

Over her shoulder, Coop's eyes met mine and when I saw the apology there the dangerous lump inside my rib cage broke apart a bit. His face was saying, "Sorry, she's…like this sometimes," and somehow just sharing a secret look with him while Satan clung to him pathetically made me feel more poised again.

"Wow," he said, when she finally loosened her grip

enough to allow some air into his lungs. "Long time no see, huh?"

"Months!" She looked at him with an appraising eye, now. "You look different."

"Really?" He stepped around her, then grabbed my hand and surprised me by leaning down and planting a firm, warm kiss on my lips right there in front of her. Not that Coop and I are stingy with kisses—it's just that we don't have much practice doing it in front of other people. Three months doesn't give you loads of PDA opportunities, I guess.

"Hey, kitten," he said into my ear. "You look so great. Love those shoes—God, what an outfit." His voice made the already half-dissolved doughnut in my chest dissolve completely. I realized then that Dannika hadn't commented on my travel ensemble. That's the genius of Satan. You don't recognize the affront until it's too late to retaliate.

"You do, you look different," Dannika repeated, sounding annoyed that he'd even greeted me. "Something's changed. What is it? Did you lose weight?"

Coop patted his stomach, barely existent. "Don't think so…"

"Shave or something?"

He touched his face, always sporting a couple days' worth of stubble. "Yeah, right," he laughed.

She shook her head, mystified. "Your aura's different," she said. "Are you getting enough vitamins?"

"Wait a minute, my aura needs vitamins?"

She slapped his shoulder. "Two separate observations, you moron!"

He looked at me. "I'm really happy for the first time in my life. That's all."

"Huh," Dannika said. "Well, it doesn't suit you."

He shot her a look.

"It doesn't! What can I say? You look underfed or something."

I tried not to gloat, but I doubt I pulled it off. "I think he looks great."

"Huh," Dannika said again, and the irritation packed inside that one syllable only added to my joy.

Right. So that's pretty much the good part of the day, in a nutshell. What followed was an arsenic cocktail with a ground glass chaser.

Where to begin?

Well, I doubt it escaped your attention: I'm in the backseat.

Which was okay, at first. I mean you know, Dannika was driving and I was hardly going to ride shotgun anymore with *her* behind the wheel—the view from up there was just too terrifying. The passenger seat isn't nicknamed "the death seat" for nothing. I was just about to volunteer when Coop beat me to it.

"I'll ride in back," he said, tossing his duffel bag in the trunk and scooting in next to the surfboard. "Sweet!" he said. "You brought your board."

"Where's yours?" Dannika asked.

He hesitated. "You think there's room?"

"Well, Gwen did bring *four* suitcases." She said it sort of jokingly, sort of not. It was like she was tattling but pretending not to tattle, which really ended up being more annoying than if she'd just tattled outright.

I stared at her, unsmiling. "A hatbox is hardly a suitcase."

Coop laughed and slung his arm around me. "Gwen's a good Girl Scout—always prepared."

Dannika flipped her hair over one shoulder. "Go get your board and suit—we'll just shove it in somewhere. We haven't surfed together in a million years! That's half the reason I even agreed to come."

Coop, being amiable and, really, so in love with surfing I could see he was salivating at the very thought, did what he was told. In a few minutes, he returned with his board under one arm and his wet suit under the other.

"I don't know," he said. "I grabbed my shortest board, but it's going to make the backseat sort of cramped."

"Gwen's got short legs," Dannika said, eyeing me.

Considering that she had long, lithe, slender legs, it seemed like a pointedly bitchy comment. When I looked her in the eye, though, she winked, like getting Coop to bring his board was this really fun mutual goal of ours—a sisterly effort—and her making me feel like a midget was all part of our coy, girlie plot.

"Gwen?" Coop said. "You going to back me on this?"

He nodded at his board. "It'll be in the way, don't you think?"

I shrugged. "If you guys want to surf, bring it." I'd be a sport. What was the big deal? I brought a trunk of shoes; he could bring his board if he wanted. "I don't mind the back. That way you two can catch up." There! I'd be generous. He'd think I was incredibly confident, not threatened in the least by the demonic blonde.

"Great!" Dannika's eyes gleamed with victory. "Thanks so much, Gwen. We haven't seen each other since…that night in Malibu?"

I felt my throat seize up. It was like a giant hand just reached over and closed my esophagus.

"Uh-huh." Coop looked at me. "Dannika's mom lives there," he said, sensing my discomfort. Maybe *sensing my imminent death due to lack of oxygen* would be more accurate.

"That was so long ago," Dannika continued, oblivious to my silent horror.

Why do the words *night in Malibu* sound so ominous when placed side by side in this context? Why couldn't Coop have a horrible, pockmarked, male, alcoholic best friend who wears vomit-stained corduroys and refers to women only in anatomical terms? Why, why, why, why, why?

Coop let me into the backseat and took special care in arranging the boards in order to provide me with the maximum amount of legroom. Not that I needed any, according to Dannika. *Yeah, don't mind the Oompa-Loompa in the back; she's just along for the ride.*

Look, I know what you would say. *Relax, Gwen. Breathe. You remember—in and out. There you go.*

But do you realize I've been in the backseat for hours now and no one is paying any attention to me? Sure, every twenty minutes or so Coop glances back with one of his vaguely apologetic, sickeningly adorable grins. Once he asked me, "What are you writing?" to which I replied, "Just catching up on some correspondence." That satisfied his curiosity a bit too readily. How does he know I'm not penning love letters to my six-foot-seven husband who currently resides in San Quentin? What does Coop care about that—he just listens to Dannika going on and on about the great times they've shared, careening wildly in and out of traffic. I can't hear much of what they're saying; random phrases drift back at me every now and then like bits of confetti, but I find little comfort in them. I hear Dannika calling out *crazy night* and *that time in Seville* and *thought I'd die.* I see her turning to him, her bright white teeth shining as she laughs, her profile so perfect and well-shaped it's sculptural. They're happily reminiscing, reliving their years of chummy intimacy, and I'm the recent acquisition, the girl-come-lately.

Okay, we're stopping. I've got to snap out of this. I'm working myself into a fuming little wad of rage back here. Smoke's coming out of my ears. If I don't regain control,

Coop is going to see I'm a possessive, pint-sized freak with no sense of humor.

More later...

Hugs and kisses from the Furious Midget,

Gwen

Thursday, September 18

10:23 a.m.

Dear Marla,

Since when is breakfast an organic banana, seven ounces of soy yogurt and a double shot of wheatgrass? This chick doesn't eat enough to sustain a sparrow. God, I hope she develops a thyroid problem soon and becomes obscenely obese. Maybe then she'd know how the rest of us feel.

Okay, that's not nice of me. I should exercise a little compassion. But do Nordic supermodels who live on nondairy yogurt and wheatgrass really deserve my compassion?

Here's the thing: she hates me. I can tell.

And she's after Coop.

Look, I know you said if they've been friends this long and they haven't gotten together they obviously don't have any chemistry. I knew at the time there was a gaping hole in your argument, but it took me this long to put my finger on it. You see, Coop's never denied or confirmed the nature of their relationship history—he's only referred to her as his "best friend." He never sat me down and said, "Gwen, in case you're wondering, Dannika and I never had sex." Actually, come to think of it, I've barely heard any mention of Dannika at all in the three months we've been dating, except as an occasional character in the stories from his college days. I thought of her as a distant historical footnote, not as a rival worth considering. I was way more concerned about the cute blond barista with the crew cut who flirts with him at Café Europa.

But now it's clear to me: they've definitely had sex. Maybe not recently, maybe not on a regular basis, but they've slept together.

I can't decide what's worse—knowing they've been intimate, or worrying that they're dying to get intimate.

Whatever. The point is, they've done the deed and now I'll have to live with it. Every time he gets me naked, I'll have to wonder how my hideous little pygmy body measures up to her smooth airbrushed curves. Okay, yes, so I have more curves than she does, actually, but my curves aren't the miles-of-flawless-skin kind; my curves have dimples and…you know…texture issues.

Is this productive in any way?

God, how am I going to get through this weekend?

Maybe if I just focus on the actual events, I'll avoid a full-on panic attack.

We're back on the road now, headed along the coast. No I-5 for this crowd—way too sterile, according to Dannika. She's all about the scenic route, even if it means extending our estimated time of arrival by at least three hours.

The brief stop in Malibu was very enlightening. Satan was kind enough to yell over her shoulder that we'd be stopping soon for "breakfast." I guess she was feeling guilty about shoving me back there like an ill-behaved pet and monopolizing my man's attention. A few minutes later I found myself standing at the counter of a chichi little juice bar, staring at several cases of bright green wheatgrass behind glass. When I'd heard the word *breakfast* I had visions of greasy potatoes, syrup-drenched pancakes, a mocha piled high with whipped cream. I was ravenous and hunger always makes me a little edgy—you know how I get. It was easy to see as soon as we pulled up that this place wasn't exactly the greasy spoon of my dreams. The menu was primarily liquid-based; there were smoothies with exotic names like Tahitian Sunrise and Arab Blue. In addition to wheatgrass, they were juicing things I never imagined you could drink, like beets and ginger, parsley and yams. In the solid-foods department there was soy yogurt, homemade granola, flaxseed protein bars and fruit salad. My stomach growled and I felt a surge of hunger-induced homicidal hysteria coming on.

"Dannika's a raw food junkie," Coop said when he noticed me staring in disbelief at the menu.

"So I gathered." My voice sounded tight and strained.

"We could—you know—go somewhere else. What are you in the mood for? Doughnuts? Waffles? Hostess snack cakes?" He squeezed my shoulder affectionately.

Coop knows I have an insane sweet tooth. Can I help it if my body demands a sugar and caffeine rush every morning? Possibly I'm an undiagnosed diabetic—well, I *could* be. I was about to tell him a chocolate croissant from the bakery next door would be dreamy when I saw Dannika glance over at us with a smug, vegan smirk. God, I hate raw food freaks. They're so righteous and *clean* looking, it makes you want to force-feed them Rice Crispies Treats until they puke.

Suddenly I was overcome with the desire to beat Dannika at her own game. Looking into her clear blue eyes, I could see my own short brunette self reflected there and I knew exactly what she was thinking; she saw me as a mere blip—a passing fancy of Coop's, nothing more. She seemed almost disappointed in the lack of challenge I presented. Whether or not she wanted Coop for herself, it was clear she didn't consider me worthy of him. In her mind, that was all that mattered. She'd already written me off. She would tolerate me for the duration of the weekend, but by Monday, I would be toast.

Well, she was wrong; I had to show her that I was a force to be reckoned with. I would demonstrate—forcibly, if I had to—that her approval wasn't required.

If there is only room in Coop's life for one of us, I'll be damned if it's me who's getting ousted. He's the first man I've ever met worth fighting for and if I have to sharpen my claws to keep him, so be it.

"You know what? I think the root juice sounds amazing," I said.

Coop looked at the menu. "Carrot, beet, yam and ginger?" He eyed me skeptically. "You sure?"

"Mmm, hmm," I said. "It sounds…cleansing."

"Okay," he said. "If you say so. I think I saw a bakery next door, though. Little mocha, chocolate croissant…" His offer was tempting and I was touched at how accurately he'd assessed my cravings, but I was determined to out-vegan the vegan, even if it killed me.

"No, really," I said, "this is perfect."

Dannika pretended not to be listening. She did some pretentious, show-offy upper body stretches as we waited for the anemic-looking woman in front of us to finish ordering. "The protein bar doesn't contain any wheat, does it?" the lady asked, dabbing at her nose with a crumpled Kleenex. The bronzed surf God behind the counter assured her for the third time that everything they served was wheat and gluten-free.

When it was our turn, Dannika stepped forward gracefully, leaned one hip against the counter and said airily, "I'll take a double shot of wheatgrass, one banana and a small soy yogurt, please."

The guy's face went from bored to astonished so quickly, it was like watching a flower bloom using time-lapse photography. "Are you—?" He blushed under his tan. "I'm sorry, but aren't you Dannika Winters?"

Her smile was radiant. "That's me."

"Wow, this is so cool. My roommate has all your DVDs. God, she's going to die when I tell her I met you. Would you mind—" he fumbled behind the counter and produced a napkin, then a pen "—signing this? It would mean a lot to her."

"No problem." Dannika bent over and the surf God eyed the cleavage revealed artfully beneath her tank top. "What's her name?"

"Huh?" He looked dazed.

"Your roommate's name?"

"Oh. Kyra," he said, "K–Y–R–A."

She wrote something on the napkin and signed it with a flourish, then pushed it across the counter.

He picked it up reverently. "She's really going to lose her shit. I mean—sorry—you just made my day, is all."

"You're too sweet." Dannika graced him with another celebrity smile.

Coop stepped forward. "Mind if we order?"

The kid folded the napkin carefully and put it in his

pocket. He managed to concentrate long enough to jot down Coop's request for an extra-large granola with vanilla yogurt and a protein smoothie. When it was my turn, I ordered my disgusting root concoction and tried smiling at the bronzed groupie with my own brand of electric charisma. He didn't even notice. He just looked over my shoulder at Dannika, who was by the window, now, performing some kind of elaborate leg stretch against one of the stools.

You'll be proud to hear that I managed to choke down my root juice without gagging. It tasted like something you'd scrape off the bottom of a lawn mower. Delish.

So now I'm in the backseat again, wedged between the surfboards and my trunk of shoes, with my self-esteem ankle-high. Plus, I'm starving. Apparently, this is where she wants me. I'm the backseat spectator, forced to watch as my nemesis undermines my relationship a little more with each mile.

All I can say is, she'd better watch her back. I may have lost the first couple rounds, but I'm not going down without a fight.

11:20 a.m.

Dear Marla,

Warning: we've entered the epicenter of Coop-and-Dannikaland. This is ground zero for college memories, which most likely include the pornographic trysts of their late teens and early twenties, when their flesh was no doubt even more supple and alluring than it is now.

Oh God, I think I'm going to be sick.

Our stop? Santa Barbara, where even the meter maids look like Pilates instructors.

12:45 p.m.

Dear, dear Marla,

Psychotic jealousy, be gone. Coop's just filled me in on the Tragic Tale of Dannika's Past, which makes it completely unnecessary to continue fantasizing about gouging her eyes out with my kitten heels. Seriously. Our entire trip (not to mention our relationship) has been saved!

Here's how it went down.

We stopped at the beach in Santa Barbara. It was this secret little tucked-away point break they used to surf all the time in college. I always wondered if anyone at UCSB actually studied; from the sound of it, the answer is *not much*.

I still couldn't hear more than a few random exchanges from the backseat, but once we got off the freeway, I could tell they were reliving a long string of surfing memories from the good ole days.

I thought we were just stopping to stretch our legs and take in the vista. I really wasn't dressed for a romp on the beach—you know how I hate getting sand in my shoes. The engine hadn't even sputtered into silence, though, before Dannika was leaping out of the car and shaking out the golden flag of her hair in the cool ocean breeze.

"God, it's so beautiful! I'm not even going to wear a wet suit. I want to feel the water." Her eyes were shining as she watched a big wave curve in on itself, crash explosively, then unfurl a long carpet of foam.

For a second, the three of us stared out at the water. Coop turned to smile at me. "How you doing back there, kitten?"

It was nice hearing him use my pet name. His hand reached back and squeezed my knee and the warmth of his fingers on my skin sent cool shivers up my thigh.

"I'm okay." At that very moment, it wasn't a lie. "You?"

Before he could answer, Dannika surprised us both by yanking her shirt up over her head and conversation became suddenly impossible. There she was, standing not three feet from us, pulling her tank top off like it was the most natural thing in the world. Her pale breasts, once freed from the tight-fitting tank, were fuller and more buoyant than I would have thought possible on such a skinny girl. Her brown belly was shockingly flat—a stretch of smooth inter-rupted only by the subtle indentations of her six-pack abs. It was one thing to be a size two, but to be that well-defined was something else—the mark of the physically elite.

My root juice threatened to resurface. I swallowed hard and fought it back down.

Of course I looked away, embarrassed. So did Coop, but not before I caught his eyes lingering just a second too long. When he looked at me again, he was blushing.

I've never seen Coop blush.

"Last one in's a rotten egg!" In a matter of minutes, Dannika had her turquoise bikini on, and she was running down to the water with her surfboard under her arm. It was a disgustingly *Blue Crush* moment.

Coop and I didn't say anything for a few seconds. Then we both tried to speak at once. I said, "Aren't you getting in?" and he said, "Beautiful day," and then we both looked at our laps, the awkwardness between us so obvious, it made it even more awkward.

"Come on," he said finally, opening the door, getting out and pushing the seat forward to let me out. "I want to show you something."

It was difficult navigating the steep, rocky path down to the beach in my kitten heels, but Coop's arm was right there whenever I needed something to balance against. For the first time in my life, I could see the appeal of sneakers or even those hideous river sandals that were the plague of the

'90s—Tevas or Geckos or whatever you call them. When we got down to the beach I took my shoes off and the sand against my bare feet was silky-warm.

"We used to come here a lot." Coop's dark hair was windblown already from the car ride, and now the ocean breeze played with it gently, swishing a few strands in and out of his face.

"You and Dannika?" I tried not to pucker my lips in distaste when I said her name.

He squinted against the sun. It was bright out and the sky was that rich, lucid September blue, marred only by a couple of patches of pinkish fog hovering near the horizon.

"Yeah," he said. "Phil and Joni, too—this was kind of our spot."

"The friends we're going to see?"

"Yeah. I think you'll like them. They're really cool."

I just nodded.

Dannika was doing a series of yoga stretches just outside the reach of the surf. We both looked at her, our eyes drawn by the elegant lines her body made as she arched and folded, performing a slow dancelike sequence, her blue bikini striking against the dark velvet of wet sand. We were the only ones on the beach besides a couple of seals bobbing out in the water and a flock of pelicans swooping low, teasing the foamy edges of the waves with their long, graceful wings.

"She's a little high-strung today," Coop said.

"Dannika?"

He nodded.

"She seems pretty relaxed to me." I tried to make it sound offhand, like I really hadn't given it much thought.

"She, um…" He paused, choosing his words carefully. "She tries to give the impression that she's confident—even cocky—but the truth is, she's pretty insecure."

I kind of snorted at that. I couldn't help it. If he wanted to make me feel sorry for her, it was going to be a hard sell.

"No, I know, it sounds crazy. People figure she's got everything—successful career, amazing La Jolla beach house—"

"Perfect body," I added bitterly.

"Exactly," he said, agreeing a little too readily for my taste. "The whole package."

We heard her whooping with excitement and turned to see her paddling for a pretty enormous wave. Her arms churned hard against the water and she rose up over the mountain of blue just before it broke, disappearing over the lip.

"The thing is," he said, "I knew her when she was just a damaged kid."

We stopped walking and stood still for a moment, facing the water. Dannika was paddling farther out, now, working hard to get beyond the breakers, where the ocean got smooth and glassy.

"What do you mean, damaged?" I asked.

"Hold on," he said. "I'll explain in a sec. First I want to show you something." He took my hand and led me down the beach a little ways. Feeling his big, warm fingers closed over mine reminded me of being a child, walking with my father, feeling safe and enclosed.

We paused when we came to a cliff that jutted clear down to the edge of the water. The waves were crashing against the slick, barnacle-encrusted point. Small pebbles popped and sizzled as the receding tide dragged them backward.

When the wave had receded completely, Coop cried, "Go now!" and pushed me forward. Without thinking, I dashed across the rocky sand, past the sharp apex of the cliff, and then the next wave was sweeping up toward me, roaring like a wild animal. But Coop had timed it perfectly and I managed to curve around the point, then run away from the water so that it only licked at my toes, the spray misting the hem of my skirt. I laughed like a little kid.

Coop appeared a few seconds later, his jeans rolled up, but his wave was bigger and he didn't quite manage to escape it. He looked so cute running hard up the beach toward me, the foam surging around his ankles, getting his cuffs wet. *If I could just look at him the rest of my life, I'd be happy,* I told myself. Before I could let the impact of that thought sink in, he ran right for me and hugged me so hard that my toes dangled in the air. He kissed me; we were both giggling and I could feel the vibration of our laughter in his lips.

"Here." He put me down and led me farther away from

the water. Scanning the beach with his eyes, he said, "There it is. God, I haven't been here in years."

We were in a little cove, surrounded by a half circle of bluffs about thirty feet high. There, at the deepest part of the crescent-shaped beach, the sheer cliffs gave way to a small, dark cave. As we got closer I could smell the damp, slightly rotten odor of seaweed decomposing in the salty air. I hesitated at the edge where the sunlight turned abruptly into a cool envelope of shade, but Coop tugged at my hand again and soon we were sitting together in the shadows.

"I used to come here all the time," he said.

"By yourself?"

"Sometimes," he said. "Or with friends."

"With Dannika?" It came out all whispery and sort of scared. I couldn't look at him.

He was studying my profile; I could feel his eyes on my face. "Yeah, or Phil and Joni." He touched my hair. "It's the pirates' hideout. Top secret."

"I'm not much of a pirate," I admitted. "I get seasick. You sure I'm allowed to be here?"

"You underestimate yourself."

We sat there for a while, watching the waves crash against the sand. We couldn't see Dannika from in there, and I was glad.

"I just really love how it feels in here, you know? Like a secret fort."

"Yeah." It seemed kind of dank and smelly to me, but I sure as hell wasn't going to say so.

Coop took out his pipe and lit it. Did I ever mention how much I love his pipe? I mean I know smoking's a despicable habit, and I should hate everything about it, but when he smokes that pipe it just pushes every anachronistic, senti-mental button I've got—and you know I've got a lot of those. I mean, how many guys under the age of eighty smoke one of these babies? Every time he lights it, I feel like we're in an Ingmar Bergman film.

"Dannika's not what she seems to be," he said. I snuck a quick glance at him; he was squinting at the horizon, a serious look on his face. He puffed on the pipe a few more times to get it going. "When I met her freshman year she was skinny and awkward and painfully shy. Her teeth were all crooked back then and she was always holding a hand up over her mouth when she laughed or ate."

"You mean she wasn't always so…beautiful?"

He shook his head and took another drag from his pipe, blowing the smoke away from me. It smelled like choco-late. "She had a really messed up childhood. I won't go into the details—she'd hate me if I did—but when her dad died he left her some money and she spent it all on her looks. She got braces and a boob job. It's like she went away one summer and she came back a totally different girl. She even changed her name."

"Really? What was she called before?"

He tried not to smile. "Donna Horney."

I winced. "Yikes. No wonder."

He nodded. "She totally transformed herself—I mean, top to bottom. Now she pretends none of it ever happened. According to her, Donna's dead. End of story." He reached down and grabbed a handful of sand, let it pour out of his fist like a grey waterfall. "People meet her and assume she's Miss Enlightened, but the truth is, she's still Donna Horney inside."

I had to fight a huge giggle. I wanted to leap into the air and do a dance in the sand, but I sat there perfectly still. Dannika Winters was a phony! I knew at least some part of me should feel sorry for her, but all my body produced was a giddy surge of relief. My nemesis was a total fake. She couldn't possibly harm me. I was real; she was just smoke and mirrors.

Coop turned to me and this time I couldn't avoid his eyes. "What are you thinking?" His brow was furrowed.

"Um…" I hesitated. It hardly seemed fitting to blurt out *Ding-dong the witch is dead!* "I'm just surprised, I guess. That's really sad." I could feel a huge, satisfied grin threatening to spread across my face, but I covered it in time with a concerned frown.

"I'm telling you because I know from past experience that she can be really…" he searched for the right word "…intimidating."

"Sure. I can see that."

"But she's super private, okay, so don't mention any of this. I mean Phil and Joni know, of course, but we're the only ones. She'd seriously kill me if she knew I'd told you."

I zipped my lips with my fingers. "Mum's the word." I squeezed his hand. "Thanks for trusting me. I've been kind of nervous about meeting your friends. It helps that I'm not completely in the dark."

He set his pipe down on a rock, leaned over and kissed me. He tasted of salt and smoke—the sweetest flavor in the world.

I guess you probably don't need the gory details of every minute we spent in that cave. All I know is, most the buttons on my suit were undone and even when the fog started reaching toward the beach with long white fingers, I didn't feel the slightest bit cold. God, Marla, he's such a crazy-good kisser. I swear I could live on nothing but the taste of his mouth.

We were pretty caught up in the moment when I heard someone saying, "Oops, sorry."

I looked up and Dannika was walking away from us, her perfect little butt still swathed in nothing but a bikini.

Coop gave me a sheepish look as we both made the necessary adjustments to our clothing. When we were presentable again he kissed me one last time, tapped out his pipe, and we followed Dannika back down the beach toward the car. The tide was going out, I guess, because it was easier getting around the point this time. We waited until Dannika was dressed and sitting in the driver's seat of the Mercury before Coop gave me a piggyback ride up the path.

"I can't believe you didn't come out there," she told Coop as we climbed back into the car. There was a pouty note to her voice. Looking at her profile, I thought I could see the ghost of the gangly girl she'd once been. "It was like double overhead, dude."

"Did you have fun?" He tousled her wet hair affectionately and it didn't even bother me at all.

"It was a blast." She definitely didn't sound happy. "You totally missed out."

He shrugged. "I was busy."

I couldn't help giggling a little, and Dannika shot me a look over her shoulder. "Whatever." She jabbed the key into the ignition violently and the car roared to life. "Your loss."

She drives even worse when she's pissed.

Every ten miles or so I have to clench my jaw and cling to my seat belt as she passes another RV on a blind curve. To add to my discomfort, her surfboard's dripping little salt water drops onto my shoulder and the fog is making me shiver. All the same, I'm smiling as I write this.

I'm pretty sure I won't need this notebook anymore. Coop's provided me with an infallible cure to my jealousy. From now on I'll be the picture of sisterly sweetness. If I feel myself slipping, all I need are those two magic words: Donna Horney.

Anyway, thanks for suggesting I write all this down. If I

hadn't, who knows how this trip would have turned out? You could be reading about me in the papers: *Jackie O Strangles Yoga Diva*. Now I can safely say my petty insecurities are behind me.

Hugs and Kisses from a New and Improved Gwen

10:10 p.m.

Dear Marla,

You're absolutely not going to believe this, but I'm writing from MY MOM'S HOUSE.

Oh, horrors.

How did this happen? you ask. *Gwen hardly ever visits her parents. She finds her stepfather inane, her mother loud and the dogs deeply depressing.*

Precisely my point. Yet here I am, at my mother's house in western Sebastopol, with my leopard-print car coat covered from collar to hem in dog hair. The parakeets are screeching off-key and Carrie, the Irish wolfhound, is drooling on my shoes. This is not my idea of a romantic weekend away.

You want to know how this happened? I'll tell you how it happened. Dannika Winters, that's how.

There we were, cruising up Highway 1, shivering in the fog. Shouldn't we take the shortcut on 101 from San Luis Obispo to Salinas, I asked. Dannika was horrified at the mere suggestion; of course we couldn't, that would mean missing Big Sur, the most dramatic, remote, beautiful stretch of coastline in California. Did she also mention *the most deadly?* At one point she was messing with her CD player, heading for a cliff that dropped at least two hundred feet straight down to the sea. After Coop saved us by grabbing the wheel just in time, he waited a discreet three or four minutes before suggesting she must be tired of driving by now. I doubt she was tired, since she never gave the road more than seven percent of her attention, but *I* found her driving exhausting. I had to keep slamming the brakes on in the backseat and my thigh muscles were beginning to cramp.

I'm sure if it was anyone but Coop, Dannika would have bristled at the suggestion, but he seems to have a magical, almost narcotic effect on her. He makes her laugh. As much as I hate to admit it, I can see why they've been friends for so long. I guess it's just that irresistible tension of opposites. Marla, you know how you and I are so different, yet somehow we work, like sweet and sour, or tulle with taffeta?

You're sloppy, I'm structured; you're go-with-the-flow, I'm paint-by-numbers? Well, that's how Dannika and Coop are, in a way. He's Mr. Steady—he smells like sawdust and pipe tobacco. He's warm all the way through, not just on the surface. She's madcap, impulsive, spoiled and self-absorbed. She smells like a very expensive health food store. I guess I'm screwing up their delicate balance and that's why my presence is making us all so nervous. It's like they're perched on opposite ends of their teeter-totter and I'm the new kid, demanding they make space.

Anyway, there we were, cruising through Big Sur, then Monterey, then Santa Cruz to San Francisco. With Coop driving, I found I could relax and the afternoon took on a dreamy quality as the road lulled us all deeper and deeper into our private worlds. The windy roar of the convertible made it difficult to talk much, so we didn't try, and after Dannika's Wilco tape CD ended nobody bothered to put in another one. The fog dissipated, and the sky turned a deep, pensive late-afternoon blue.

I found myself remembering, for some reason, a night when my father didn't come home. I was seven, and my mom was cooking meatloaf. I remember that, because when she took it out of the oven, she burned the inside of her wrist on the loaf pan. She was standing there by the freezer with a piece of ice pressed to the blue veins on the inside of her wrist and I was crowding her, going, "Let me see, Mom. Let me see." I was sort of a morbid kid, fascinated by injuries, especially burns—I spent hours with my father's book on Hiroshima—but she wasn't in any mood for my dark curiosity and I remember her saying, "Jesus, Gwen, just get back. Fuck." Hearing that edge in her voice, hearing her swear, which she never did, made me feel suddenly cold. There'd been something in the air all night, but in that moment it went from an amorphous sadness that might dissipate with a joke or a really good episode of *Murder, She Wrote* to a black force that had to be reckoned with.

Wow, that was weird. Don't know where that came from. I guess that's why I never come back here. The farther north I get, the more memories assail me. By the time I hit Sonoma County, they're coming at me like bloodthirsty bats.

Anyway, as I was saying, we were driving along in silence for hours. I'd been scribbling furiously, trying to keep you updated, and every once in a while Coop would glance over his shoulder, saying, "What you got going there, kitten, the great American novel?" to which I'd reply, "Just notes." Once Dannika said, "At this rate, she's going to have *War and Peace* by the time we hit Mendocino." I guess she thought that was funny. I speculated about whether I could "accidentally" dig my kitten heels into her surfboard. At least she'd have something to remember me by.

When we finally crossed the Golden Gate Bridge, the sun was sagging toward the water, soaking the ocean and the cars and even our skin in tangerine light. Coop and Dannika looked like movie stars with their sunglasses on and the red, curving lines of the bridge swooping past them. The left-out feeling that had haunted me most of the day started to creep back in. They just looked so perfect together up there—so natural and salty and wild. It was hard not to imagine how photogenic their little surfer children would be. Everyone driving past us must have wondered what I was doing in that picture. They probably assumed I was the wacky cousin visiting from some obscure Eastern European country that hadn't yet discovered denim or Lycra.

When we got across the bridge and were getting closer to the turnoff for Highway 1, I was astounded when Dannika said, "Let's take the coast again." I mean, God, the sun was halfway down and we still had a couple hundred miles to go. Even if we took 101 and headed northwest at Cloverdale, we were still looking at four, maybe five more hours in the car, depending on traffic. Taking the coast would mean five or six, at least, most of it in the dark on hellish-curvy roads.

I couldn't help it; I leaned forward and said, "Why don't we just take 101?"

She looked at me with disdain. "I don't believe in freeways."

"You live in San Diego and you don't believe in freeways?" I punctuated the remark with one raised eyebrow. There were things she could learn from me.

"I don't," she said. "They're evil. Coop, don't you think we should take the coast?"

We both looked at him.

"If it were up to me, I'd go for 101. It's twice as fast." He shot Dannika his don't-be-mad-I'm-only-being-honest look.

She shook her head and laughed. "You're just siding with her."

"It's only logical," I said. "Why take the scenic route in the dark?"

"Well, sorry, folks, but it's my car and my car doesn't take freeways. End of story. Here's the turnoff." Her tone was brusque, but underneath it you could hear the warning: *my way or the highway*—which in this case turned out to be the same thing.

When Coop turned off obediently I wasn't surprised. I mean yeah, it was a little wimpy, but we all knew if he didn't we'd have a major tantrum on our hands and I don't think any of us were up for it.

Of course, the gods of Highway 1 had a few surprises in store for us, so if we were looking to get off easy, we could forget it.

We were just passing Point Reyes Station, getting close to Tomales Bay. The sun was long gone but there was still a fiery pink clinging to the underside of a few smudgy clouds—the leftovers of a messy sunset. The air was turning a harsh, coastal-cold against our faces. I'd been debating for the past twenty minutes about asking if we could put the top up, but I hated to be the hothouse flower amongst tough native shrubs. The irony here was that *I* was the native. I'm the one who comes from apple country; Coop's from Philadelphia and Dannika spent most her life in Ventura—what do they know about the strange, hostile territories north of the Golden Gate Bridge?

As I sat there freezing my ass off in my wool chemise suit and my yummy little leopard-print car coat, I kept dreaming about the full-length mink I'd almost run back to grab this morning. If I had that, I could bury my face in its silky depths until the numbness in my nose and ears went away. Again, it was Dannika who had kept me from following my instincts. All day we'd been bending to her will—why? Because she had a perfect, perky little nose, gleaming blond hair, a supple, pinup girl body? And what part of all that wasn't store bought? Even if it wasn't—even if she was as all-natural as that gag-inducing juice I'd choked down earlier—what right did that give her to call every shot?

Suddenly, I didn't care if it was her car or if they thought I was a total city girl. I was going to ask them to put the damn top up. What was this, some kind of naturalists' boot camp?

I was just leaning forward to make my request when two things happened at once. Coop turned his head slightly and said, "You cold, kitten?" The words weren't even out of his mouth when the engine coughed a few times, sputtered briefly and died.

Coop guided it onto the crumbling, almost nonexistent

shoulder and stared at the dash. "That's weird," he said. "Sounded like we ran out of gas, but the gauge says we're still half full."

There was a pause.

Dannika broke the silence. "Actually, the gauge is sort of…broken."

I leaned back and sighed.

Coop just looked at her. "You're kidding me."

"No," she said. "It's busted. It hasn't worked for months."

He ran a hand through his hair. "Why didn't you mention this before we got all the way out here?"

"I thought you knew!"

His voice turned incredulous. "How would I know this, Danni?" I didn't like the nickname, but I relished the tone of their conversation. They were bickering and if they kept it up the exchange would escalate into a proper fight. Usually I hate violence, but in this case, I thought I could make an exception.

"Jesus, I'm sorry, okay?" Her voice didn't sound very apologetic. "I forgot you haven't driven my car in a while." The subtext was complicated but clear: *I forgot you've been so wrapped up with the little bitch in the backseat that you've neglected me and my precious car for months.*

Coop backed off. "Never mind, it doesn't matter. Who's got a cell phone?" We all looked at each other blankly. "Dammit," he said, slapping the steering wheel, but he was laughing a little now. "A couple of technophobes and a retro purist. Why couldn't we have one normal, mainstream American on board?"

It was kind of funny. I laughed with him.

Dannika didn't even crack a smile. "Great. So what now?"

"You have a map?" he asked.

She shook her head, no.

"Shit." Coop wasn't laughing this time.

"It's a straight shot up the coast," she told him. "Why would I need a *map?*" She was whining now, and I thought, *careful, girl, your Donna Horney's showing.*

We all looked around at the sloping hills turning rapidly darker. There were a few stars out, now. The stretch of highway disappeared around curves both ahead and behind. There were scraggly coastal trees, bent over like old people from all those years of wind. We were truly out in the sticks. The air smelled of cypress and salt—clean and cold. In the distance, I could hear seals barking.

I closed my eyes and visualized where we were on a map. Remember how you used to call me Navigation Girl? You always said it was my superpower. This time it was easy, since you and I used to drive this stretch a lot in high school, although usually we'd head south at Point Reyes Station so we could sit on the beach in Bolinas and watch the hippies surf, scanning the waters for sharks. We were maybe four miles north of Point Reyes Station now; the stretch ahead was pretty desolate.

"Our best bet is to backtrack to the last town we passed," I said.

They both looked at me in surprise, as if they'd forgotten I was back there.

"We haven't passed anything for miles," Dannika snapped.

"Yeah, we did," I said. "Point Reyes Station. It's easy to miss, but I'm pretty sure they have a gas station."

"I would have noticed," she said.

Coop smiled at me in the lengthening shadows. "That's right. You grew up around here, didn't you?"

I nodded reluctantly. "Yeah."

I know you're proud of being a Sonoma County girl, but for me it's a lot more complicated. I never talk about the past with Coop if I can avoid it. I know it's beautiful up here, rustic and quaint and all that shit, but in my mind it's a big tangle of memories and misguided impulses, most of which I'd rather just put behind me. You were the best thing Sebastopol ever gave me and I got to take you with me when I left. Everything else I'd just as soon never talk about again. I guess that's why Coop had half forgotten—didn't even really know—that we were only about fifteen miles from the town where I was born and raised.

"So, what's the plan?" Dannika was the princess waiting for her incompetent advisors to suggest a solution. I suppose it didn't occur to her that our current situation was entirely her fault.

"How far back is Point Reyes Station?" Coop asked me.

Before I could answer, Dannika barked, "There wasn't any town."

I forced myself to stay calm. She was really starting to get on my nerves. To Coop I said, "Maybe four miles back."

"I swear to God there was nothing back there." She sounded close to a meltdown. "The last town I saw was Stinson Beach, and that's not far from San Francisco."

"Well," I said, "it's back there. Trust me."

"Right." Coop got out of the car. "I guess I'll try to hitch a ride and get us some gas. If worse comes to worst, I can probably walk there and get a ride back." He leaned against the driver's side and looked at the surfboards. "If we all go, our gear might get stolen. Then again, I hate to leave you two here…"

"Yeah, but think about it," Dannika said. "We can't all three hitch a ride—it's easier if you just go. Besides, is Gwen going to walk four miles in those shoes?" She shot a bitchy look over her shoulder at my kitten heels. I wanted to tell her if she didn't stop whining I'd happily plunge one of these sharp little heels deep into her heart (provided I could get past the silicone) but I bit my tongue. In some ways, I liked it better when Dannika was a pouty little wench. It made her even easier to hate.

"Kitten?" Coop put his hand on my head. His warm fingers made me want to curl up in his arms—more than that—I would have curled up inside his lungs right then, if it were possible. "What do you want to do?"

As much as I hated the thought of spending the next hour or three stranded on the side of the road with the satanic blonde, I couldn't come up with a better solution. "I guess Dannika's right," I said. "We'll just stay with the stuff. But be careful about who you get a ride with. There are some freaky people out here."

"Can't be worse than L.A., right?" He grinned.

"You'd be surprised," I said.

One of the reasons I never go back to Sonoma County with you is because the land itself is polluted by my childhood. When I drive through Sebastopol, it's like navigating a minefield. The deli on the corner reminds me of the time my dad and I went in there for Junior Mints and he left with the salami slicer's phone number. I can't drive past the old ballet studio on Valentine Avenue without thinking of my mother acting rude and tight-lipped with Miss Yee, my favorite teacher there; later, in the car, she blurted out that Daddy was sleeping with "that Chinese slut in the legwarmers."

I never took lessons there again. How could I concentrate on my pliés, when images of my father doing vague, obscene things under the covers to Miss Yee were burned into the eight-year-old folds of my brain?

Sebastopol is riddled with these traps. Every store and restaurant, every open field and parking lot, every strip mall and house can be traced through an intricate mesh of connections back to some messed-up snapshot from my childhood. I can see the whole town in my mind; it's a vast, convoluted topographical map. Remember Mr. Colwell telling us about the experiment with spiders on acid—how their webs were all wonky and haphazard? The lines of my map are like that—way too complicated and crazy to follow.

It's sad, really, because I know that good things happened here, too. I mean sure, most of the kids at school thought I was a certifiable nutter, which made at least eighty percent of my adolescence excruciating and torturous, but after I met you, everything changed. I was still considered a freak, but when you signed on as my friend I could feel the rest of my life opening up and beckoning me forward. You were an ambassador to the future sent to remind me that there was so much beyond that myopic, claustrophobic little high school. Remember that night when we snuck out and drove your mom's car to Salmon Creek? We stood in the dunes, staring out at the water. The moon was so bright that our shadows were etched into the sand. You sang that Cat Stevens song "Moonshadow," and I called you a hippie and then we ran down to the crashing waves and closed our eyes and let the mist pour over our faces in the dark while the cold foam licked at our bare toes.

You see what I mean? Get me within county lines and I become a font of nostalgia. Actually, that's not accurate. I become more like AM radio; every once in a while there's a good song that comes soaring out of the static, but mostly it's just a bunch of lame, reactionary crap.

Enough careening down memory lane. Suffice it to say,

I'm not happy that this dog-hair infested couch I happen to be writing you from is the epicenter of all those bad memories.

So there I was, trapped in the '57 Mercury with my gorgeous nemesis. As I snuck glances at her profile, I couldn't help thinking about the bags of silicone inside her boobs. Do they still use silicone—isn't it like saltwater now? If she had it done eight years ago, what did they use back then? I was overcome with an irrational impulse to ask her about the surgery. What did it feel like, rising from the operating table like a sexed up Frankenstein? Did it take her long to adjust to her new proportions—did she run into things for a few days? What did people say when they first saw her? Were they too polite to comment on her new cleavage or was it so in-your-face they couldn't help but blurt out something inappropriate?

"Sure is dark." Dannika's voice in the front seat was surprisingly squeaky. "You want to sit up here?"

Was the queen actually inviting me out of the servant's quarters? "I'm okay," I said.

She turned around to face me. "You're not cramped back there?"

Gee, I've only been wedged between two surfboards and a steamer trunk for eleven hours, now—how kind of you to notice. "It's not too bad."

An awkward silence ensued. The barking seals started up

again, so far away you could barely hear them. It comforted me, knowing we were close to the water, even though we couldn't see it from here.

"It's getting kind of cold," she said.

"Yeah," I replied.

An owl let out a high-pitched, lonely hoot. Dannika shivered and pulled her sweatshirt together at the throat. "Why don't you come up here?" she said. "That way I don't have to turn around when I talk to you."

It's all about you, isn't it? I thought, but I went ahead and climbed over the seat into the front. She was sitting dead center and I climbed into the passenger side so she had to scoot over behind the wheel. I couldn't see any reason why I should contend with the steering wheel—not when her surfboard had been dripping cold, waxy blobs on my beautiful car coat for the past two hundred and fifty miles.

Freed now from my confining second-class accommodations, I realized that the car was so immense it was like a mobile couch. All three of us could have ridden in the front, easily. She leaned against the driver's side door and stretched her legs out on the seat. I let my head fall back and looked up at the growing assembly of stars.

You're totally going to force-feed me Zoloft when I tell you this, but for one dizzying second there, I considered what it would be like to kill someone—namely, the leggy bombshell beside me. I mean it's not like I thought it was a good idea. I knew it was sick. But a truck barreled past us just then, a huge logger with a mammoth pile of lumber, and I just thought, *we're alone; I could lure her into the road somehow and act all horrified when she's flattened.*

Do you think I should seek professional help?

I was slightly aghast, but at the same time it made me realize something: I really, really want Coop in a way I've never wanted anyone in my life and whoever gets between us better watch herself.

It was chilling, but also weirdly uplifting. In other words, I knew I was in love.

"You always this quiet?" Dannika asked.

"No." I started wracking my brain for something else to say, but it was a total blank. Actually, it wasn't blank so much as clouded with an impenetrable fog of resentment. I'd been right there, barely two feet from her, all day. Had she shown any interest in making conversation before now? I wasn't going to be her backup entertainment, called onto the stage because her star had gone to get gas.

"So, how did you meet Coop?"

"At the Laundromat," I said. "Stars Wash-n-Dry. Everything in L.A. is about stars—especially places where no celebrity would be caught dead."

When I didn't offer anything else, she asked, "What was his pick-up line?"

I chuckled. "It was really crowded and I was waiting for his washer. He left a pair of his boxers in there, so I went over and returned them. I guess I was blushing—he said I was turning pink and could he buy me a beer for my trouble." I paused.

She must have sensed my hesitation, because she said, "And…?"

I shrugged. "That's it."

There was no way I was going to tell her the rest—about the delicious, giddy beer buzz we nursed, even though it was only eleven in the morning on a Sunday. How we dropped his laundry off first, then mine, then ate at this random hole-in-the-wall Korean barbecue place we found in Venice. We tried going back there a few weeks ago, but we couldn't even find it. It was like we slipped down an elusive rabbit hole that day, into a land of fleshy noodles, sweet, tender pork, duck that dissolved on the tongue. I was drunk on the afternoon, on his dimples and his cheekbones and the penetrating warmth of his muddy hazel eyes. If she thought I was going to tell her all that, she was crazy.

"We met in the ocean," she said. "At that beach we stopped at today." I realized with irritation that her silence wasn't a sign that she was patiently waiting for more details. She'd been recalling her own meeting with Coop.

Again, I wondered very briefly about the best way to get her into the road before the next semi came around the corner.

She laughed softly at her private little memory.

"What?" I prompted, unable to stop myself.

"Oh, nothing. Just—he told me I surfed like a sumo

wrestler. I'd plant myself on the board and nothing could throw me off. He nicknamed me Poonha."

"Poonha?" I echoed weakly.

"After Conrad Poonha—this three hundred-pound Hawaiian surfer guy they show for like thirty seconds in *Endless Summer.*" She lifted her hair with her forearm and flopped it over the car door. "We totally hit it off. For a little while I thought we were in love." She let out a deep, throaty laugh that sent shivers up my spine. "Shows you what I know."

I swallowed hard and forced myself to adopt a casual tone. "Did you ever date?"

She tilted her head back and forth and pursed her lips; it was the noncommittal look a doctor gives you when you ask, *is it going to hurt?* "We never really *dated,*" she said. "We just…hung out."

The ambiguity made me want to throttle her. "Hung out?"

"You know how it is." She didn't look me in the eye. I wondered how much it would hurt if I took a pair of needle-nose pliers to the diamond twinkling in her nose and yanked as hard as I could. "When you've been friends for ten years, there's not a lot you haven't experienced together."

"I've known my friend Marla for twelve years." I cleared my throat. "Of course, we've never had sex."

"Really?" she said. "Why not?"

I was still puzzling over this comment when I heard the

crunch of tires on gravel behind us. I was hoping it was Coop already back with gas, but it seemed unlikely. When I turned around I saw the next best thing, under the circumstances: a CHP officer sizing us up through the windshield of his patrol car.

"Dammit," Dannika said. "God*dammit*." Apparently she didn't share my enthusiasm.

"What's wrong?" I whispered.

"It's a cop!"

"Yeah, I know. And we're stranded. Don't we need a cop?"

"Just, don't let him into the trunk, whatever happens," she said, glancing furtively over her shoulder.

"What do you have back there, a body?"

She shot me a withering look. "Let me do the talking, okay? I know how to handle pigs." She sat up very straight and gripped the wheel with shaking hands. She looked like a little kid playing "car" in her parents' garage.

"Hello, ladies." The officer sidled up to the Mercury. His hairline was receding slightly, but still he was mildly handsome in a squeaky-clean lanky way. He had a rather mammoth mole on his left cheek; the overall effect was very John-Boy Walton. "What seems to be the problem?"

Dannika was staring straight ahead, a zombielike expression on her face. In spite of her insistence that she would do the talking, she appeared to be incapable of speech.

"Hi, officer," I said. "We just ran out of gas. My boyfriend went back to Point Reyes Station to get some."

"He the big guy hitchhiking, ma'am?"

"That'd be him." I smiled winningly.

Dannika made a weird sound in her throat. It reminded me of the sound Audrey makes when she's getting ready to hack up a hairball. It was apparent she was trying to suppress it. She was still white-knuckling the steering wheel and staring through the windshield, rigid as a statue.

"Everything all right, miss?"

Miss—he called her miss. Why would he call her miss and me ma'am? Are my crow's feet getting worse? Dannika wasn't responding. Again, I could see it was time to intervene.

"She's deaf." For some reason I found it necessary to add, "Can't hear a word."

He looked concerned. "Should she be driving?"

"Oh, no, she doesn't drive. She just likes to pretend… when we're not moving. It's her little game." My tone implied her hearing wasn't the only part of her that was damaged.

"Uh-*huh*." It seemed to me the officer was gazing rather longingly at Dannika, even though the lengthening shadows of twilight made it impossible to really appreciate her perfect features and her luminous hair, which was practically holographic in full sun.

"Um, do you think you might be able to give my boyfriend a lift? I mean, if he hasn't already hitched a ride?"

Officer John-Boy tore his eyes away from Dannika and looked at me like a man just waking from a long, morphine-induced dream. He clearly had no idea what I'd just said, so I repeated it. Finally, he nodded.

"Sure. We'll be back in a few. Go ahead and lock all the doors."

I thought about this for a second. "Would that really help with the top down?"

Like I said, the light was fading, but I could see him blushing just the same. He glanced at Dannika, as if expecting her to sneer at him, but she was still playing corpse-at-the-wheel.

"Just—exercise caution. I'll be back as soon as I can."

When he got in his car, he actually turned on the siren before speeding down the road. I watched the spinning light disappear around the bend. It was sad, knowing that siren was for Dannika who, even as a mentally feeble deaf girl, inspired grown men to do and say stupid things. I felt like the infinitely less attractive sidekick in a romantic comedy— the one who gets the funny lines but never gets the guy.

"What was that all about?" I sounded overly irritated, even to myself.

Dannika sighed and let go of the wheel at last. "I'm sorry. I lost it."

"You played dead."

"Because if I didn't I was going to say something really, really stupid." She wiped her forehead and unzipped her sweatshirt halfway. It was getting steadily colder and there she was, sweating.

"Why?"

She looked exasperated. "What do you mean, *why?*"

"I mean, what was the big deal? He wasn't even giving us a ticket."

She looked around, a cagey gleam in her eye. "He's coming back, isn't he?"

"What's in the trunk?"

She turned to me, wide-eyed with panic. "You think he'll search the car?"

"Maybe you should just tell me what's going on."

She popped the trunk and opened her door. "I'm getting rid of it."

"Getting rid of what?"

I got out and followed her back to the trunk. She was unzipping her backpack, pawing past brightly colored cottons and hiking boots. "It's really none of your business."

"Okay, fine," I said, throwing up my hands.

"It's blow."

"What?" I spun around.

"Coke? Cocaine?"

"Oh my God, really? In there?" I stared at the backpack she was still rifling through, feeling horrified.

"If I can just fucking find it," she muttered.

"You're a yogi! You can't be a cokehead."

She finally produced a Ziploc baggie filled with white powder. "Want to do a couple lines?"

"Dannika!"

"It's really good stuff." She held up the baggie and gazed at the powder with hungry affection.

"You've got to get rid of it."

She caressed the plastic. "Right this second?"

"Yes, this second."

"I'll just hide it," she said, stuffing it into the bodice of her tank top.

"Are you insane?"

"I paid good money for this," she whined.

"Look, no offense, but if your performance a minute ago is any indicator, you're not that great under pressure. I'd hate to see how you'd act with a few grams of coke in your bra."

She pulled it back out. "Shit," she said. "What do I do?"

"I'm going to say three words, and I want you to listen to me very carefully." I employed the tone I reserve for intimidating unruly toddlers in my store. "Cop. Coming. Back."

In a panic, she tore the bag open and let the powder fly. At that moment the wind must have shifted, or maybe she was just too terrified to factor its direction, and the next thing we knew everything—the backseat of the Mercury, the surfboards, the trunk, our clothes and even our faces—was covered with a fine dusting of coke.

"Fuck," we said in unison.

It was the first time we'd agreed on anything all day.

By the time Coop and Officer John-Boy got back, the twilight had given way to full-on night and we had cleaned most the coke off ourselves and the car. It was a good thing our friendly copper didn't travel with dogs, though, I'll tell you that. We were in no mood to be sniffed.

Once the coke was gone, Dannika gave up her rigor mortis routine and managed to turn on a little charm. All she had to do was smile in Officer John-Boy's direction and he went positively twitchy with delight.

"You guys okay?" Coop asked as he poured the gas into the tank. "You're so quiet."

Dannika started to answer, but I kicked her foot, hoping Officer John-Boy wouldn't notice. She sort of squeaked, but didn't actually speak.

"We're fine," I said.

Dannika smiled sweetly at John-Boy, illuminated by his headlights. The harsh white glare would have made anyone else look ghoulish, but she managed to work the effect as if they were twin spotlights. John-Boy fidgeted with his belt, his radio, his billy club, a gawky kid at a junior high school dance—albeit an armed one. Watching from the shadows, I just rolled my eyes and fought the urge to gag.

When we were on the road with Coop at the wheel, Dannika riding shotgun and me (surprise, surprise!) in the back, I leaned forward so my face was in between them. "Dannika," I said, "have you ever gotten a ticket?"

"Parking ticket," she said.

"What about a moving violation?"

I noticed Coop was grinning a little in the dashboard light.

"I've been pulled over," she said. "Lots, actually. But I've only gotten one actual ticket."

"And was the officer a woman?" I asked.

Coop's grin deepened.

"Yeah, actually. How'd you know?"

"Just a lucky guess." I leaned back in my seat to watch the stars.

I realize, of course, that I haven't yet covered how we ended up here, at my mother's house, Chateau de Dog Hair. I'm getting to that, I swear.

What happened is this: it was getting late, we were inching our way toward the Sonoma County line, when out of nowhere this fog rolled in that was so thick you couldn't see two feet in front of you.

"This is crazy." Coop sounded edgy, and it occurred to me that the running-out-of-gas episode had been even more trying for him. After all, he was the one who had to hitch-hike—a pretty scary thing to do, even if you are six foot four. Sure, we were nearly arrested for Schedule II narcotics, but he was the one who had to stick his thumb out and make himself easy prey for random serial killers cruising down the coast. And let's face it, a wildly disproportionate number of serial killers end up in northern California.

My thoughts were interrupted when a huge deer, wide-eyed with shock, emerged from the fog like a ghostly, over-grown Bambi. Coop turned the wheel sharply and missed hitting it by inches; it shot off into the darkness, a blur in the corner of my eye. My heart was pounding wildly and, from the silence in the car, I sensed they were similarly shaken.

Coop sounded a little weak when he said, "Gwen, do you know if there's a road that cuts inland? We've got to get out of this fog."

I closed my eyes, and a map of the coast came into focus. The obvious choice was Bodega Highway, of course, but the fact that it goes right past my mom's house made me hesitate. The catch was that there really wasn't a better way east for quite a while and the fog was likely to get worse from Salmon Creek to Mendocino, since the highway hugs the coast that whole stretch. "Yeah," I said. "It's not far from here."

"Great. Let me know when you see it, okay?"

"Sure."

Dannika sat up straighter. "Where are we going?"

"I'm heading inland."

"Why?"

Coop sighed. "Because, Dannika, this was a really stupid plan. It's late, we're hungry, there's no place to eat out here, and the fog is so thick I can barely see the road."

"And your point is…?" She brushed a strand of hair back from her face and glared at him.

"I'm going back to 101."

"Wait a minute! This is my car."

"Look, stop being such a spoiled brat, okay? It's not safe to drive in this." He nodded at the swirling shroud of mist beyond the windshield.

"It's right up here somewhere," I said, still watching for the turn. "Oh, there it is." I pointed at the road veering off to the right.

Dannika scowled as Coop turned inland, but she knew it was no use; she was outnumbered. I was proud of Coop for standing up to her, even if it had taken him all day to work up to it. I wondered if he'd put his foot down very often during their ten years of friendship. I had a feeling this was more the exception than the rule.

We rode a few miles in moody silence. The fog wasn't thinning much. A possum darted into the road, pale and confused. Coop swerved, but instead of moving away from the car, it scurried blindly toward it. We all listened in horror to the sickening thud–crunch of first the front, then the back tire making contact. I couldn't help swiveling around to check it out. The tail lights illuminated a pulpy mess of fur; I could see its rodent feet still clawing at the air.

"Gross," I said, turning back around.

Dannika shook her head. "Is that all you can say? *Gross?*"

"What, should I prepare a eulogy?" I was in no mood for an animal rights lecture.

Coop intervened. "Gwen, how much farther to Mendocino taking 101?"

I did some mental mapping and calculations. "Realistically? We're probably looking at three or four hours, at least."

"You know, I hate to be a whiner, but I'm so wiped out," he said.

"Fine," Dannika snapped. "I'll drive."

"Mmm," Coop said, "I think that's kind of a bad idea."

"Why?" She said it in two syllables, like a pissed-off teenager.

"I just think you're tired, too. We all are. And this fog isn't really getting much better."

"See? We should have just stayed on the coast."

Coop let that one pass.

Dannika turned around to face me. "Gwen, you want to drive for a while? You should be fresh as a daisy."

"She doesn't drive," Coop said.

Dannika looked amazed. "You live in L.A. and you *don't drive?*"

I shook my head. I was used to this reaction. "Never have."

Coop looked at me in the rearview mirror. "What do you think, G? Should we stop somewhere and spend the night, or am I just wimping out?"

"What, like a hotel?" Dannika asked.

"Yeah, I guess," he said. "Something along 101. We could get dinner, chill out, have a drink. We haven't eaten much all day."

"I don't know," she said. "I hate hotels—especially hotels

along the freeway. And what would we *eat?* Big Macs?" She made a sort of half scoffing, half gagging sound. "Let's just keep going. It's only a couple more hours."

"Three hours," Coop corrected. "Probably more if the fog doesn't break up."

"Yeah," I said, "and the road back out to the coast is pretty gnarly." We were only about six miles from my mom's house at that point, and as much as I hated to admit it, staying there made sense. I agreed with Coop—it was dangerous to keep going when we were starving and tired and the conditions were so sketchy. The hotel idea was mildly appealing, but I had a feeling Dannika would make us drive around Santa Rosa for hours, trying to find a place to stay that wasn't morally or aesthetically offensive. I found myself reverting to my old standby: WWJD (What Would Jackie Do)?

"Actually," I said, "my mom's house is only a few minutes from here."

Coop's face lit up. "You're kidding! That's amazing."

"Yeah," I said, trying hard to match his enthusiasm but ending up about seven notches below.

Dannika twisted around in her seat and eyed me carefully. "Are you saying you want to stay there?"

I shrugged. "We could. I'm sure she wouldn't mind."

"What about you?" Dannika said. "Do you mind?"

It was a rare break from her normally self-absorbed state. Maybe all women share an instinctive understanding of the melancholy gravitational field that surrounds our mothers' houses.

I held her gaze. She was backlit by the dashboard lights, so she wasn't much more than a silhouette, but even in the semi-darkness, I could feel something shifting. "It's not my first choice," I said, "but I guess it's okay. I can deal."

"Cool." Coop was oblivious to the fragile telepathy passing between his two passengers. "Just tell me where to go."

When my mother opened the door, she was wearing an enormous orange fleecy *thing* that looked, more than anything, like a sleeping bag with sleeves. I'd seen that sort of thing in a catalogue somewhere, but I didn't believe that anyone actually *wore* one. I think it's modeled after those little sleep suits people put infants in, before they're old enough to protest. Her brown hair was streaked with gray, which seemed to have a different texture from the rest of her hair, so that her usually sleek brown bob was marred by slightly horsy, fraying stripes. All in all, she looked quite awful, but when she saw me her face went from an old-lady suspicious frown to a huge childlike smile. Instinctively, I took a step forward and let myself be wrapped up in her warm, fleecy hug.

"Gwenny, Gwenny, Gwenny—look at you, too adorable! What are you doing here? I see you brought your friends." Her eyes moved past me to Coop and Dannika, who were still lingering on the front step, looking vaguely apologetic and disoriented. "Come in, come in!" she called, before I could answer her question. Coop stepped forward first.

"Uh, Mom, this is Coop," I said.

"Coop! What sort of name is that?"

"Actually, ma'am, it's Arthur Milton Cooper, officially."

"Arthur—that's a lovely name. Why would you let anyone call you Coop?"

I rolled my eyes. "Mom…"

"Well," Coop gave her a sheepish grin, "by the time I was three even my own mother could see I was never living up to Arthur Milton. So she started calling me Coop, after my old man." He shrugged, and I was seized by a violent urge to kiss him.

Mom opened her mouth and let out a huge, horsy laugh. "That's too cute." When she'd recovered from his hilarity, her gaze moved on to Dannika, who was standing near the door with her hands in the pockets of her sweatshirt. "And who's this?"

"I'm Dannika, a friend of Coop's." There was an awkward pause. "And Gwen's," she added.

"Great. Welcome." My mother's look was so transparent, I wanted to cover her face with both hands. She clearly didn't trust this Amazon and she was trying to decide who the cute guy belonged to—the blonde or me. I didn't want to know which way she'd place her bets.

Coop must have read her expression just as easily, because he slipped an arm around my shoulder and said, "Gwen's told me a lot about you." This, of course, was a total lie, but I didn't care. He was claiming me as his, and that's what mattered. "It's great to meet you at last."

Her eyes lit up. "Well, wonderful, wonderful. Come in, make yourselves comfortable." She sort of hobbled backward in her orange bag. I saw what was coming seconds before it happened, but my reflexes weren't good enough to prevent it. Her fleece-encased foot stepped back toward the sunken living room stairs and then all at once she went over, like a big orange tree chopped at the base.

Coop was helping her up again before I could even move. Luckily, the living room was carpeted and she'd fallen rather gracefully, considering. "Mrs. Matson, are you all right?" He helped her to the couch and sat her down.

"My God," she said. "How embarrassing. I don't even drink."

"Mom, maybe you should…change? That suit seems a little hazardous."

She stroked her fleece lovingly. "Isn't it great, though? I love this thing. I never take it off when I'm at home. Once I had to drive Steven to the airport and I wore it the whole way."

"You can drive in that thing?" I noticed now that there was something yellowish and crusty on the sleeve.

"Oh, yeah. See, there are zippers at the bottom to let your feet out, if you want. It's just warmer this way." She snuggled into it happily. "My goodness, look at you! I haven't seen you since Christmas. I love what you're doing with your hair."

"Mom, I've worn it this way since the third grade."

"I know that! I'm your mother, you think I don't know that?" She shifted gears for a moment from ecstatic to indignant, then back again. "What I mean is, it looks shinier now. Did you do one of those whatchamacallits? Cellophane wraps?"

"No."

The sliding glass door opened, then, and Steven walked in with the dogs—all five of them: the two Irish wolfhounds, the black Lab, the spotted mutt and the very nervous Chihuahua that always looks like it's in the process of freezing to death. "Ooooh, come to Mama," my mother cooed as the Chihuahua leaped up and cowered in her lap, staring at us with glassy-eyed horror.

"These are the children," Mom said in that cutesy baby voice she always uses around the dogs. "Carrie and Larry," she said, pointing to the wolfhounds, "O.J." she pointed to the Lab, "Pokey, the mutt, and this—" she lifted the Chihuahua's chin with one finger "—is Aurora. Say hello, honey." To my horror, Mom lifted one paw and made Aurora wave at Coop.

He smiled at the nappy little creature, then at my mother. I was sure he was thinking, *is this Gwen in twenty-five years?*

"And I'm Steven." We all looked at Steven, then. He always looks the same—I've never seen him without that silly beret on. Who wears a beret? He must imagine it looks artistic and intriguing, but in combination with his moth-

eaten sweaters and baggy, shapeless sweats, the effect is more
homeless guy than modern day Picasso.

As Dannika and Coop introduced themselves to Steven
and the collective stench of dog filled my head, I started
getting anxious. I wiped my sweaty palms on my wool skirt
and wondered what had possessed me to make this detour.
I wished to God I'd let Coop find us a hotel, even if it did
mean cruising through ten lobbies before Dannika was satisfied with the feng shui of this or that Holiday Inn.

I snapped out of my nervous inner monologue when I
heard Steven saying, "Dannika Winters? From *Dannika
Winters Makes Yoga Easy?*"

"That's me," Dannika admitted shyly.

For some reason I looked immediately to my mother,
who was eyeing her husband and the shapely blonde in her
living room with naked hostility. I wondered if my face was
that openly bitter when I watched Dannika with Coop. The
Holiday Inn, with its plastic ice buckets and soda machines,
was sounding more and more utopian every second.

"I do yoga with you every day." Steven was looking more
animated than I'd ever seen him.

My mother scoffed. "More like once a month, Steven!"

He barely even glanced in Mom's direction. "I really
admire your work. It's so wonderful that you make yoga ac-
cessible to uncoordinated old goats like me."

For a horrible half-second, I flashed on what Steven and
thousands of old guys like him actually *do* when they watch

Dannika's tapes and I seriously wanted to heave. It was one of those irrepressible visuals that makes you wonder about your own mental health.

"Thanks." Dannika tucked a strand of hair behind her ear and looked at the floor. I flashed on the sycophant at the juice bar in Malibu and how she basked in his attention. Even with the cop, she was perfectly willing to flirt once she'd disposed of all incriminating evidence. But now she seemed self-conscious and uncomfortable. Maybe being a goddess is a job, like anything else; at the end of the day you're ready to get off duty, sip a vodka tonic and zone out for a couple hours so you can get up the next day and do it all again.

"Are you kids starving?" Mom got up from the couch. "I'll just change my clothes and rustle up some burgers or something."

Dannika smiled weakly (*sorry, honey, no root juice and soy yogurt at this pop stand*). Coop, on the other hand, beamed at Mom, and when she saw his eager man-who-is-dying-for-a-burger look she actually tittered. "Coop, I believe you're hungry," she said, sounding all at once like the Southern belle she once was.

"Mrs. Matson, if you fried me up a burger, I'd pledge my loyalty to you for life."

Mom giggled some more, but Steven frowned. "Her name's Mrs. Sherman," he said.

"But Coop can call me anything he likes," Mom said, and

sashayed (well, as best she could in her sleep sack) to the bedroom to change her clothes.

Signing off from Chateau de Dog Hair,

Gwen

5:24 a.m.

Dear Marla,

Okay, I'm writing. Breathing, writing, writing, breathing. If I weren't carving these words with a ballpoint pen into these pages right now, I'm afraid I'd be carving my initials into Dannika's little line-free forehead. (Side note: she's twenty-eight. Why doesn't she have a single wrinkle?)

I'll back up a little, tell you what happened. Maybe writing will calm me down and cool this dangerous mood I'm in.

After Mom made hamburgers for Coop and me, offering Dannika a handful of carrot sticks and a bruised apple as her vegetarian option (I was half mortified, half exhilarated by

Mom's rudeness) the issue of sleeping arrangements came up. You and I spent most of our time at your house, of course, since you had a better stereo system and your parental units didn't fight; then again, yours didn't speak to each other, but that's another story. The point is, maybe you don't remember my Mom's house much, so I'll give you a minirefresher course: it's small. When you factor in the ever-mounting collection of dogs and Steven's fascination with at-home exercise equipment, it's a wonder the two of them can even move around in there.

But you know my mom—forever the optimist. I think Coop had her thinking she was Scarlet O'Hara, living in a house with an east and west wing, wearing a satin gown and petticoats. After dinner, she graciously offered to show us to our rooms. I was thinking *rooms?* Did they slap together an addition since Christmas? Clearly, she was a little befuddled, because she led us down the hallway to my old room, opened the door, and said, "Oh." I guess at this point it occurred to her that:

a) She did not have "rooms" to offer us but *a* room.
b) It hardly seemed appropriate to shove all three of us into the double bed where I'd lost my first tooth.
c) She was not, in point of fact, Scarlet O'Hara.

There was an awkward pause.

"This is great," Coop said, sizing up the situation with

remarkable speed and accuracy. "The girls can have this room and I'll take the couch."

I was torn between loving Coop's mother-friendly ways and hating that he'd just condemned me to a night in bed with Dannika. It was torture, but there was no way around it. I comforted myself with the reminder that Mom and Steven sleep like logs, so I could always sneak out to the couch after lights-out. I told myself it might even be more fun that way—more high school.

So, Mom made Coop a cozy little bed on the dog hair-covered couch and gave him her best down pillow dressed in a fresh flannel case. We all brushed our teeth, washed our faces, said good night, and by eleven everyone was in bed.

It was very strange, getting under the covers with Dannika. As we lay together side by side in the dark, I felt weirdly self-conscious. Worse, I worried she could tell I was lying there stiffly, staring at the ceiling, too awkward for sleep. I became painfully aware of my own breathing and the placement of my body in relation to hers.

After a few minutes of this, she turned onto her side so she was facing me. "This was your room?"

"Yeah." I remained flat on my back, staring into the darkness. "We moved here when I was four."

"Does your dad always wear that beret?"

"He's not my dad," I said quickly.

"Oh—stepdad?"

"Yeah."

Her tone was gentle. "So your parents are divorced?"

"Yes." The word hung there between us, awkward in its brevity. I knew my lines. I was supposed to give a quick synopsis of my parent's messy breakup, explain my father's whereabouts and marital status, maybe throw in a cliché about how it had all worked out for the best. I just wasn't up to it. Things hadn't worked out for the best. My father was a sad Peter Pan who couldn't keep it in his pants and he'd broken my mother's heart. After he left her, she'd settled for a pedantic, weird, financially unstable shithead in a stupid beret; he was unattractive in just about every way and therefore totally safe. That was the naked truth—or part of it, anyway. I couldn't see delving into all of that with Dannika, who had so far proven herself about as trustworthy as an ill-tempered rattlesnake.

"You don't want to talk about it," Dannika said.

I sighed. "Not especially."

"My family's way fucked up, if it's any consolation."

For some reason the phrase, *keep your friends close, your enemies closer* popped into my brain. I wasn't in the mood to spill my family secrets, but if she felt like talking, the least I could do was listen. "What are they like?" I asked.

"Well, my dad's dead. That's the most important thing to know about him." Her voice was distant, removed, like she was narrating someone else's story. "Then Mom married a plastic surgeon in Malibu. She went from waiting tables at Denny's and clipping coupons to spending every Christmas in the Swiss Alps." She made a breathy sound of disdain. "But she's not happy."

I wanted to ask if her stepfather had done her boob job, but I bit my tongue. "I guess everyone's family is weird." I sort of hoped that would end the conversation on a benign we're-all-human note, at which point I could dash out to the couch and have sneaky don't-wake-the-parents sex with Coop, but Dannika wasn't done with me yet.

"Where's your real dad?" she asked.

"He lives farther north," I said.

"Like where?"

Why was she asking all these questions? "Outside Fort Bragg."

She sat up on one elbow. "Isn't that where we're going?"

"Pretty much," I said.

"Are you going to see him?"

I turned onto my side, my back to her. "No. There won't be time."

"I'm sure we could, if you wanted."

"No." It came out louder than I meant it to. "I mean— whatever—we're not that close. I don't plan on telling him I'm there."

She lay back down and neither of us spoke for a minute, but I could tell she was thinking about what to say next. "The thing is," she whispered. "No matter how messed up he is, once he's dead, it's like *game over,* you know? You don't get another chance to work it out."

I didn't respond.

"Not that it's any of my business," she added.

When I still didn't say anything, she fluffed up her pillow and said, "Well, good night. Sweet dreams."

"Yeah," I mumbled. "You, too."

I didn't have sweet dreams. I fell into a chaotic montage with a plot as linear as a French film; every image was cryptic, yet inexplicably melancholy. There was my father in a wool sweater, smoking a joint; then there was Coop, riding a bike away from me. At the same time it wasn't Coop, it was my father, and though there were a hundred other pictures that sluiced through my brain like cards being shuffled (Dannika in fur boots and an Eskimo parka, my third grade teacher getting mad because I'd thrown away my milk) the dream kept circling back to that strange duet between my father and Coop. What does it mean? I've got no idea. And I won't subject you to any more of it because we both know there's nothing more tedious than having to hear about someone else's dreams.

The point is, I woke up sweaty and disoriented. The dream had filled me with a potent cocktail of sadness and dread. It took me a good ten or twenty seconds to remember where I was. A quick glance at the clock told me it was almost four. Miraculously, I'd fallen asleep before I could sneak out to Coop on the couch and surprise him with a stealthy seduction. My dreams had drained me of any desire for sex; now all I wanted was to curl inside the hot, protective circle of his arms.

That's when I realized: beside me, where Dannika should have been, there was nothing but the wrinkled expanse of sheets and blankets.

I felt my heart throbbing in my throat.

I got up and, very quietly, tiptoed into the living room, listening all the while for sounds of betrayal: muffled giggles or amorous sighs coming from the vicinity of the couch. All I heard was the toilet running and the phlegmy rattle of Steven's snores. As I stepped out of the hallway into the living room, I spotted the empty couch, and for a split second I could picture them with terrible clarity stretched out in the backseat of the Mercury; Dannika would be on her back, her hair splayed out in a white-blond fan that spilled over the edge of the seat. Coop would be above her, sweating and— Oh God, it made me want to heave just thinking about it.

That's when I heard the low murmur of voices and saw an orange flame flicker to life out on the porch. I crept to the edge of the sliding glass doors and, hiding behind Mom's ailing ficus, managed to spy on them through the sickly yellow leaves. It wasn't very gratifying. The moonlight was weak, and through the double-paned glass all I could make out was the vague sound of their voices.

A part of me really wanted to go out there. I missed Coop, suddenly—craved him with a bone-deep need even though I was furious with him. I didn't know exactly what his crime was; couldn't he hang out with his best friend in the middle of the night on my mother's porch? All the same, I felt betrayed. I wondered how it had happened. Did Dannika slip out of bed and wake him? Did he knock softly on our door and she was the one who answered? Or were their internal clocks so perfectly synced up, even their insomnia happened simultaneously?

Obviously, I couldn't go out there. It was just too humiliating. I'd feel like the naggy wife. I flashed on a memory that made my already anxious stomach churn with nerves. We were having dinner in this very house. My mother had cooked pot roast and mashed potatoes. Our guest was a woman with flaming red hair and earrings that caught the light, casting prisms onto her neck and shoulders like some sort of faerie queen. She was beautiful, and I hated her. I don't know who she was or what she was doing there, but I remember how she and Dad kept laughing and raising their glasses in toasts while my mother cleared the dishes and scowled. I remember looking at the wine in their glasses and imagining it was blood; I told you I was morbid. Again and again, I wished the woman with the copious red hair would just put down her fork and leave. She hadn't eaten enough of her dinner to deserve dessert. The roast still sat on her plate, a meaty pink, barely touched.

God, the things my mother went through, all in the name of keeping my restless, self-absorbed father from leaving.

Nothing she did worked. She could go on cooking pot roasts and ignoring his flirtations, she could give him his freedom, his "open marriage," but none of it made any difference. He was a man made for leaving and in the end that's exactly what he did.

Thinking of all this, my stomach knotted inside me, as if my mother's burger was preparing to turn on me. Maybe it was mad cow, I thought. Soon I'd be scratching wildly—wasn't that the first sign? Maybe Dannika had the right idea, living on roots and soy products. I pinched my thighs, feeling fleshy as I monitored her slim shadow bent near Coop's, the two of them leaning against the porch railing side by side. I watched a single plume of smoke snake through the watery moonlight, rising between them; it was impossible to tell if it had come from his lips or hers. What were they talking about, anyway? It was that deeply intimate time of night—the last hours before dawn—when the specter of death touches everything and you'll cling to whatever's near. Especially, I thought, if it happens to be a glamorous, pencil-thin sex goddess with pneumatic boobs.

Suddenly they turned toward the sliding glass doors and I felt a brand-new panic rise inside me—could they see me? I shrank farther into the shadows of the ficus, pressing myself into the corner. Then I heard footsteps out on the porch. Peeking through the branches, I saw them heading straight for me. Oh God—oh *God*—I stumbled back toward the hallway. As the doors slid open behind me, my foot caught the edge of Steven's ab machine and I sprawled onto the carpet.

"G? You okay?" Coop was kneeling beside me. "Danni, turn on a light, would you?"

In a matter of seconds, the merciless glare of track lights illuminated my shame. I wanted to curl into a fetal ball and will myself dead.

Coop helped me sit up. He brushed a few strands of hair out of my eyes with surprising tenderness. "You okay?"

"Yeah." I blinked a little in the bright room, hoping to appear half asleep and vulnerable. "I got up for a glass of water and I guess I tripped." It was a fairly ineffectual lie, flimsy as cellophane, but I knew it would make the moment pass more quickly than a confession.

Coop chuckled with the indulgence one usually reserves for toddlers and kissed my forehead. "You poor thing," he said, helping me up. "Did you bruise anything?"

I looked down at myself. I was wearing that whisper-pink satin nightgown I bought from the Countess of Albania— remember her? Under normal circumstances, I thought it guaranteed me Alluring Siren of the Night status, but at the moment I was struck by just how many acres of chubby thigh it revealed. My knees were rug-burned and I thought I could see the beginnings of a potbelly protruding from beneath the satin drape.

Coop lifted my chin with one finger and looked into my eyes. "Kitten, are you all right?"

To my horror, seeing his warm, hazel eyes studying me with such sweet concern made my bottom lip quiver. Instead of answering, I looked instinctively over at Dannika, who was standing across the room watching us with her arms folded over her chest. Our eyes met and hers were icy-cold, glinting at me with a look I can only describe as hateful.

The second Coop glanced over his shoulder at her, though, her expression lost all rancor and transformed into a bland innocence.

"Hey, Danni," he said, "mind if I talk with Gwen a minute?"

She shrugged. "Course not. I was going to bed, anyway." She unzipped her sweatshirt and took it off, revealing a filmy little lime-green tank top that showed off her perky nipples shamelessly. "Don't stay up all night." She winked at me with a coy grin, then padded past us and was swallowed whole by the shadows of the hallway.

Coop led me to the couch and we sat down together. I could smell smoke on him, but it wasn't his usual chocolaty pipe smoke smell. I sniffed again. "Were you smoking pot?"

He nodded. "Uh-huh."

Just like that—like it was the most natural thing in the world. He's never smoked pot around me, but there he was, acting like it was no big deal.

"Does that bug you?" he added, when he saw my expression.

"No, I just—I didn't know you smoked. Pot, I mean. Do you?"

"Sure, I used to."

"What, like in college?" I told myself to stop sounding like his mother.

"Yeah, mostly. These days I don't buy it, but when someone has it, I don't mind sampling."

"Is it Dannika's, then?"

He nodded. "She always has the best shit money can buy."

I was wondering why she hadn't gotten rid of it when she unloaded the coke earlier tonight. If the cop freaked her out so thoroughly, wouldn't she just toss everything?

Coop put a finger in between my eyebrows, smoothing the lines there gently. "What's with the furrowed brow, kitten?"

"Um…" I didn't want to mention the coke, for some reason. God knows I had no reason to keep secrets for the girl, but somehow it just seemed wrong. "I was just wondering, wasn't she worried when the cop showed up? I mean, what if he'd searched the car?"

"She's got a medical card."

"Like, medical marijuana?"

"Yeah."

"Does she have…a disease or something?" I tried to keep the hopeful edge out of my voice.

He grinned. "No, not really. She just got some doctor to give her a card, like for migraines, or something." He studied me for a moment. "Is that what's bothering you, us smoking herb?"

Why should I be bothered, Coop? So what if you're sneaking off at a quarter to four in the morning, indulging in illicit substances with a perky-nippled supermodel? Why should that worry me? "Nothing's bothering me."

He scooted closer to me. "Come on, kitten. What is it?"

"I just miss you, I guess." I shot him a sideways glance and wished I'd remembered to brush my teeth. "I'm used to having you all to myself."

He nuzzled my neck. "I'm all yours, now."

I turned toward him and he kissed me. Maybe it was the dangerous taste of illegal substances, but when his tongue touched mine a white-hot vein of electricity moved through my bones and I was instantly aroused.

"Have I been neglecting you?" His hand moved over the satin bodice of my nightgown and all the angry confusion that had been running wild in my system for the past twenty hours dissolved like sugar in hot coffee.

"Not really," I mumbled, barely able to get the words out before he kissed me again.

"I know you're high maintenance," he teased as he kissed my neck slowly. I couldn't help sighing in decadent pleasure. His thumb moved over my nipple and I have to say at the moment it was perky enough to rival even Boob-Job-Blonde's. "You need constant supervision." He was speaking in that bad-daddy tone that undoes me.

Abruptly, he pulled back and searched my face like it contained an elusive code he intended to crack. "Really though, Gwen, are you okay? You seem a little…uneasy."

Reluctant to come back to earth, I closed my eyes again and whispered, "At the moment, I'm perfectly at ease." I tilted my face toward him, offering my lips to be kissed.

Still, he hesitated. "You sure wrote a lot today. What was that all about?"

"Just—you know—recording my thoughts."

"You're not mad or anything?"

"Not right now." I was being straight with him; it's amazing how a rush of blood to the erogenous zones can completely negate even the powerful force of psychotic jealousy. Hormonal distraction never lasts, but what the hell? I'll take my delusions where I can get them.

Evidently, Coop agreed, because he bent down and kissed me with his whole mouth, probing my teeth with his tongue. When the kiss ended, he leaned in to the curve of my neck and sunk his teeth into the sensitive spot right above my clavicle. He knows that makes me totally insane. I squirmed against him, stifling a squeal.

He looked up at me through his lashes with a sly, wolfish grin. "It's been too long."

I laughed. "You're telling me. When was the last time? Tuesday?"

He pressed against me until I was flat on my back on the couch. "You wicked girl," he said. "You've been intentionally driving me wild with those little outfits of yours."

"What 'little outfits?'" I pretended to be indignant.

"Your adorable travel suit and now—" he ran a finger

along the crease of my cleavage, letting it trail under the plunging neckline of my nightgown "—this little number."

Duly noted: travel ensembles a smashing success!

He slipped one hand under the elastic of my underwear and explored the warm, fleshy wetness of—

God, do you really want all these details? Actually, I know you, and the answer is a gleaming-eyed, greedy little yes. I can just see you sitting in your *trés* chic Parisian café, devouring this notebook like it's one of your coffee-stained, dog-eared bodice-rippers with a horribly seventies-esque Fabio flexing on the cover. Just don't expect any throbbing members or secret clefts of womanhood, here. It's all anatomically accurate in my world.

"For your information," I told him, trying not to cry out as his finger pushed easily inside me. "I am a fashion professional and I choose my clothing not to drive men wild, but to revive the aesthetic impulses of a bygone er—" But I couldn't finish my sentence. He was spreading my thighs and the warm, damp curve of his tongue against my flesh made it impossible to conjugate verbs.

I closed my eyes. Colors streaked around in a psychedelic light show under my eyelids. Surrendering to Coop's mouth is like Venice tiramisu, a bottle of Mumm de Cramant, and the first morning of summer vacation, all rolled into one. As his tongue worked its magic, I eased my fingers into the dark nest of his hair and pulled gently, murmuring, "Oh God, Coop," under my breath.

Just as I was starting to pant and sweat, he slid his tongue up the center of my belly, over my navel, between my breasts, pushing my nightgown aside and kissing me hard on the mouth. I could taste myself on his lips and in the hot wetness of his tongue; it was a strange, intoxicating flavor— the tang of my body mixing with the heat of his.

When I pulled his shirt off, he produced a condom from his wallet and sat it carefully on the arm of the couch. I watched the muscles of his back, sweaty and glistening as the track lights pooled on the glossy surface of his shoulder blades. I just couldn't believe I was actually with this guy— he was so made to order—with his rock-star hair and his cut shoulders. Why would he bother with me when he could have the bionic blonde?

Before I could muddy the moment with worry, he unbuttoned his fly and dropped his jeans to the floor. I sat there Indian-style on the couch and he touched my hair with the tips of his fingers; I pulled his boxers down slowly and slipped his—okay, okay!—his throbbing member between my lips. I glanced up to see how I was doing and his eyes were closed in a look of total bliss. I slipped him in and out of my mouth until he was slick with saliva, glistening and hard, plum-colored. I've never really considered anyone's cock beautiful, but Coop's is different. Usually, sex is such a tense transaction for me, I'm just happy if it's not gherkin-sized or flaccid. With Coop, I feel like I could fondle and caress it forever. The first time I saw it, I remember thinking, *this is the one.* Isn't that weird? Like I'd been looking for something and I didn't even know it until right then.

After a long, slow blow job, he let out a soft groan and bent over me, searing my mouth with another famished kiss. The next thing I knew the condom was on and he was inside me, the full length of him pushing in, deeper, moving slowly, watching my face like he wanted to memorize every inch of it. I leaned back against the cushions of the couch and smiled with dizzy pleasure as I felt my body making way for him, yielding like warm river sand. Outside, one of the neighbor's dogs howled and a gust of wind rattled the sliding glass doors. I could still hear Steven snoring his long, rattling snores, but I tried not to think about that. I wanted to tell Coop something—I didn't know what. I ached for words as nuanced and delicate as what he made me feel, but my lips wouldn't cooperate and it was too late for talking, anyway.

He kept moving, faster now, finding his rhythm, pushing against me and into me, his eyes closed in concentration. I felt the familiar climb, the roller coaster slowly cresting the hill, one excruciating moment building on the next, and then the drop was visible, the plunge just around the bend, and his moan unleashed a great white heat inside me. My mother's house flew apart in a blinding flash and in my head the scream I let out was primal, electric, terrifying, but the sound that actually slipped through my parted lips was barely more than a breathy little gasp.

★ ★ ★

Just so you know, I'll probably take a Sharpie to all the above before sending this. It'll look like World War II correspondence after the censors had a crack at it. Don't take this the wrong way, but at this point you've become sort of irrelevant. I mean writing all this down is starting to transcend the usual aim of a letter—to entertain or inform or whatever. Now it's therapy, and we're talking high-crisis treatment like shaved heads and electric shock. When you handed me this notebook I thought the whole idea was pretty daft, but now I see the method to your madness; if I weren't committing this shit to paper, someone would have been hospitalized by now and there's a good chance that someone would be me.

At the risk of sounding presumptuous, I know what you're thinking. *How did Gwen go from a blinding orgasm to nearly carving her initials into Dannika's annoyingly wrinkle-free forehead?*

I'm getting to that.

Coop and I had a quick, post-coital snooze. I awoke to the sound of a flushing toilet and figured I should get back to the bedroom for appearance's sake. It's not like my mom thinks I'm a virgin and certainly Steven's got nothing to say about what goes on in this house, but waking up to my mother's coffee grinder with the smell of recent sex still hanging in the air just sounded a little creepy. So I kissed Coop gently, left him there unconscious and slipped back into the bedroom.

To my surprise, Dannika was bent backward like a horse-shoe, balancing precariously on her hands and feet. She didn't acknowledge me as I came into the room, she just morphed effortlessly from the horseshoe shape into a one-legged balance pose, her hands folded as if in prayer. The clock on the nightstand read four fifty-eight.

"Morning," I said.

"Hi," Dannika whispered, but her tone said don't-bother-me-now-I'm-becoming-enlightened, so I didn't make another attempt at conversation. Instead I crawled back under the covers. I was hoping to catch at least two hours of blissful, post-orgasmic sleep. I lay there flat on my back, eyes closed, my body so pliable and relaxed I felt like a stick of butter that's been softened in the microwave. The river of semi-consciousness was pulling me along, getting ready to release me into the open ocean of dreams, when I heard a little voice saying, "He's pretty good, isn't he?"

My eyes fluttered open. For a second, I thought it was one of those weird hallucinations of half-sleep, but then she spoke again.

"I've been with plenty of men and I have to say, Coop's in a class all his own."

Forget fluttering—my eyes popped open and my head snapped to the left. "What did you say?"

She was on the bed beside me, lying on her back outside of the covers, hugging her knees to her chest. "I'm sorry—were you trying to sleep?"

"Not really." I sat up. "What were you saying?"

Her pink lips formed a pert little *O* of surprise. "Shit, he didn't tell you, did he?"

I winced involuntarily. "Tell me what?"

"No—God, I'm such an idiot—forget I said anything. I totally assumed you guys had talked about it."

"Talked about what?" I was speaking through clenched teeth. I forced myself to relax my jaw.

"Just—you know—our history." She released her hold on her legs and sat up beside me, leaning against the pink satin headboard of my childhood. "It was such a long time ago. I never should have mentioned it."

"Can you be a little more specific?" I was having an uncomfortable déjà vu; weren't we having this conversation just before Officer John-Boy appeared on the scene? How many times did she intend to torture me with vague allusions to their sexual past?

"Well, if he didn't tell you, I probably shouldn't."

I fixed her with my stare. "Get real. You have to."

She sighed and swept her hair into a waterfall that cascaded gracefully over her sculpted shoulder. "It was one hot week, that's all." She paused. "Are you sure you want to hear this?"

"Go on," I said, feeling masochistic.

She massaged her neck and gazed into space, remembering. "We were twenty-four, both in the midst of a quarter-life-crisis. It was before I started my yoga studio, and I was still trying to use my degree—marine biology, totally useless at the B.S. level in the real world. Everyone thinks majoring in science is practical, but what are you going to do when you graduate? Unless you want to move to bum-fuck Canada and work for some dick with a piss-poor grant, taking notes on sea cucumbers, forget it."

She glanced at me, and I have a feeling my expression was not exactly sympathetic.

"Anyway," she said, "I was in crisis mode and he was dating some girl. What was her name?" She studied the ceiling. "Victoria, I think. He wasn't happy. She was hearing wedding bells, but he just wasn't into it. We house-sat for my mom in Malibu and—" she licked her lips, a wicked grin taking over "—had a totally amazing time." She stared into the distance, lost in a private reverie. "The guy's incredible," she said, more to herself than to me. Then, as if suddenly remembering my presence, she patted my leg like a chummy aunt offering advice. "The point is, you're a very lucky girl. And I speak from experience."

"Why did it only last a week?" My voice sounded surprisingly steady.

She waved a hand dismissively. "Oh, he felt guilty about Vicky, for one thing. He tried to make it up to her by pretending nothing had happened. Plus, I didn't have my shit together. I moved to Spain for a couple months and had a torrid affair with a sculptor who was old enough to be my father." She cast another wistful glance at the ceiling. "Coop and I had really hot chemistry, but our timing sucked."

I studied my lap, smoothing my nightgown. "Did you ever think about getting back together?"

She sighed. "Oh, sure, we toyed with the idea. But somehow the timing was always off—it's our curse, I guess. And then there was the whole honesty issue."

When she didn't elaborate, I croaked, "Honesty issue?"

Folding her legs into lotus position, she studied my face. "Here's the thing, Gwen, and I only say this because I like you and I think you deserve to have all the information up front: Coop's great in bed, but he's not the best communicator. If you ask him about our past, he'll deny it. That's just the way he is. He thinks it's better to offer someone comfort than to slap them with the truth. He never told Vicky about us—in fact, I'm sure he's never told anyone. He's into revisionist history. If you can deal with that, you can deal with Coop, but for me the whole thing was just a little too slippery." She grinned. "As lovers, I mean. As friends, it doesn't really matter. He can sleep with whoever he wants and lie about it till he's blue in the face—it's none of my business, so what do I care?"

I felt like she'd punched me in the solar plexus.

Her hand reached out and rested on my shoulder. "I hope I haven't upset you," she said. "I just think you should know what you're getting into."

"Sure," I managed to mumble. "I appreciate that."

"I'm going to do a few sun salutations. Do you want to join me?" Her offer was all sweetness and light. "It's a great way to greet the day."

"No, thanks," I said. "I'm going to write for a while."

"You sure do write a lot, don't you?"

"It's a new thing," I told her, lunging for my notebook like an alcoholic going for the bottle. "It relaxes me."

The roosters are crowing. Sun is streaming through my bedroom windows, illuminating the accumulated cobwebs and muddy paw prints on the glass. Dannika is taking a long shower, which no doubt pisses Steven off, who guards the house's finances with stingy diligence. It gives me a tepid surge of pleasure knowing Dannika's irritating the shit out of someone else for once. I can hear Coop in the kitchen chatting up my mom, offering to help with breakfast, complimenting her coffee.

I can't decide who I hate more right now: Coop for wrapping me in a cotton-candy confection of lies or Dannika for turning my pink cloud into a sticky, gritty mess.

I considered catching a plane back to L.A this morning, but I've decided to see this trip through to the end.

From here on out, I'm in it for the revenge.

9:04 a.m.

Dear Marla,

First, a fashion update.

The magic words today are understated, fetching, femme fatale. It's neither the first day of the trip (which requires more fortitude and formality) nor is it the day of the wedding (for which I've reserved my secret weapon, to be revealed at a later date, i.e. tomorrow). Thus, I've carefully chosen my elegant shirtwaist dress in off-white acetate rayon with French cuffs, rhinestone-jeweled buttons and matching cufflinks set off by bracelet-length sleeves. I've got a string of pearls at my throat, cat-eyed sunglasses with rhinestone details and, of course, my signature leopard-print kitten heels. Over my shoulders I've draped my favorite Norwegian blue-fox stole, which I'll admit seemed a touch dressy for the occasion, but I couldn't resist its silky depths once I dared to try it on. All in all, I'm perfectly prepared for the weather here in the backseat which is, frankly, cold as shit.

While arctic winds blast us with gale force, the sun is shining and the sky is a clear, cloudless blue. Dannika won this morning when she sweetly suggested we continue on our coastal route. We were eating eggs and bacon—well, I should qualify that. Coop and Mom were shoveling in eggs and bacon, I was toying with mine, Steven was drinking coffee, gazing at Dannika with puppy-dog eyes, and Dannika was eating a banana and sipping her peppermint tea. She said, "I guess we'll stay on the coast, since we're so close."

My mother looked at her with cold eyes and a tight smile. "Honey, you don't want to take the coast. That road winds around so much, it'll take forever."

Dannika smiled back, her eyes equally hostile. "I know. I like it that way."

"Well, it might be fine for the driver," Mom said. "But whoever's in the back is going to be sick as a dog. The curves on that highway make me queasy just looking at them."

First, Coop looked at me, then Mom did, followed by Steven. Dannika just stared into her peppermint tea.

"I don't get carsick," I said, looking at Mom. "You know that."

Mom was right, though—a lesser woman would be puking up her three bites of scrambled eggs, half a piece of bacon and coffee by now. I guess it's a minor miracle that I'm so immune to motion sickness I can write to you back here and not get nauseous at all. Of course, it's a little hard to concentrate when I'm having a near-death experience every time we hit a curve; Dannika's driving has not improved overnight. But in some ways, I'm glad we chose this route. This stretch of highway is mind-blowingly scenic. To our left, the ocean is sparkling in the sun like a sheet of crumpled tinfoil, and when we rise up on a dramatic cliff and get a glimpse of the panoramic view, it feels like we're skirting the edge of the world. Also, I needed the extra car time to mull things over.

Coop keeps turning around in his seat, flashing me his secret little crooked grin and reaching over to give my knee an affectionate squeeze. Sometimes he lets his fingers slip under the hem of my dress and graze my thigh suggestively. He's so incredibly sexy. Why does he have to be the only man I've ever met who's perfect in every way? (For now, let's table the alleged tendency toward pathological lies.) Even the things that shouldn't be perfect become perfect on him. I mean, just look at his hair—it's a mess. Why do I adore that mess? When he wears something mildly stupid, like the faded, threadbare The Nerve Agents T-shirt he's got on today, I swoon. Why? I'm the woman who said I could never love a man who didn't wear cufflinks and a flannel suit at least five days a week. Do you think Coop has ever worn cufflinks or a flannel suit? Yeah, right. Coop's idea of dressing up is tucking his T-shirt into his jeans.

Oh God, Marla, I'm so confused. Who am I even talking about? The Coop I'm thinking of—the one I kissed for the first time on Venice Beach, the one I had sex with this morning—is now dead. Dannika killed him when she touched my arm and said in that pious, condescending tone, "I just think you should know what you're getting into."

I abhor dishonesty. You know that. No one's ever cheated on me because I refuse to give them the opportunity. The slightest indication of a wandering eye or a spotty relationship résumé and I'm out of there. And yes, in the past, I'll admit I had a tendency toward hair-trigger responses. My shithead radar was, perhaps, a little too finicky and subject to faulty readings. Sometimes my tactics were downright preemptive. But even by normal standards, the information Dannika dumped in my lap this morning should have sent me screaming back to L.A. He was practically married to Vicky—who I've never even *heard* of, by the way—when he spent a week filled with searing-hot yogi sex in Malibu. And then (you know this is the sin among sins, for me) he didn't even fess up. He went on pretending nothing had happened, when he knew the girl was aching to walk down the aisle in a big, poofy meringue of a dress.

So by my own logic, I shouldn't be here. I should be back

in my apartment in Los Feliz, ripping up pictures of Coop and getting slowly hammered on dirty martinis.

But I'm not. See, that's the weird thing. And I have to wonder, is this how it happens? Is this the first step down the slippery slope of *I know he's an asshole, but I love him?* You know when you see women in airports or malls or—oh, say, a dog hair-infested house in western Sebastopol—who are married to men so much beastlier than themselves, you're forced to wonder if they've been subjected to some bizarre form of hypnosis? Maybe it's not hypnosis at all, but the systematic denial of facts due to excessive amounts of whatever-that-chemical-is-in-orgasms-and-chocolate flooding your bloodstream.

I'm beginning to think this is how it goes: You're crazy about someone. You discover a skeleton in his closet; maybe it's a week in Malibu, maybe it's a history of recreational cannibalism. The details are unimportant. The point is, you discover that your prince charming is flawed—not leaving-his-boxers-on-the-bathroom-floor flawed, but flawed in a way that threatens the very fiber of your being. What do you do? Flee like a sensible girl? Hatch a diabolical plan that will humiliate him in front of all womankind, thus making it impossible for him to have sex even with the bucktoothed checker at Wal-Mart? No, you don't. Because you're in love. So you tell yourself his tendency to gnaw on human femurs is endearing or the week in Malibu was just a blip and you go on as if nothing's happened. And the next time, when even more damning and repugnant evidence bobs to the surface, you continue to tell yourself that love is about forgiveness and compromise and, yes, your coffee table is made of human bones and okay so you had to sacrifice your left forearm, but what's so wrong with that, if you're really nuts about the guy?

You see, I'm inching into dangerous territory, here, but I can't seem to stop myself. Riding behind Coop under a brilliant blue sky, I'm horrified to discover that I still want him. I could try to tell you it's just my body responding to the sight of him—a stupid, hormonal reaction to his cheekbones and his eyebrows, his sensual, full lips—but I'd be lying. The feelings I have for Coop run all the way down to the chemical makeup of my toenails, the spongy center of my bones. With guys before him, the very hint of disloyalty turned my affections sour. That's why it was always so easy to bail; once I saw them as scamming womanizers (whether or not they were), I didn't even crave them anymore. Remember Tom Jepson, the lawyer with the Porsche and the cat and the gorgeous flannel suits? I was so into him, but the minute I learned he'd cheated on his ex-wife, I was out of there. Amazingly, I suffered no withdrawals, even with him. I could kick the habit of any man cold turkey as soon as he gave me the slightest reason.

I'm afraid those days are gone. Right now, watching Coop's hair blow this way and that in a wild tussle of brown and dark honey hues, my heart's aching. I always thought that was just a figure of speech, not a physical sensation, but watching his profile, I can feel this dull pain inside my rib cage, like my heart is swollen and throbbing in the too-tight space. My mind is spinning with images of Coop and Dannika. I see him leaning in to kiss her in front of a massive stone fireplace. I see him gazing at her sundappled face as she sleeps, brushing his fingers lightly along her peach-colored cheek. I watch their limbs intertwine as they make out in the frothy Malibu surf like the black-and-white models of a Calvin Klein perfume ad.

Coop just turned around and said, "Kitten, you're going to rip the paper if you keep pressing so hard."

I offered a faux-serene smile. "Almost out of ink, I guess."

"Looks like you're almost out of pages, too."

He's right. I've already burned my way through all but two pages of the journal you gave me. And why is that? Because if I don't, there's going to be blood on my hands. Blonde blood. Every once in a while I try to comfort myself with the words *Donna Horney,* but they don't help. If anything, her tragic past, her ability to transform herself so thoroughly, only makes her a more formidable foe. Besides, the problem now transcends Dannika and her perfect size-two ass. The problem now is epic. I'm grappling with Coop's fundamental ability to be honest. If Dannika's story is true, Coop is alarmingly capable of deceit—not just capable, but good at it. To date a liar is one thing, but to date a master liar is to find yourself in the worst sort of paranoid schizophrenic hell. Those sort of men make you doubt your own name—they make you second guess your very existence. You and I have both dated enough actors to know just how treacherous trained liars can be.

I know what you're going to say. *What if Dannika's the one who's lying?*

There you are, sitting in your Parisian café, sipping your third cappuccino. Your eyes are all bugged out from the excess caffeine and you're dying to throttle me for assuming the worst about the man I adore. You're saying, *Jesus, Gwen, get a grip. Should you really believe a girl with silicone tits, bleached-white teeth, $200 highlights, a coke habit and a pseudonym?*

And yes, you have a point. Maybe there was no sizzling week in Malibu. It's possible there wasn't even a Victoria, though I'll bet she's clever enough to have used the name of a girl Coop once dated, even if she exaggerated how serious they were. Maybe Dannika is bent on sabotaging our relationship because she wants him for herself. Or maybe she's just one of those girls who doesn't like to share.

It's possible.

But don't you see, Marla? There's no way to know. If I ask Coop about Dannika's story, he'll deny it, like she said. He's either an amazing liar, in which case there's no hope, or he's perfectly innocent—there's no in between. The only way for me to sniff him out, here, is if he's a bad liar; then I could confront him with Dannika's claims and he would naturally give himself away. He'd be unable to look me in the eye, or I'd catch him on some minor detail as I cross-examined him. But that just can't be. Coop is good at everything he does. If he's a liar, I'm willing to bet money he's a talented one.

Besides, suppose he's innocent? There we are in idyllic Mendocino. Out of nowhere I start ranting about a secret fling he and Dannika supposedly had years ago and some imaginary almost-fiancée he lied to. If it's all fabricated, I'll seem like a jealous, unstable, possessive bitch. Dannika might even deny having told me anything. They could have me wrapped in a straightjacket before the weekend's through. I could be writing my next letter from inside a padded cell.

Marla, help! I'm caught between the proverbial rock and the hard place, flooded with a confusing mixture of rage, doubt and hormones. I'm struggling madly but remain perfectly still, my complete confusion mistaken for vacuous calm.

I have to find out who's lying, and to do so I'll need to work undercover, watching at all times. From behind my cat-eyed, rhinestone-studded glasses, I'll note every move, every twitch, every glance. I'm the spy in kitten heels.

And when I root out my villain, beware....

Stealthily yours,

Matson.

Gwen Matson.

11:11 a.m.

Dear Marla,

We're getting closer to Mendocino—we just passed Gualala, where we stopped for gas and I bought this new, considerably inferior notebook. When I slapped it onto the counter with a backup pen, Coop gave me a funny look. "I had no idea you were such a prolific writer."

"Neither did I." I produced what I hoped was the mysterious smile of a budding artiste and not the mad grin of a neurotic letter addict.

Okay, so my compulsive scribbling is a little weird. I can see that. You set this in motion, Marla, and suddenly I can't stop. I'm fixated on the idea that this weekend will seal my fate and if I don't record every moment of it, like Gretel scattering breadcrumbs, I'll lose my way. I don't even know what that means, exactly, but the thought is haunting me around every curve, through patches of fog and orange bursts of sunlight, through everything.

When Coop first brought up this weekend about a month ago, I believe his exact words were, "Come to Mendocino with me. My best friends are getting hitched."

"To each other?" I'd asked.

"Yeah. What could be better, huh? I only have to use one page for them now in my address book."

I'd been thrilled at the intimacy of the invitation and the casual way he threw it out there, like it was nothing. I got the feeling this would be the first in a long series of such adventures—trips we'd take to celebrate the change of seasons, promotions, anniversaries, whatever the hell we felt like. It would be us out there in the world, together, peeing in grubby gas station bathrooms and discovering perfect little out-of-the-way bakeries with the most amazing chocolate chip cookies.

Anyway, the point is that this trip took on epic proportions in my mind. I spent long hours at the shop steaming wools and taffetas, dreaming of our romantic getaway to the north coast, land of rugged, remote beaches, pristine redwood forests, supple, satiny wines and patchouli-soaked hippies. I envisioned long walks on the beach in bulky sweaters (well, he'd be in a bulky sweater, I'd be in my elegant wool trapeze coat). The wedding would be packed with beautiful, fresh-faced vegetarians and we'd all throw rice in front of an old-fashioned white clapboard church.

Then one day, about two weeks before we were supposed to leave, Coop was cleaning the burnt crumbs from my toaster when he said, "I talked to Dannika last night."

"Oh," I said brightly. "How is she?" He'd mentioned her enough for my antennae to rise, but I wasn't making sketches of voodoo dolls or anything.

"She's fine. I guess she wants to come up north with us."

I said, "Uh-huh...?" trying hard to sound neutral and open-minded.

"I told her she was welcome to ride up with us, but then this morning she called to say she checked her schedule and she's got to teach at some conference in Ojai that weekend."

"Mmm," I said. "Too bad."

Oh God, if only that stupid guru hadn't died. Then the conference wouldn't have been canceled and she'd be demonstrating downward dog for flabby housewives in Ojai instead of torturing me with her brilliant blondeness. Of course, staying with Coop would mean crossing paths with Dannika eventually, but it would have been nice to drift in ignorant bliss for at least another couple of months.

Sometimes I wish I had a map of my future, something I could stick in my wallet for quick reference. There'd be a roving star with the words You Are Here and then the paths ahead could be viewed in miniature, labeled clearly—a sort of portable GPS tracking device for potential destinies. Eastern route: treacherous self-deception, premature gray, brief marriage with Coop resulting in one child, ugly divorce, insufficient child support and severe emotional scars. Later years involve ungrateful daughter with prescription drug addiction, string of well-meaning but ultimately unfulfilling boyfriends, and untimely death by number-five bus. Western route: Brutal honesty with self and Coop resulting in cathartic breakup, journey to Taos, scorching affair with alcoholic English professor followed by reunion with contrite and reformed Coop. Glamorous, jet-setting life springing naturally from the publication of cowritten relationship book, *Letting Go for Love;* death at age ninety as a result of well-publicized tandem skydiving accident.

Instead I have to stumble forward blindly, getting ambushed by the Dannikas of the world, never knowing what's around the next hairpin turn. Will I like Phil and Joni? More importantly, will they like me? Will this weekend prove to be the first of many for Coop and me or will it be our swan song, our final number before the stage goes black?

Only time will tell,

Gwen

September 19

1:46 p.m.

Dear Marla,

I've completely alienated everyone around me within my first forty minutes on Mendocino soil. This is good. If I stick to this path, I'll be a full-on social pariah by dinnertime.

Coop hates me.

Right, okay, I hear you—back up, calm down, tell you what happened. I will, just let me perform minor oral surgery here to extract my big foot from my even bigger mouth.

So we got here a little after noon, completely famished. I guess being bludgeoned with ice-cold wind for hours works up an appetite. In spite of my ongoing confusion about whether or not I'm sleeping with a liar, I was allowing a thin trickle of optimism to seep into my system, something along the lines of *until he proves himself a total dick, let's have a good time.*

As we came around the corner and caught a postcard-worthy glimpse of Mendocino, I caught my breath in surprise. I haven't been up here for years—since I was a teenager, at least—and the sight of those quaint little weather-beaten pastel buildings holding their own on the wind-ravaged bluffs made me suddenly, unreasonably happy. The layer of clouds above the ocean was sliced into thin wedges like the exposed rib cage of a whale, and that made me happy, too. I looked from the clouds to Coop's dark hair growing ever-messier in the wind and somewhere beyond logic a little flame flickered to life inside me—a tentative promise to myself that everything was going to turn out just fine.

Dannika almost missed the turn, but at Coop's urging she swung a hard right onto Ukiah-Comptche Road and sent us cruising inland. The street was lined on either side with dripping ferns and towering redwoods. There were houses here and there, but most of what I saw as I peered past the huge, hairy trunks was the deeply shadowed world of forest. I rested my chin on Coop's surfboard and squinted at the scenery flying past. I'd forgotten what a fairyland it was up here. Columns of dusty gold sunlight slanted through high branches, illuminating miniature cosmos of frenetic bugs. The farther east we went, the more we got whiffs of warm, oak-scented air competing with the ocean breezes pushing at our backs. I was struck by just how far we were from the sprawling parking lot of L.A. I felt fully immersed in the adventure, then; I wanted nothing more than to make Coop's friends love me and to return home on Sunday with his lifelong devotion tucked into my hatbox for safekeeping.

We drove at least fifteen minutes inland, another ten or so on a narrower side street heading southeast, then spent another twenty navigating a muddy, unpaved route through an even darker, denser forest. In places the road was barely passable and I had to just stare straight ahead and pray we wouldn't plunge down the steep, forested grade that loomed in my peripheral vision. At last we curved our way into a clearing, where lemony sunlight poured lavishly over a small orchard of gnarled apple trees. When I'd stopped breathing dust, my lungs were rewarded with sharp, clean air thick with the sweet, cloying perfume of decaying apples.

We got out of the car, yawning and blinking in the sunlight. Dannika did a somewhat involved series of neck stretches while Coop peed in the apple trees and I applied a coat of lipstick. Next to the orchard there was a two-story house shrouded in nasturtiums, hollyhocks and morning glories. It was a modified A-frame made of redwood, with big glossy windows and upstairs balconies facing north and south. As I took it in, a woman surged through the front door, down the steps and toward us, her reddish-brown dreadlocks bouncing as she moved.

"Joni!" Dannika sprinted for her, almost knocking her over with the force of her hug.

"Hey, girl," I heard Joni say. "Long time no see."

Coop finished peeing, came over and wrapped an arm around me. I shrugged off the mink stole and left it on the backseat, feeling a little self-conscious as my kitten heels made sharp indentations in the soft, damp earth.

"Hey, Cooper—what's going on?" Joni and Coop greeted each other with a long, warm hug; I noticed that she was standing on her tiptoes and he had to crouch down, just like he has to with me. She was short—maybe even shorter than me by an inch or so—and when they pulled away from each other I saw she had a pretty face with well formed cheekbones and rich, caramel-swirled eyes. There was a quarter-sized, beige birthmark on her forehead, but even that looked sort of good on her.

"You must be Gwen." I was relieved when she offered a hand instead of hugging me. I hate it when strangers want to skip the handshake and go straight to the embrace; it's an aspect of California I've never quite gotten used to, even though I'm native. "I'm Joni. Welcome to FUBAR Ranch."

"FUBAR Ranch," I said. "Interesting name."

She rolled her eyes. "Phil's invention. Never hook up with an ex-marine-turned-anarchist."

"Where is he, anyway?" Coop asked.

"In the studio." Joni tilted her head vaguely behind her, to where the dirt road disappeared around a sharp bend. "He should be back any minute. Come on in; I've got lunch."

We filed into the house two by two, Dannika and Joni followed by Coop and me. Dannika was full of animated sounds—girlie squeals and whatnot—touching Joni a lot and making a fuss. I got the general impression that she and Joni weren't really that close and that Dannika was making up for that by being extra solicitous.

"Cool digs, huh?" Coop nudged me, and I nodded.

"Really cool," I agreed. Everything about Joni and Phil's house was deeply bohemian. Even the way it smelled—like yeast and pot, dust bunnies and good coffee—evoked an artistic, rugged, off-the-grid lifestyle. The downstairs had a completely open floor plan. From the entryway we could see four separate living spaces, partitioned artfully with plants, furniture and counters. To our right was a spacious living room filled with ferns and trees and orchids, a cushy red-velvet couch, three huge suede beanbag chairs in buttery yellows and a long, low, tile mosaic coffee table. There was a large counter behind the couch that looked like it was used as a workspace, and behind that was a big pool table surrounded by more cozy chairs and a somewhat abused-looking loveseat. Jutting off to the left was a beautiful kitchen, also cordoned off with work counters, and in front of that was a casual dining room with a big oak table lit by a domed skylight. The hardwood floors were a smooth, satiny amber and there were thick jewel-toned Persian rugs here and there. On the walls were big, colorful paintings of twisting flowers and crooked little beasts that evoked, more than anything, Dr. Seuss. In the center, at the nexus of each separate space, was a wrought-iron spiral staircase curling up to the second floor. It wasn't my style—you know me, I prefer white picket fences and porch swings—but there was no denying that the place had a charm all its own.

"So," Joni said, handing us each a Corona. "How was the drive up?"

"Great," Dannika chirped just as Coop said, "Long."

I smiled weakly, sensing it wasn't wise to add what I was thinking ("Torturous"). Joni caught my eye, though, and a knowing look passed between us. Her golden eyes seemed to say that thirteen hours in a car with Dannika couldn't be easy; I suddenly wanted to hug her, even though minutes earlier I'd been relieved about the handshake.

"Yo, Homes, Dan, whattup?!" A tall, gangly guy in ragged jeans and an orange striped sweater exploded through the back door.

"Scrappy!" Dannika pounced on him, nearly strangling him with her hug. When she released him, he and Coop exchanged a hip, hand-slapping-bicep-squeezing sort of guy greeting.

He turned to me, assessing my outfit with a quizzical once-over. "You gotta be Gwen," he said. "Awesome fucking threads."

"Thanks," I said. "I guess."

He laughed a loud, explosive laugh that was part AK–47, part horse. I couldn't help but smile at that. He was a skinny guy, a little older than the rest of us, and as he pulled off his stocking cap I could see his head was shaved totally bald. He had on horn-rimmed glasses and something about him made me think of Elvis Costello.

Over a delicious lunch of Joni's Thai coconut soup, chopped salad and chicken wings, I listened as they caught up. Joni was writing poetry and teaching a night class at the local community college; Phil was recording bands in his studio, which was only about twenty yards from the house; Dannika told them about her latest DVD and a morning show that was in the works; Coop gave them a modest account of his furniture-making business. Joni asked me questions about my shop and my work in costume design, which I answered between bites.

By the time we got to Joni's incredible chocolate brownies and big, rough-hewn mugs of honey-sweet chai, the catching up was more or less completed—at least, the abridged version—and Dannika started talking about the wedding.

"I just think it's so wonderful that you guys are getting married." She reached over and squeezed Joni's wrist. "At least someone from our circle is taking the plunge. Coop and I will probably be single forever."

I glanced up and saw Phil looking at me. His face was hard

to read; his expression hovered somewhere between sympathy and amusement. "I don't know," he said, turning to Dannika. "Coop's the settling-down type, if you ask me."

Coop's eyebrows arched. "I'm right here. No need to use the third person."

"Seriously, man. I can totally see it: you got the pipe, all you need now is a worn-out pair of slippers."

Dannika laughed. "Yeah, and a girl who'll put up with you." Her eyes slid over me dismissively.

Coop squeezed my knee under the table, changed the subject. "You guys got everything set for tomorrow?" he asked Joni and Phil. "Need any errands run?"

Joni shook her head. "It's okay. We've got it under control."

"What I don't understand," said Dannika, "is why you guys decided to actually get *married*—like, legally. I mean, don't get me wrong—I'm not criticizing—I just thought you were sort of against the institution or whatever, back in college."

Phil downed the last of his brownie. "We figured, what the hell, you know? We like to party, we want to bring our friends together, why not just go for it? Plus, we want to pop out a kid or two…."

Joni started clearing the dishes.

Dannika made a high-pitched sound of delight. "Really? That's so exciting!"

Phil watched Joni's back as she stood at the sink. "Yeah. We're pretty excited."

Dannika jumped up from her chair and bounded over to Joni, squeezed her tightly. "That's so great, Joni! You're going to be a mom!"

"Well, someday." She allowed herself to be hugged, but as soon as she was released she turned back to the dishes. "We're not sure when, exactly."

Coop said, "The important thing is, we get to party tomorrow and Scrappy here's got to buy the champagne."

"Yeah. I paid good money for that shit and I don't even drink it. Does Jackie O here smoke?" He jutted his chin in my direction. I might have been insulted, except that behind his horn-rimmed glasses his eyes glittered with impish affection.

Coop wrapped an arm around me. "She travels with her own cigarette holder, but no, she doesn't smoke."

Joni laughed as she came back to the table for more dishes. "I love your style," she said to me. "You're like a walking anachronism."

It was a relief that Phil and Joni didn't mind talking about my attire. Often, my clothes make people uncomfortable— I know that. It's impossible to walk into a room and say, "Hey, I'm Gwen and all my clothes were created between 1952 and 1963. No, you can't touch my mink. What's your name?"

"Coop," Phil said, standing and pulling a pack of American Spirits from the pocket of his baggy jeans. "Let's go." He jerked his head toward the kitchen door.

"No way!" Coop shot a look of disbelief at Joni. "You finally got Scrappy to smoke outside?"

"It was gross." She made a face. "Our house smelled like a bar."

"Now you can't even smoke in the damn bars!" Phil tapped a cigarette out of the pack and stuck it between his lips. "You coming, or what?"

Coop put on his coat and foraged in his pocket until he produced his pipe and tobacco. "Yeah, yeah, yeah, just relax."

Dannika put her fork down and stood up. "Anyone want to smoke a bowl?"

Phil cackled. "That's my Dan. Sure, it's only—" he glanced at the clock "—one o'clock, but what the hell? Let's start the party right now."

"Phil," Joni said, "did you call about the tables?"

"Everything's set up, babe." Phil pulled Joni to him and for a moment his jaded persona fell away, leaving a look of naked adoration behind. I tried not to stare, but the closeness between them was palpable right then and it made me happy just to see it. "It's going to be great, trust me," Phil told her. "Don't you worry about a thing. All you got to do is show up and say *I do.*"

"Or, *I do, as long as nothing better comes along,*" Coop said, opening the door.

"Shut up, man," Phil told him before kissing Joni and following him outside.

When the boys were gone, Dannika went to the big backpack she'd slung onto the couch and unzipped a side pocket. She pulled out a small black film canister and a delicate glass pipe that reminded me of the miniature animals I used to collect when I was little. "You want to smoke?" she asked us.

I stood and started helping Joni with the dishes, hoping she wouldn't take Dannika up on her offer. The last time I got stoned was at that Halloween party in college, when I ended up cowering in the arms of a towering Greta Garbo in drag. You know I become a paranoid idiot with one hit, but I didn't want to be the only one abstaining.

"No, thanks." Joni squeezed Dannika's arm as she passed. "Get Phil high, though. He needs to chill."

"Roger that." She slipped out the door.

There was a pause, filled only with the sound of dishes clunking around in the sink. I shuttled plates and cups from the table to the tile mosaic counter beside her. "How did you two end up here?" I asked, picking up a dishtowel to dry while she scrubbed.

"I'm from here," she said. "My parents actually live on the property. They've got an old Finnish farmhouse down the road about half a mile—the house I grew up in." She looked out the window, wistful. "Never thought I'd come back, tell you the truth." Her smile was a little sad. "But here I am."

"Brave girl," I said. "I could never live within a hundred miles of my parents."

"Where are they?" she asked.

"My mom's in Sebastopol. That's where I grew up."

She looked at me. "And your dad?"

Oh, God, why did this keep coming up? I'd have to learn to steer conversations more carefully. "He's up here somewhere," I said evasively.

"Up *here?*" she echoed.

"Yeah, this area. I haven't talked to him in four years." Somehow, saying it, I felt the weight of those years in the pit of my stomach. I lost my grip and the dish I was drying shattered into tiny pieces as it hit the terra-cotta floor.

"Shit," I said. "I'm so sorry."

"No problem." Joni got out a broom and dustpan; within minutes, she'd whisked it all off into the garbage and had her hands once again in the sudsy water of the sink. She might look like a Rasta-hippie, but she was efficient. I liked that about her.

When the dishes were all dried and put away, she said, "You want a tour? I can show you the recording studio, the farmhouse, the sauna—the entire *estate.*" She said this last word mockingly.

"Sure," I said. "Sounds great."

She cast a dubious glance at my shoes. "It's a little muddy out there. You want to borrow some boots?"

I looked down at my kitten heels. Already, they were a

little dirty just from walking to the front door. It dawned on me then that I'd been encased in L.A. for nearly half a lifetime, now. I mean yeah, I went home on occasion, but I made it a point never to stay more than a day or two and we limited our activities to holiday meals or the occasional rented movie. In my world—the one I lived in day to day—it was all sidewalks and carpeting, marble foyers and taxicabs. Seeing the mud staining my leopard-print heels reminded me of being little and wanting to wear things I couldn't because my mother insisted I feed the dogs or rake the lawn. I always despised tennis shoes. To me, they were hideous symbols of mediocrity, the antithesis of elegance.

"What size shoe do you wear?" Joni asked, rousing me from my thoughts.

"Size six."

"Perfect!" she said, clapping her hands together. "Me, too." She pursed her lips and squinted at me thoughtfully. "I think I have just the thing," she said, and ran up the spiral staircase to the second floor.

I was sure she'd return clutching a pair of clunky hiking boots, probably in something practical and weatherproof like Gore-Tex, for God's sake. I shuddered at the image. When I heard her footsteps pattering down the stairs again, I was surprised to see her holding pale clothing in one arm and a beautiful pair of English riding boots in the other.

"It's my Nana's old riding outfit," she said. "Very Katharine Hepburn. What do you think?" She put the boots on the floor near me and held up first a crisp, white cotton blouse with mother-of-pearl buttons, then a well-preserved pair of tan riding pants. I reached out to touch them, fingering the extended tab double-button closure. If I had to guess, I'd say they were from the early 1950s.

"Wow," I said. "Lovely."

"I bet they'll fit. Try them on."

"Oh, I couldn't…"

"Sure, you could!" she enthused. Then she paused, a new thought dawning on her. "Oh, wait—do you hate this look? Coop said you're very particular about clothes. I don't want to force—"

"No!" I interrupted. "They're really gorgeous. But God, these were your Nana's. What if I get mud on something?"

She put one hand on her hip. "Gwen, come on, you think this is my style? Nana would be thrilled to see a beautiful girl like you wearing her clothes. No one else is going to. Seriously, go try them on."

I didn't need any more encouragement. The outfit was a bit of a stretch for me, but only because it was all wrong for the streets of L.A. If I was going to don country garb, by God, this would be it. Plus, I was incredibly touched by the gesture. After almost thirty hours of dealing with Dannika's sadistic form of girl-bonding, I was misty-eyed at the kindness of strangers.

Once I was dressed, I checked myself out in the full-length mirror that stood next to the claw-foot tub. The white blouse was a perfect fit, and the riding pants hugged my curves in a way that flattered from every angle. The shiny, chestnut-brown knee-high boots were utterly delicious—so thoroughbred and classy I found myself adopting a haughty stare unconsciously in the mirror. Joni was right. The whole getup was pure *Bringing Up Baby*.

When I came out of the bathroom, Joni let out a wolf whistle. Just then Phil came in the kitchen door, followed by Coop and Dannika. Coop smiled at me, shaking his head.

Dannika covered her mouth with two fingers and tried to choke down giggles. "Are you going riding?"

I could feel my face starting to burn. All my life, people have been laughing at my clothes. I should be used to it by now, but hearing it from Dannika, I felt a fresh wave of humiliation, as if it were happening for the very first time.

"You look amazing," Coop said, after shooting Dannika a warning glance.

"Doesn't she?" Joni was excited. "These are my Nana's old clothes."

"Oooh, let's dress up Gwen like a little doll." Dannika wasn't laughing anymore, and her tone had an unmistakably nasty edge to it.

"What is your problem?" I stared her down. I think the boots were giving me courage; I felt suddenly very capable of kicking someone very hard, if need be. Possibly in the head.

"*My* problem? You're the one with a problem, okay, so don't hang it on me."

My jaw dropped. "Me?" was all that came out.

"Yeah, you." Every trace of the benevolent yoga goddess was gone; her anger was making her skin turn splotchy and her face looked less sculptural, more rodentlike, tensed for a fight. "Don't give me that innocent look, okay, Kewpie doll? I've had just about enough of your shit."

"Cat fight," Phil said under his breath.

Coop started to say, "Dannika, what the—?" but I interrupted him.

"No, let her get it off her chest," I said. "She's obviously been dying to call me childish names for quite a while."

"Don't get all condescending," she spat. "I saw your mother's house—I know the mediocre bullshit world you come from. So don't cop this holier-than-thou attitude."

I looked her right in the eye. "Sure," I said evenly. "Anything you say, Donna."

She took a step back, wobbling slightly, as if I'd slapped her. Then she shot a look at Coop, wheeled around and ran out the door, slamming it behind her.

I cast a quick, furtive glance around the room. Phil was groping again for his cigarettes. Joni was gnawing on her bottom lip, her eyes on Phil. Coop was staring at me like I was a complete stranger. After an unbearable silence, Coop shook his head once as if waking himself from a dream and followed Dannika out the door, calling her name.

So there you have it. My first assignment as an undercover agent and what do I do? Spill my secret code word, blow my cover and piss everyone off in the process.

Now I'm upstairs in the cozy guestroom all alone, writing in my little diary like a sulky teen while Coop and my nemesis are out there somewhere in the backwoods of FUBAR Ranch. If I know Dannika, she's leaping through the forest like a spooked gazelle while Coop chases after her; when he finds her, he'll have to physically stop her, trying to be gentle as he grabs hold of her arm, only she'll thrash about and the next thing you know we'll have a *Call of the Wild* sex scene on our hands.

Shit. I hear footsteps on the stairs. More later.

Dishonored and disgraced,

Gwen

3:10 p.m.

Dear Marla,

The footsteps on the stairs were Joni's. She knocked softly and when I responded she poked her head in and said, "You ready for that tour?"

I winced. "I was sort of thinking I'd be evicted soon."

She let out a low, throaty laugh. "It takes a lot more than that to get kicked out of FUBAR."

I stood up and put my leopard print coat on. "Glad to hear it."

We walked downstairs together. The house had seemed festive and lively just twenty minutes ago; now it was steeped in the silence that follows an argument. When we stepped outside, there were two crows cawing at each other midair, swooping erratically, but it was hard to say if they were playing, mating or attacking. To me it looked like they were out for blood, but maybe it was just my mood. The air was cool but the sun on our faces was warm and the breeze carried the scent of blackberries. We walked for a couple of minutes in silence, which is a long time to resist babbling with someone you barely know, but something about Joni made it easy to say nothing.

When we reached a little wooden shack with a chimney and an outdoor shower Joni said, "Here's the sauna. The Fins who first came here built it."

"You guys use it?" I asked.

"Phil does. I get kind of claustrophobic. I don't really like to get so hot, but he's into extremes. We're sort of opposites in that way."

We walked a little farther and she pointed to a pile of flat rocks at the edge of the forest with clumps of calla lilies sprouting around it. "Our family dog is buried over there. Sam. We got him when I was three."

"Wow," I said, "you go way back here, don't you?"

"Yeah." She sighed. "Sometimes it feels like living with a bunch of ghosts. But Phil and I built our house, so that's fresh territory. The studio's all new, which my dad's really psyched about. He's a bluegrass guy, so now he gets all his friends up here to record—bunch of hayseed hippies with banjos and washboards."

"Cool." I always feel a kinship with people dedicated to a bygone era.

We kept walking. The sun was behind us, sagging slightly westward; our shadows, etched into the dusty road before us, looked absurdly tall and thin. Her Nana's pants were comfortable and the boots seemed to cushion my feet with every step. I wondered what it would be like to dress this way every day—to walk with your feet so close to the earth, instead of clicking along a city sidewalk in dainty heels.

There was a swath of open, grassy meadow on either side of the road. To our right it stretched about forty feet before the forest of pine, oak and redwoods took over. On our left, it only extended about ten feet before it was swallowed by huge tangles of blackberry bushes, which butted up against more forest. I wondered again if Coop and Dannika were somewhere in those woods, and if words failed them, would they resort to the language of limbs and tongues and teeth?

"I totally messed up, didn't I?"

She shoved her hands into the pockets of her peacoat. "Dannika's just uptight about her past. Coop told you?"

I nodded. "That's the worst part. Now he won't trust me."

"Oh, he'll get over it." She reached over and plucked a penny from the dust. "Here," she said, "it's only good luck if I give it away."

I took it from her. "Are you and Dannika pretty close?"

"Honestly? Not really."

I raised my eyebrows. "She seems to like you."

"I don't know why. We've just never really clicked. I've known her ten years…it's weird. She's a bit of a cokehead—her energy's too scattered for me. I'm surprised she's not doing lines yet."

I stifled a giggle. "We had a little run-in with the law. She had to ditch what she had."

Joni laughed out loud. "No shit?"

"It was pretty funny," I said, letting myself laugh with her. When we were done giggling, I asked, "If you're not that close, why did she come all this way for your wedding?"

"Because of Coop. He's the only reason we even know her anymore. I mean Phil thinks she's sweet—we all feel kind of bad for her—but Coop's the one she goes to when she's in trouble."

"You think he's her only friend?"

She didn't even hesitate. "Absolutely. And her only family. Her mom's the most asinine, shallow person you'll ever meet, her dad's dead, no siblings. She's totally alone." She picked up a stone from the road and tossed it into the blackberry bushes. Three or four quail darted out into the open, then followed their leader back to the safety of the brambles. "She's threatened by you. You know that, don't you?"

I stopped walking. "Please. The woman's flawless. How could I possibly threaten her?"

Joni widened her eyes at me as if I was being dense. "Because Coop's crazy about you."

"He's crazy about her, too."

She scoffed. "Not in the same way."

"Do you know that for a fact?" I stared at the road, now, suddenly shy.

"Wait a minute—are you under the impression that Coop and Dannika are *into* each other? Like, sexually?"

I shrugged. This was getting complicated. If I told Joni the story Dannika had dished this morning, wouldn't she be tempted to tell Coop? If she did, Coop would be on his guard, arranging his defenses before I could get to him— I'd never know the truth, and before long I'd be pushing forty with crow's feet, stuck in Van Nuys with three toddlers, fetching sippy cups while Coop cruised the city in a big SUV, getting his fill of nubile blondes. Besides, what was the advantage in telling Joni? She and Phil had been up here five years—she probably wouldn't even know about the bodily fluids being swapped in Malibu.

When I didn't say anything, Joni rested her hand on my shoulder. "Let me just tell you, Gwen, I've never seen Coop so happy, okay? Don't let Dannika screw that up."

I felt tears suddenly stinging at the back of my eyes. "Except now…" I hesitated.

"Now what?"

"I'm just confused. I have a few trust issues, I guess, and this trip hasn't exactly been reassuring in that way."

Joni picked up another rock and fired it at an old, mossy fir. She hit the trunk dead center, so hard that small bits of bark went flying.

"Wow," I said. "Good shot."

"I used to play fast-pitch in high school," she said. "Now I write poems and cook soup." Again, there was something melancholy in her tone—wistful or nostalgic or something. I wondered if she was happy with her life or if she'd just sort of washed up here, corralled by the currents back to her childhood home, like a bottle washed out to sea then ferried back again by the tides.

"I'm going to tell you a story," she said, shifting gears. "I'm not telling you this to be gossipy, okay? I just think you should be armed with information, because there's no telling what Dannika will do or say to confuse you."

"Okay…" This sounded promising—knowledge is power and all that—so I put on a neutral, receptive face, all the while thinking, *Secret Agent Gwen, back in action.*

"About four years ago, Coop was involved with this girl named Victoria. She was somehow related to the Rockefellers, I think. Very blue blood, aristocratic, classic good looks. Sort of looked like you, actually, but tall and skinny."

Ouch.

Joni saw my face. "No—bony skinny. Gross. No boobs, nothing."

I gave her a *whatever* look.

"Anyway, she wasn't my cup of tea, but Coop was really

taken with her. She was the first girl in years he seemed serious about." Her caramel eyes found mine and I could tell by her face we were getting to the important part. "Dannika lost her shit. She'd call us every night complaining about what a bitch Victoria was, how wrong she was for Coop. One night she let herself into his apartment, got really drunk and passed out in his bed. When he and Vicky got home from their date, there she was, shit-faced. Not long after, Victoria broke up with Coop. Tell you the truth, I think it was about money. Coop could never make enough to keep a girl like that happy. But Phil thinks she didn't want to deal with a *Fatal Attraction* psycho."

"What did Coop say about it?"

Joni smirked. "Well, he didn't really say anything. That's Coop for you. Even with us, he's secretive."

I mulled this over. "So maybe he had something to hide."

She looked puzzled. "Like what?"

"Like…" This was thin ice; I'd have to tread carefully. "Maybe he cheated on Victoria."

"I doubt it," she said. "He really liked her. Anyway, that's never been Coop's style."

My heart surged at this, but I didn't want to jump to conclusions. "Have you ever known Coop to cheat on someone?"

She didn't even pause. "Nope."

"But if he's secretive…" I let the sentence dangle, unfinished.

"Coop's not trying to cover his tracks, he just hates

gossip—I mean, *hates* it. He doesn't talk about something if he thinks it'll come back to haunt him. I'm sort of shocked he told you the Donna Horney story."

"Tonight at ten," I said, in a mock news anchor voice, *"The Donna Horney Story."*

We both giggled, but I was feeling terrible. I'd betrayed Coop, turning our private communication into a big public drama. "I can't believe I did that," I said. "God, I'm such a moron."

"I'm guessing Dannika's mostly mad at Coop. It's one thing that you know, but it's worse that he told you. In her mind, that's pure betrayal. It means he's asked you into the inner circle."

I swallowed and tried to keep my voice light. "So you don't think he and Dannika ever…?"

She smiled. "You and your ellipses! Ever what?"

"Ever got together?" I said with effort.

"No."

"Come on, they're both obscenely attractive…."

She picked up another rock and tossed it gently from one hand to the other. "Just because they're beautiful doesn't mean they're destined to get it on," she said, "if that's what you're thinking."

When she said it like that, it did sound sort of juvenile.

"Coop really likes you, Gwen." She gave me a funny look. "You're unusual. He likes unusual girls."

I rolled my eyes. "Is *unusual* code for *freaky?*"

"We're all freaky," she said. "But you're a freak with flair. Not everyone can pull that off."

When we got back to the house, Phil was in the kitchen, talking on the phone. "Look," he was saying, "I don't care if your mother died, your woman left you, your dog shit in your car—I don't *care*. You made a commitment, here, and you don't call me the day before the wedding to tell me…" He paused, listening, rolling his eyes at Joni. "I told you, Conrad, I don't give a shit about your personal dramas. We rented a sound system from you and you're going to deliver or I'm personally going to destroy your piss-poor excuse for a business. You got me?"

Joni went to him and pressed her hand flat against his chest. "What's he saying?"

He just shook his head at her, offered a weak smile. It died as soon as he started talking again. "Okay, okay, so have your brother deliver it. Fine. And remember, I know my speakers, so don't try to slip me your jerry-rigged bullshit knock-off brands, you got me? All right, later, man." He hung up the phone and rubbed his forehead. "Fucking amateur."

"Conrad?"

"Yeah, says his girlfriend moved to China and he can't get out of bed. Shit. He's sending his brother with the gear tomorrow."

Joni looked alarmed. "Isn't his brother like fifteen?"

"Yeah. Whatever, man, we just can't worry about it." He

looked at me. "Who would've thought getting married would be such an administrative nightmare?"

Joni slipped an arm around his waist. "It'll be fine, babe."

He bent down and kissed the top of her head. "I know. Who cares? It's just a party."

She looked up at him. "Just a party? Hello, it's our wedding."

He smiled. "Exactly. And you're going to make me the happiest man alive, even if they deliver Peavey speakers."

She frowned, nibbling on a cuticle.

He rubbed her shoulders. "You okay?"

I sensed they needed a moment, so I wandered into the living room. Coop and Dannika were sitting on the couch, talking in low voices. When I walked in they both stopped talking and looked up at me. Coop's face was unreadable, but Dannika's was openly hostile. Her pink nose and blood-shot eyes made it clear that she'd been crying.

"Sorry," I said. "Didn't mean to interrupt." I headed for the spiral staircase and started up.

"I'll be up in a minute," Coop said.

"Take your time." As I glanced over my shoulder, all I could see of Coop was the back of his head, but Dannika was watching me, her eyes tightened in a slight squint, her mouth set in a hard, flat line.

6:50 p.m.

Dear Marla,

I sat upstairs in the guestroom for about twenty minutes before I heard Coop making his way up the spiral staircase. His conversation with Dannika had been in hushed tones and though occasionally I could make out the rise and fall of their voices, I couldn't distinguish any specific words. I'd considered sneaking into the hallway to listen from the top of the stairs, but I was afraid someone would catch me and, besides, my secret agent zeal was on the wane. At first, investigating covertly had seemed like the only way to get at the truth, but now skulking in the shadows of the stairwell sounded acutely humiliating. Was Coop really worth all this? If I couldn't ask him straight up what was going on, how long would we last?

When I heard his footsteps making their way toward our room, I ran to the mirror and wiped away all traces of my supposedly waterproof mascara. Then I dashed for the bed, swiping a book from the nightstand, which I propped up on my knees.

He knocked softly.

"Yeah?" I stared coolly at the page and tried to look engrossed as he let himself in, closed the door behind him and lingered for a moment. I could see him in my peripheral vision leaning against the doorjamb. When I looked up our eyes locked and though his expression wasn't warm, exactly, I still felt myself melting under his gaze, going just as liquid as I did that day when I'd handed him his boxers at the Laundromat.

Still standing near the door, he said, "How you doin'?"

"Okay." I turned a page in the book, affecting total absorption.

He walked over to the bed and tilted the paperback away from my knees so he could get a look at the title. "*Edible Mushrooms of the Pacific Northwest,* huh?" He raised his eyebrows. "Sounds mesmerizing."

I put the book down. "This trip isn't going very well, is it?"

He sat down on the edge of the bed. We weren't touching, but he was so close that I could feel the warmth of his body against my legs. "Things are complicated."

I sighed. "I shouldn't have called her Donna. I'm sorry."

He pinned me with his eyes. "It takes a lot for me to trust someone. You know that, don't you?"

I nodded. "Coop, I completely screwed up, I'm—"

He interrupted me with a searing-hot, tear-off-my-clothes-and-fuck-me-this-minute kiss. The world spun around and before I knew what was happening I was underneath him, intensely aware of his erection as it pressed against the crotch of my borrowed antique riding pants. I arched my back and he planted a trail of blistering kisses along my throat. I started to tug at his shirt, dying to feel his skin against mine when he pulled away abruptly and sat again on the edge of the bed, raking a hand through his hair.

I sat straight up and said, "Coop, God, what is it?"

"I'm so attracted to you," he whispered, not looking at me.

"And that's a problem?" I was a little dizzy from the whiplash-inducing shifts in mood, here. All the blood had left my brain and was now throbbing between my legs, making it very difficult to think.

"I just don't want to use sex to avoid what's really going on." I could see the little muscle in his jaw flexing, which excited me, but I forced myself to focus.

"Of course not." I brushed a strand of hair from my eyes. "So…what *is* going on?"

"Look," he said, turning slightly toward me. "Dannika's been a real friend to me. We've got a long history together.

I've always promised I won't abandon her when I find someone I want to…"

"You want to what?"

"Be with. You know. Long term."

My internal Greek chorus started in on a rapid-fire debate. *Is he saying he wants to be with me long term? I don't know—it's Dannika he made the* promise *to. It's like they're married or something! Yeah, but didn't he just imply—? So what? Implication means nothing. People imply things all the time, it's a chickenshit way to cover your tracks. If he wants to be with you long term he should come out and say that. Yeah, but maybe he's testing the waters, here—he's human, he doesn't want to be rejected. You've got a lot more to worry about than his pussyfoot confessions. See what you can find out about Malibu, for God's sake. Malibu-Shmalibu. Who cares what happened then if he can be mine now? Shut up and listen, you needy cow.*

"Gwen?" He rubbed his thumb across my cheek. "Was that a yes or a no?"

Shit, he just asked you something important and you weren't even listening! You suck, Matson.

"Absolutely." I had a fifty-fifty chance, right? When he looked a little taken aback, I added, "Not. Absolutely not."

His grin was mischievous. "Is that your final answer?"

I nodded, feeling like a gawky second grader at a spelling bee.

"I see. So your reply to 'Are you listening?' is 'Absolutely not.'"

I covered my face with my hands. "I'm sorry, Coop. I got a little distracted."

He laughed and rubbed his hand over my back. "I know this isn't easy for you." His smile faded as he looked out the window. "I guess I was sort of naive, thinking we'd all just get along. She doesn't make friends easily, especially female friends. I mean, she *is* beautiful…"

Okay, so she's a supermodel, does he have to say it? Can't we pretend she's a hatchet-faced ho?

"I know she's difficult," he went on, "but you're so disarming and…"

Disarming. Read: "Not sexy enough to be threatening."

"…I thought we could just have a nice weekend. I didn't realize it would be this tense." He studied me. "But she *is* one of my best friends, so eventually—I mean, we'd all have to hang out—if we're going to be together. You and me, I mean." He looked at the ceiling. "God, I'm really screwing this up, aren't I?"

I put a finger to his lips. "No. I'm the one who screwed up. I betrayed your trust."

"She pushed you. I know she pushes people. But it's just a defensive thing. She can be a real bitch when she wants to be, but normally she's a lot of fun."

Yeah, if you're a six-foot-two, deliriously gorgeous stud. Otherwise, she's about as much fun as colon cancer. "You know what, Coop? I can totally handle this. It's not a problem. Really."

He cut his eyes at me and they were filled with such hope,

such sweet relief, like a kid who'd just been informed he wasn't getting a spanking, of course not, and would he like a cookie?

"I admire your loyalty." I traced my fingers over his gently. "It's part of who you are."

"I just worried things were spiraling out of control, here."

I leaned toward him and touched my lips to his, just barely. "Everything's going to be fine."

He kissed me with his eyes closed, a gentle, searching kiss. As soon as I felt him relaxing, though, melting into me, dipping us almost imperceptibly toward the mattress, he stopped and sat upright again. "I just—you know—I've had sort of negative experiences with her in the past. That's why I'm gun-shy. I don't want the same thing to happen again."

I nodded, my face grave.

He gazed at me a moment, and then his eyes moved to my throat. He ducked his head and started a long, slow line of tiny, hot kisses starting just below my earlobe, working his way down to my clavicle. I closed my eyes and felt shivers spreading in slow, swirling whorls across my body.

"I don't want her to come between us," he said, gently nibbling the side of my neck. "Like she did—"

"With Victoria?"

I'd mumbled it, not thinking, my eyelids still full of swirling, kaleidoscopic shapes, as the shivers continued to travel across my skin. The second it was out of my mouth, though, I felt his body stiffen and pull back.

"What did you say?"

I winced. "Nothing…"

He opened his mouth, closed it again, started over. "Joni told you about that?"

Technically, I'd heard the story from two sources, with distinctly different perspectives, but at the moment it seemed better to keep things simple. I nodded.

He looked at his lap. Our bodies, moments ago entwined, were no longer touching. "You know, I would have told you that story myself. I just didn't want you to have preconceived ideas about Danni."

The nickname lodged like a softball in my gut.

He went on, still not looking at me. "I was hoping she'd grown up a bit since then. I guess the jury's still out on that."

I wanted to ask him about Malibu, about how he felt when he looked at her white teeth, about whether he'd ever pictured her when he was inside me. I longed to sit in his lap and listen to him saying I was the only woman he'd ever really wanted—not just in a hot-stab-of-lust way, but wanted with such fervor he longed to curl up beside me night after night and listen to me breathing.

Just then the front door slammed downstairs and Phil's booming voice called out, "Yo, Coop! We got to get going, man. We got some hell to raise."

Coop just stared at me, and something in his face told me he was retreating, pulling away from me so fast it was like watching the taillights of a speeding car. "Yeah, okay," he called to Phil over his shoulder. "Hold on a sec."

It hurt, thinking he was going to leave me like that, right in the middle of things. I felt raw, exposed, sitting there on the bed in a strange house while Coop's eyes grew more and more distant every second. It didn't help that I was several hundred miles from my own apartment, where at least there was a medicinal stash of Stoli and Chunky Monkey in the freezer.

"Where are you going?" It came out part squeak, part whisper.

"Phil's got some crazy idea about a stag night." He laced his fingers in mine. "I don't want to go, really—I hate these things—but he'll freak if I let him down."

I nodded. Once again, I could feel my arms and legs prickling with goose bumps, only this time it was from loneliness, not pleasure. "No big deal." I forced myself to produce an encouraging smile. "Go on. Have a good time."

He looked doubtful. "It feels weird—I mean, you just met these guys—I don't want you to think I dragged you up here and threw you to the wolves."

Just hearing him say that made me feel less abandoned. "Joni's great. Seriously. We'll have a good time."

"You sure?" He squeezed my hand.

"Yes. Go."

He went to his duffel bag and pulled out a pair of brown wingtips—my favorite. He sat in the old leather chair near the window, unlaced his muddy boots, pulled them off, and exchanged them for the dress shoes. As he was lacing them up he said, "Are you going out with the girls?"

"Don't know," I said. "Nobody's mentioned it."

He finished tying the laces, stood up and touched his hair a couple times while looking in the mirror. "Listen, kitten." He pulled a silver gum wrapper from his pocket, then bent down and scribbled something on the blank side. "If you need anything, this is Phil's cell, okay? Even if you just want to say hi."

I stood up and went to him. "I'm a big girl," I said, wrapping my arms around his neck. "I think I can handle a night out with the girls. Or a night in with the girls. Or a night by myself, if the girls ditch me."

"I doubt that. Joni really digs you."

I grinned. "See? I'll be just fine."

"Coop! For God's sake, get down here, man. It's my last free night on earth." Phil was obviously getting restless.

Coop touched the back of my neck so softly I felt all the lust he'd stirred up earlier kick back into high gear. Right then I wanted nothing more than to tear his clothes off and force myself on him, to meld our bodies into one permanently fused entity.

But he headed for the door. "We'll talk more later."

"Right." I nodded, trying to look brave.

He threw a heartbreaking glance over his shoulder and mumbled, "I miss you already," before closing the door.

8:00 p.m.

Dear Marla,

Now that Coop's left, the silence in the house buzzes like a thousand cicadas. I'm still sitting on the bed in the guest-room, clutching a batik pillow and brooding. Something about the smell in this place, the cold Northern California damp in the air, reminds me too much of being little. I stare out the window as the sky does its slow fade from a cheery blue to a dusky violet to star-sprinkled indigo; against this backdrop, the specters of my childhood slide into view, three-dimensional and way too real.

What happened between my parents—the avalanche of

their marriage—took place when I was a kid, so it's hard to
see it clearly sometimes. Then again, the memories I do have
are so finely etched with details, they seem more real than
the room I'm sitting in right now. I was nine when they
finally split up. A lot of people assume the divorce itself is
the hard part on kids, but for me it was the years leading up
to it that sucked. It was like watching your home buckle and
give way in a surreal, slow-motion demolition; the worst
part was, we were stuck inside, watching the rafters split and
the windows shatter—at least my mom and I were. For
awhile I wondered where Dad was, why he wasn't helping,
but now I know he was the guy outside with the wrecking
ball.

The crazy thing about being a kid stuck in your parents'
mess is that you're not really lucid enough to call them on
their shit, but you're right there in the midst of it, just the
same. I think that's why I was so fascinated back then with
wounds and burns and skin diseases. Mom thought it indicated a predilection for medicine, but I realize now it was
simply a fascination with pain that showed. Inside our family,
the injuries and the infections were all hidden within the
folds of our silence. It seemed like a relief to wear your suf-
fering out in the open, even if it meant sporting angry red
boils or having your flesh sliced down to the bone.

I know I haven't told you any of this. By the time I met
you, I was deep into the process of reinventing myself and
I had no desire to look back. My obsession with vintage

clothing blossomed soon after my parents' divorce. I wanted to blot out the era I was raised in and become someone from an uncontaminated time, when men were men, women were women, and dinner was served at six. I loved the clean, antiseptic feel of the fifties—the mincing innocence of a Peter Pan collar, the haughty aloofness of pure white kid gloves. In the starched and pressed world of vintage fashion, I found the road away from home and I took it without a glance back at the wreck I'd left behind.

But before there was you and before my closet was lined with pillbox hats, there was me and my parents and the failed experiment of their open marriage. At the time, of course, I didn't have anything to call it; nobody bothered explaining it to me. All I knew was that right around the second grade my mother became obsessed with Lindsey Baylor.

Lindsey was a girl I hardly noticed before my mom pointed her out. I guess you never met her; the Baylors moved away just before I started junior high. Lindsey had white-blond hair that was so silky and fine, her little pink plastic barrettes were forever slipping out of place. She was skinny, with scared little-rabbit eyes and a pale, slightly freckled complexion. She wasn't even in my class; she was in Mr. Durden's, and I was in Mrs. Franklin's, but suddenly my mom was quizzing me about her while we ate French fries and salad in front of the news. Dad was never present during these meals; he was often gone, anyway, but during that time he only popped in for brief guest appearances and even then he seemed preoccupied, distant. Mom's peculiar fascination with Lindsey Baylor grew and Dad's absence became more and more conspicuous.

Anyway, as it turns out, my dad was having an affair with Lindsey Baylor's mom. There you have it: mystery unveiled. Evidently Mrs. Baylor used to cut his hair, and I guess it just happened. Dad may have been a womanizer, but he was also compulsively honest and intellectually overdeveloped. He told Mom all about it and suggested that monogamy was a worn-out bourgeois value, that they should consider trying a more modern marriage (or maybe a more old-fashioned one, depending on how you look at it). And because she wanted a family, not a child-support payment that probably wouldn't even be regular, she told him okay, you sleep with whoever you want, just tell me where you are and get your ass home before Gwen gets up in the morning.

Just like that, they transformed themselves. One minute they were Mr. and Mrs. Matson, wrestling coach and home-maker, the next they were swinging bohemians, pioneers in the uncharted territory of sexual freedom.

Except the thing is, my mom didn't swing. It was pretty much a one-sided experiment in non-monogamy. Dad did the messing around. Mom did the mothering.

That's the abridged version—the one I was able to piece together as an adult—but that's not the one I lived. Now I can see it all miniaturized, like peeking into a dollhouse, but when I was eight and my dad was staying out late and my mom was nursing a nervous breakdown, the forces that guided us were murkier, more opaque and sadder. Half of those scenes I can barely remember, but there is one that haunts me and that's the one struggling to take shape now as I sit here on Joni and Phil's bed in the guestroom, holding tight to a batik pillow like it can somehow protect me.

Don't be mad, Marla. I just can't write it down. Putting it on paper is too ugly. I had to live it; why should I have to make it real all over again, resurrect it with ink? Besides, you're in the City of Light. It hardly seems fair to mail you all my shadows.

Signing off from FUBAR Ranch,

Gwen

4:12 a.m.

Dearest Marla,

As you can see, I finished off that little spiral notebook like it was nothing. Joni lent me this legal pad until I can get to town and buy something with a cover. I left the top page blank as a precautionary measure, but it makes me feel sort of exposed, like wearing one of those paper gowns at the doctor's office. Now I see why they make diaries with locks; it's amazing how much you can tell a blank page, isn't it?

Anyway, it's a good thing she lent me something, because so much happened tonight, it's dizzying. I'm afraid if I don't get it down now, the details will be surrendered to the deep, dark void that swallows wild nights, leaving behind only alcohol-blurred snapshots and tiny, disposable mementos like matchbooks and crumpled cocktail napkins.

I guess it was about eight-thirty when Joni knocked softly on my door, saving me from myself for the second time since I'd met her that afternoon. I'd been writing and stewing for too long and I was so wrapped up in my childhood when she pushed the door open a couple inches, I had to blink a few times before her face came into focus.

"Gwen? Can I come in?" Her voice stirred me from my trance.

"Yeah." I slammed the notebook shut and put it down on the dresser, knocking a glass of water over on accident. "Shit," I mumbled.

"Do you want the heater on?" she asked.

"Goddammit. What?"

"The heater. It's freezing in here."

She was right. I hadn't noticed that my feet and hands were practically blue. "Oh, yeah, please."

She spun the dial on a small space heater, then flipped the switch on the overhead light. A golden glow filled the room and exposed the puddle of water cascading over the bedside table and onto the tiled floor. I hunched over it, embarrassed, looking around for something to wipe it up with.

Joni said, "No big deal—I'll get a towel," and returned quickly with a thick blue terry-cloth one that absorbed the water on contact. For some reason—I guess I'd been sifting through the wreckage of my family for too long—even the spilled water made me sad and I sank back onto the bed, feeling lost and depleted.

Joni sat in the leather chair near the window. "So I guess you're a writer?"

"Me? No. It's just a few letters."

"Be careful," she said, "that's how it starts. Next thing you know you're collecting rejection letters."

"I don't think so." I sighed. "I'm not very good with rejection."

She twisted one of her dreads around her finger and studied me. "You okay?"

"Yeah." I tried a perky tone, but it fell flat. "No," I admitted. "I'm sorry. This is the weekend of your wedding. I shouldn't be dragging my own troubles into it."

She propped her chin up on her fist. "Commandment number one at FUBAR Ranch: Thou shalt not fake an emotion for the convenience of yourself or others."

I laughed. "That's cool. I like that. What are the other commandments?"

"I don't know, I just made that one up. It's good though, isn't it? Maybe I should give up poetry and try my hand at bibles...."

"You may be onto something."

A silence fell over us, but it wasn't awkward. It was like the moment before snow falls; you feel a shift in the air, a change in climate. "Did you and Coop have an argument?"

Normally, I'd find it presumptuous for someone I'd known for seven hours to pop such a question, but with Joni it was welcome. "I don't know. We had something."

"Something…delightful?"

"No, not exactly. It was confusing. I think he was trying to tell me not to screw things up between him and Dannika."

She guffawed. "Gwen! You have to get off that."

"How can anyone compete with all that history? And all that blond," I added under my breath.

"He's loyal to Dannika, like brother and sister. That's it. End of story."

"Hmph." I wasn't convinced, but I loved hearing it, anyway.

"I'm serious." Her buttery eyes were even more intense than usual as they bore into mine. "Coop is crazy about you. Stop obsessing about Dannika, okay? It'll only create problems."

I looked away. "I just don't trust people very easily." I picked at the quilt on the bed compulsively. "Men, specifically. I've never been with anyone for more than three months."

"How long have you and Coop been dating?"

I swallowed. "Three months tomorrow."

"Aha. So we're at a turning point, here."

I nodded. "You might say that."

She leaned forward, resting her elbows on her knees.

"Well then, we're both about to commit tomorrow, aren't we?"

"Maybe…"

"What good is a commitment if it's only 'maybe'?"

"It's just that I don't know if he's going to come through." A touch of whininess had seeped into my voice. "Men rarely do."

"Gwen, I don't say this lightly, okay? Coop is one of the rare keepers. Believe me…he's worth taking a chance on."

I grinned. "You really think so?"

"I know so." She paused, watching my face as if to make sure her words had sunk in. Then she slapped her thighs abruptly and stood up. "Since we're both going to the guillotine tomorrow, I say we party hard tonight."

I giggled. There was something magical about Joni. Who would've guessed I'd ever be so entranced by a hippie chick with dreads? "What's the plan?"

"First stop is Dick's."

"Ominous name," I quipped.

"No kidding. After that, your guess is as good as mine."

"Who's going?" I tried to make the question sound innocent.

"You, me, the blonde downstairs."

I tried to keep my face neutral. I told myself that having her in plain sight was definitely better than sending her off with the boys. Still, I was sick of her. "Anyone else?"

"My friends Portia and Miranda."

"Is that a coincidence? That they're both named after Shakespearean heroines?"

She laughed. "No, they're twins. Their father's Henry Rhymes."

My eyes went wide. I designed for one of his plays a couple years ago—a comedy set in the late 50s. "The playwright?"

She nodded. "I grew up with them. Mendocino's full of eccentric artist-types. And then there's Ohm."

"Ohm?"

"Yeah, Ohm Nix—I know, weird name—he was conceived in a meditation hut."

I raised my eyebrows. "Are boys allowed at bachelorette parties?"

She waved a hand at me. "He doesn't count, he's gay. So come on, let's get cracking!"

Miranda, the designated driver, picked us up in her dust-coated Subaru, her twin sister riding shotgun. They were redheads, and though Miranda wore her hair short and Portia's hung to her waist, their pale, freckled faces and pouty bee-stung lips were identical. Dannika, Joni and I piled into the backseat and listened as they argued about which novel they should try to adapt for the stage, *Wuthering Heights* or *Pride and Prejudice.* Miranda favored the former, while Portia was partial to the latter.

"How the hell are we going to convey the *moors* in

Cotton Auditorium?" Portia was saying. "For *P&P* you get a couch, a couple chairs, you're set."

"Bor-ing," Miranda sing-songed.

"Hardly! Austen's the master—her dialogue can carry the whole thing."

"Where are we going to get all those hoop skirts and petticoats?"

"The high school just did *The Misanthrope*. We'll borrow from them."

Joni leaned toward me. "They're obsessed with adaptations. They did *Ulysses* our junior year and they've been totally into it ever since."

"I was in a play one time," Dannika said. *"Gentlemen Prefer Blondes."*

I watched Miranda and Portia exchange looks. "Let me guess," Portia said. "Were you the blonde?"

Dannika looked delighted. "How'd you know?"

Portia smirked. "Just a lucky guess."

Dick's turned out to be a tiny, old-fashioned dive right in the middle of Mendocino that seemed startled by its posh surroundings. All the other businesses on that oceanfront street were clearly expensive, arty and decadent, with finicky window displays and calculated lighting. The clientele at Dick's ranged from crusty old beer-bellied fishermen to tourists decked out in cashmere pashminas and tasseled loafers. The large, tinted windows looked out over the bluffs and, beyond that, where the fog thinned, you could see patches of the sea shining with an abalone luster in the moonlight. The contrast between the plain, brown interior of Dick's and the rugged romance of the view was striking. I looked from the half-moon above the fogbank to the aging vinyl stools and the TV mounted on the wall. All in all, it looked like a decent place to start.

When we got there, Joni, Portia and I all ordered Heinekens. Miranda ordered a 7-Up. Dannika propped her elbows on the bar and asked for a vodka mangotini. The bartender leveled his gaze at her, his bloodshot eyes peering out from under white, bushy brows, and said, "You're not from around here, are you?"

She threw her head back and laughed while his eyes soaked her in: the pale, sculpted throat, the inch of cleavage showing beneath her thin white blouse, her skinny hips in faded jeans, the radiant swirl of blond.

"Just Stoli, neat, then," she said.

He delivered her drink like a man in a trance. Portia cleared her throat, saying, "Hey, Mack, think you can handle getting *our* drinks, too?" He tore his eyes away from Dannika and hurried to serve our beers, but had to be reminded about the 7-Up. I saw Portia and Miranda exchange another look.

When Dannika went to the bathroom, Portia said to Joni, "Where'd you meet Malibu Barbie?"

Just the word *Malibu* was enough to set my teeth on edge, but I have to admit, I was sort of enjoying the twins' cattiness. It made me feel like less of a loser.

"She's an old friend from college," Joni said.

Miranda raised an eyebrow. "You want her at your wedding? Twenty bucks says she tries to upstage you."

Portia nodded. "She'll wear something see-through and white."

Joni waved a hand at her. "She's okay. Mostly, she came because of Coop—Gwen's boyfriend. They're tight."

Both twins looked at me with pity.

"God help you," Portia said.

"If you need a good hit man, I'll hook you up," Miranda added.

Just then Ohm swept into the bar, turning heads. I knew it was him even before Joni pounced on him, squealing his name. He had a chiseled, theatrical face: bright blue eyes fringed in dark lashes, a regal nose, jet-black hair, high cheekbones.

"Ohm," Joni said, pulling him by the arm over to me, "I want you to meet Gwen. You're going to adore her."

"Is that an order?" When he saw me, he stopped dead in his tracks and touched a hand to his cheek. "My God," he said, "it's Audrey Hepburn."

I couldn't help grinning at that. I'd put on my orange trapeze dress—the one I always seem to wear when I'm about to get violently drunk—and a few of Dick's patrons had snickered when I'd walked in. It was gratifying to see Ohm's eyes light up with impish glee. He was wearing an old-fashioned tailored tweed vest, and though it wasn't exactly set off by the striped shirt he'd paired it with, I appreciated the effort.

I stuck out my gloved hand. "Nice to meet you," I said, "love your vest."

"She's Holly Golightly in the flesh," he murmured, nudging Joni.

"That's possibly the nicest thing anyone's ever said to me," I told him.

"A woman who recognizes a compliment. I like that." His eyes gleamed as he looked me up and down, taking in everything: leopard-print car coat, matching clutch, gleaming white go-go boots, a double strand of pearls.

"She's exactly your type," Joni said, "elegant, exotic and pathologically original."

"You're right," he said, "I adore her."

They were still talking about me in the third person, but I didn't mind. I felt an instant kindred spirit-thing with Ohm. I studied his face. Though his complexion was radiant and his posture exemplary, there was also a slight whiff of sadness about him—just a tiny creasing around the eyes and mouth that said he knew what disappointment tasted like. Or maybe I was reading into things. Joni had told me quite a bit about him already. Apparently, he'd tried his luck in New York after a dazzling high school career playing every leading role available up and down the coast, including a campy Desdemona in drag. But Broadway hadn't flung open its doors the way he'd hoped it would, and after a bad stint living with a controlling sugar daddy, he'd packed it in and come home. Now he waited tables in Fort Bragg and took care of his arthritic grandmother. He hadn't acted in more than a year.

Ohm was just greeting Portia and Miranda when Dannika emerged from the bathroom. She held out a hand and flashed her perfect teeth at him. "I'm Dannika." She had a fresh coat of lip gloss on and she looked beguiling. "You must be Ohm. I've heard so much about you."

Ohm gave her a quick once-over. "Pleasure's mine," he said, but it was gratifying to see that his face didn't light up for her the way it did for me.

"Great," Joni said in her matter-of-fact way. "Now we're all acquainted. Let's get drunk."

After we left Dick's, the six of us wandered around the corner and up the street until we landed in a cheerful little Irish pub filled with a pink-faced, slightly rowdy crowd that looked to be well on their way to inebriation. There were peanut shells all over the floor and a rotund man in suspenders pouring pints of Guinness behind the polished mahogany bar. It was warm inside from the many bodies. We were lucky enough to nab a booth just as four dour-faced German tourists were leaving.

Looking around the room, I decided the coastal uniform was depressingly pragmatic. Tennis shoes or hiking boots, bulky sweaters, down vests and waterproof parkas were everywhere. An occasional jewel-toned scarf or an off-the-shoulder sweater were the only concessions made to fashion. Some of the patrons were obviously visitors; even if they'd aped the locals' jeans and sweaters, their hair was too expensively cut and their shoes too urban to quite fit in. The coastal hairstyle was the ubiquitous long gray ponytail. Every man and woman for miles seemed to be sporting one and even the youngsters looked like they were just biding time until they could sprout their own.

Ohm went to the bar and ordered a pint for each of us except Miranda, who asked for Perrier. While he was standing there, waiting for the Santa Claus bartender to finish pouring, a cute little blonde in hip-hugger jeans sidled over and started laughing hugely at everything he said. Joni saw me watching, leaned in close and said, "The guy's a chick magnet."

"But don't they know?"

She shrugged. "Pickings are slim out here. They figure he can be converted."

"Does he have a boyfriend?"

She pursed her lips, thinking. "Not really. There was a guy who'd fly out from New York every now and then, but I think that's cooled off."

"He shouldn't be here," I said. "I should abduct him, drag him down to L.A."

Joni scoffed. "Great—just waltz right in and steal my best friend."

"You know it's true," I said.

"Yeah," she admitted, "he's not exactly thriving here."

Her expression was a bit gloomy, so I changed the subject. "How are you enjoying your last night as a free woman?"

She looked around the room. "Honestly? I'm panic-stricken."

"No, you're not."

She turned and looked me in the eye. "Yes. I am."

"What are you panicky about?"

"Put yourself in my position. Just look around the room at all these men."

I did as I was told. The breakdown at the pub was roughly seventy-thirty in women's favor, and some of the guys were decent-looking. There was a tall blond guy sitting at the bar with great forearms, and a lumberjack type in a nearby booth who happened to be a dead ringer for Elvis—before the bloated years, of course. Though their fashion choices were disappointing, at least three or four of the specimens in that room probably had *the smell*. It's weird, you know, because intellectually and aesthetically, I'm attracted to clean, crisp forms, but when it comes to men, they've got to have a specific, slightly dirty smell, or my pulse stays as calm as a corpse's.

Coop's got the most amazing smell.

Somehow he takes the essence of sawdust, pipe tobacco, varnish and wool, then mixes them together with his own secret ingredient and—voilà! You have la crème de la crème of *the smell*.

"Now," Joni said, when she was satisfied I'd assessed the room thoroughly. "Tell yourself: *I'm going to have sex with just one man for the rest of my natural life.*"

Ohm reappeared with our beers before I could reply. Anyway, I don't think Joni expected me to comment. The look she gave me just before she picked up her pint and downed half of it indicated that she'd just summarized everything I needed to know about her current state of panic.

The disconcerting thing: this thought *didn't* make me feel like gulping my beer in one swig. For the first time in my life, having sex with just one man forever seemed almost natural. I mean, sure, if I had to pick one of these guys— even the well-built Elvis in the black T-shirt—I'd be hyperventilating. But when I told myself, *I'm going to have sex with Coop and only Coop for the next half a century,* the prickly sensation it left me with was more like pleasure than panic.

As Joni and Ohm gossiped about mutual friends, I looked around the room again, and this time my gaze fell on Dannika. She was sitting across from Joni, staring vaguely toward the bar. Her long fingers toyed absently with the red straw in her drink. Miranda and Portia's heads were bent toward one another, locked in conversation. Dannika looked completely alone. I suddenly felt sorry for her.

As if she sensed a shift in the air, her eyes found mine and she studied me for a moment. I'd like to say we exchanged a look of mutual understanding and sisterly bonding, but that would be a lie. Her eyes were shining with cold, reptilian calculation. She reminded me of an alligator in a National Geographic special, luring the prey closer through stillness but preparing all the while to attack.

"Idn't that right, Gwen?" Joni was starting to slur a little.

"Sorry?"

"You little scamp," Ohm scolded. "You haven't been listening to a word. I swear L.A. girls have the attention spans of gnats."

"Oh, please," I said, rolling my eyes. "Don't even start with the NorCal SoCal thing. I was born and raised in Sebastopol—I'm totally native."

"But you chose L.A., didn't you?" Ohm raised a scolding finger. "And now look at you. You're L.A. to the bone."

"And I should be ashamed of that?" I sipped my beer. "I live in the middle of the only city on earth where the major exports are sex and illusions. I love that. Nobody cares who you are, as long as you're *somebody.* You can reinvent yourself every single day, if you feel like it."

Joni turned to Ohm with a little sulky turn to her mouth. "Gwen thinks you should move there."

Ohm laughed uneasily. "Really? Why?"

"Your talents are wasted here," I said. "You need a bigger pond."

"You don't even know if I can act," he said.

"I'm not talking about acting—I'm talking about living."

"Great," Joni said, "so what's that say about me? I'm a little minnow who's only good enough for this Podunk puddle?"

Her tone was vaguely belligerent and irrational; I could see she was on the fast track to drunk, with no signs of turning back.

"You can move there, too!" I assured her. "I just thought you were happy here. I don't think Ohm is." It was an odd thing to say about someone I'd only known a couple hours and as many rounds—for that matter, I'd only met Joni this afternoon—but something about them made me feel so at ease.

"I see you're married," I said to Ohm, nodding at the ring on his left hand. "Any advice for the bride-to-be?"

He flashed a wicked grin. "Just lie back and think of England."

"Seriously," I said, "why do you wear that?"

He held out his hand and studied the plain gold band. "It's supposed to keep the girls from hitting on me."

"Does it work?" I asked.

Joni snorted. Ohm shook his head. "Hardly. I'm beginning to think it *attracts* them."

"Maybe you should wear more pink, or leather chaps or something," I suggested. "Pink leather chaps, maybe?"

He cringed. "Too subtle for the girls I meet. They'd think I'm being ironic or sensitive or something."

Joni said, "You could get a tattoo of a couple guys doing it."

"Yeah, where? On my forehead?"

We laughed. The beer was making the whole room glow

with a warm, golden sheen. Voices lapped against each other gently in the background. A couple wearing his-and-her leather coats came in through the glass doors and a cool tendril of foggy air drifted in then was swallowed by the steamy warmth of all those bodies. I could feel a happy little buzz starting in my brain, inching its way down to my limbs. For a moment, the awkwardness of my stay at Chateau de Dog Hair, the cramped drive up Highway 1, even the weirdness between Coop and I this afternoon all seemed distant and small—miniaturized, even—like images on postage stamps.

Just as I turned my head in search of the ladies' room, I caught another glimpse of Dannika. Her eyes were narrowed to slits as she sat watching me. Her face was quietly malicious. I told myself I was just getting paranoid. Still, I couldn't shake the sense that she was stewing in her own ylang-ylang scented juices, planning my imminent doom.

On the way north, crammed uncomfortably into the twins' backseat, Ohm explained to me the difference between Mendocino and Fort Bragg.

"Mendo's the beautiful, older, bitchy sister—classy, arty, postcard-perfect. Fort Bragg's the shit-kicking stocky chick with crooked teeth."

"Which do you prefer?" I asked.

"Fort Bragg. I'll take dirty fingernails over latte-swilling, pinot-loving tourists any day."

"I'm surprised," I told him.

"Why?"

"You just seem too sophisticated to be into dirty finger-nails."

He shrugged. "It's kind of a 'pick your poison' situation."

When we got to the Tip Top, a seedy little bar two blocks off the main drag in Fort Bragg, I could see what Ohm was talking about; the ambiance was noticeably different from the cheerful Irish pub we'd just left. We made our way past a clump of gray-faced, stringy-haired smokers huddled on the sidewalk and stepped inside. It was a decent-sized place—not huge, but at least twice the size of Dick's—and you could tell it was popular. To our right was a large, horseshoe-shaped bar. Behind the chunky barmaid were several signs: Avoid Clean Living; Jägermeister and Complaint Department; 69 Miles Out, 2 Floors Down. There was a touch-screen jukebox blaring Shania Twain and a couple of pool tables where burly guys competed under cheesy lamps emblazoned with Miller Genuine Draft.

We got our drinks, and immediately a couple of hopeful bachelors in flannel shirts started chatting up Dannika. A flock of twentysomething women absorbed Joni, Miranda and Portia, squealing hellos. I decided I'd challenge Ohm to a game of pool.

"Ready to get your ass kicked?" I asked.

He smirked. "Whatever you say, Holly."

Miraculously, one of the tables was free. We flipped a coin

and he won the toss so I racked, arranging the balls carefully, solid-stripe-solid-stripe, the way my father taught me years ago. We used to play every night in the basement when I was a kid. It had been a while, but I was pretty sure my old shark instincts were just dormant, not dead. I sat down on one of the vinyl-padded benches that lined the walls, resting my feet. The go-go boots weren't exactly my most comfortable footwear.

Ohm took a seat beside me, sipping his drink. "I'm actually a champion pool player," he said. "No one in this town can touch me."

"Small pond," I said, "big fish."

"I'm just warning you."

"Fair enough."

When he broke, he sent every ball flying in a burst of color. He sank a solid on the break, another on his first shot.

"So, Joni tells me you lived in New York." I had to speak up so he could hear me over the Metallica blaring from the jukebox.

"Yeah." He bent over and took a shot at the three. It was a difficult angle, but he sank it anyway. "Lived in the Village for three years."

"Did you love it?"

He squinted at the five, lined it up and drove the cue ball straight at it with surprising force. The five slammed into the pocket. "It's the greatest place on earth." He tilted his head, considering. "Of course, it's also hell."

"Did you have a hard time there?"

He tried a tricky bank shot and made it. He was running the table. I'd have to work hard to catch up—if I even got a chance. "It was the best of times, it was the worst of times." He slid his cue behind his back and took aim at the seven. I just shook my head when it slid into the corner pocket without a sound.

"And what's it like to be back home?" I asked.

He paused to rub chalk on the bulbous blue tip of his stick. "You want the truth?"

I nodded.

"I feel like a trapped animal."

"Maybe you should bolt, then."

He smiled sadly. "I'm afraid I'll have to chew off my own leg to do it."

"Why? What's stopping you?"

Turning back to the table, he said, "Me, I guess. I'm stopping me."

"But why?"

He took a shot at the four and missed. It was an easy one, compared to most of the ones he'd made so far. "You see that? I screw up when things are simple. That's why New York was good for me. Everything was really, really complicated there." He took a sip of his scotch. "Then again, that's why I couldn't take it anymore."

"Maybe you need a balance of the complex and the straightforward," I suggested. "L.A. for example."

He scoffed. "I need L.A. like I need a hole in the head."

"No, really!" I enthused. "It's big and it's sort of complicated—the freeways are, anyway—but it's also pretty simple.
Everyone wants eternal youth, an ocean view and perfect
tits. That's not exactly rocket science."

"Interesting," he said. "Something to consider. Now take
your shot, so I can finish you off."

I proceeded to sink every ball on the table, including his
lonely four. "See? I'm a genius. You should listen to me."

He raised his glass to me, smiling broadly. "Holly, baby,
where have you been all my life?"

The jukebox was pounding out Vanilla Ice and the Tip
Top was packed with a sweaty, enthusiastically inebriated
crowd when Joni started taking off her clothes. The patrons
at that point were overwhelmingly male. They lacked the
youthful dewiness of the regulars at the Irish pub we'd
come from; their faces were eraser-pink, their noses oily red,
their eyes bloodshot. They radiated the grim recklessness of
men who worked hard at soul-sodomizing jobs and
expected a little bloodshed before daybreak. Whether she
was inspired by this audience or simply felt it was time to
get naked, I couldn't tell you. All I know is, Joni jumped
up on the bar and started swiveling her hips to the refrain,
"Ice, ice, baby," releasing an animal roar from the men
below. Encouraged by their fervor, she pulled off her
waffled Henley and started busting some serious moves in

nothing but her faded Levi's and a lacey black push-up bra. The crowd went wild.

"We've got to get her out of here." Dannika was at my elbow, suddenly. "She's sideways."

"She's so…" I searched for the right word as Joni unbuttoned her jeans slowly, looking like each movement brought her excruciating pleasure, "…professional."

"Yeah, well, she *was,*" Dannika said, as if this was obvious. "She used to be a stripper."

My eyes widened. "You're kidding."

"Look at her." Joni was now inching her jeans off, revealing polka dotted panties. The men below screamed and whistled until they were hoarse. "She made good money at it."

Ohm came over, looking alarmed. "We have to get her out of here," he said. "She'll start a riot."

"That's what I said." Dannika tossed her hair over her shoulder impatiently.

"But *how?*" I was eyeing Joni's thick-necked fans as they raised their hairy hands to her in supplication. I wasn't quite sure how the three of us were going to free her of that mob without violence. I looked around for Miranda and Portia.

"They're outside smoking up," Ohm said, reading my mind.

"Great," I mumbled, rolling my eyes. My SWAT team consisted of a D-list celebrity and a fairy who looked like a Calvin Klein model. The three of us were about as threatening as a bridge club.

I looked back at the bar, trying to formulate a plan. Joni was now slowly, teasingly starting to unhook her bra. Her hips continued to gyrate with the relentless grace and efficiency of a well-oiled machine. There was a guy who looked like a linebacker screaming, "Joni Greenfield! Baby! Come to me!" over and over. His face was purple with the effort and his big, hammy fists kept flying into the air in a vague gesture of victory. There was another guy planted directly below Joni whose face was so hairy, he could easily be mistaken for Sasquatch. He said nothing, just gazed up at Joni with worshipful bovine eyes, but didn't hesitate to shove anyone who dared to infringe on his space, sending them flying back like torpedoes into the crowd. Joni was still toying with them, inching her bra straps lower as she batted her eyelashes and slowed her hips to a sinuous writhing.

Miranda and Portia appeared just as a plan was starting to crystallize in the dim corners of my brain. It wasn't a good plan—I was perfectly aware of that—but under the circumstances, expedience was more important than brilliance and nobody else seemed to be stepping forward with the blueprints for another, more foolproof escape. We formed a quick huddle.

"Right, this is how it goes: when this song is over, Dannika and I will climb up on the bar while Ohm and Miranda drag Joni away. I don't care how you do it, just get her out of here. Dannika and I will distract the crowd so they won't complain too much when she disappears."

Portia looked hurt. "What about me? What do I do?"

"I'm getting to that. We're the red herrings, but then we'll need to get down off the bar and out of here without incident. You know where the lights are?"

Miranda nodded. "They're back there," she said, nodding to the far corner, "by the bathrooms."

"Did you hear that?" I said to Portia. "Your job is to trip the lights, then run for the door. We'll climb off the bar in the dark and meet you all by the car, which Miranda should have started by then. You got it?"

"Fine," Dannika said, unbuttoning her blouse one button and smoothing her glossy blond hair into place. "Let's get this over with."

When the final refrain of "Ice, Ice, Baby" started to fade and The Rolling Stones kicked in with "Emotional Rescue," Dannika and I clambered up on the bar. Thank God I was wearing my white go-go boots—there's nothing worse than being humiliated out of costume. As soon as we were in place, Ohm and Miranda yanked Joni off the bar none too gracefully and she cried out in protest as they carted her toward the door in her bra and panties. A few forlorn fans followed her with their eyes as she was carted kicking and screaming out the door, but then I saw their faces turning back toward us—or, more specifically, toward Dannika, since I was just standing there, frozen in place, wearing my car coat over my orange dress and looking, no doubt, more like a PTA mom than a stripper.

Dannika, on the other hand, was taking to her role quite enthusiastically. Eschewing Joni's gradual, teasing style, she immediately ripped open her blouse, sending buttons flying and exposing a lovely blue silk bra that displayed her silicone wonders to great effect. One of the guys yelled, "Show us your tits!" and just like that she undid the front clasp, letting everything pop out. She slung her bra out into the crowd; only then did she start to dance.

That's when things got truly surreal.

The ceiling was pretty low, so she had to hunch over slightly, and a couple times she almost whacked her head against the exposed beams. None of this stopped her from taking go-go dancing to an all new, totally manic level. Her hips became frenetic pistons that jerked spasmodically with no regard for the languorous rhythm. She shimmied her shoulders so her breasts jiggled, but the movement was more Easter Seals than burlesque. I cringed. The faces of the men below went from awe to confusion to cringing embarrassment in a matter of seconds.

Where was Portia with the damn lights? I looked over toward the bathrooms and spotted her talking to a rat-faced hippie in a striped rugby shirt. She looked like she was arguing with him, and each time she moved for the switch on the wall, he blocked her, smiling sadistically.

I had no choice; I had to intervene.

Against my better judgment, I started to dance. I stood there with my coat on, closed my eyes, and let my hips find the beat. Once I felt the bass line reverberating off my pelvic bones, I let the song travel up into my chest. Mick Jagger's predatory growl was throbbing inside my rib cage by the time I took my coat off, folded it neatly, and placed it behind me on the bar.

Dannika was attempting some wildly arrhythmic hip-hop moves that lent her the air of a palsied mental patient in the midst of electric-shock therapy. The men were all looking to me now for some kind of relief. Though the social consciousness in that place was barely ankle deep, I really think they felt guilty about watching the retarded blonde take her clothes off, no matter how nice her tits were.

Suddenly I heard a dull thud beside me, and saw Dannika rubbing the back of her head with one hand. She must have hit it on one of the beams. She looked around the room in bleary confusion, as if trying to recall where she was. Sasquatch offered her a hand, and she crawled down off the bar. It was just me now and still Portia was trying to get around the vile hippie, to no avail.

You know I have to be in a certain mood to dance. Well, tonight I learned that in an emergency I can force that mood. By the time I got around to slowly unzipping the front of my dress a few inches, the electric guitar was in my bloodstream and my pulse was pounding in time with the snare. Those go-go boots were planted firmly on the bar, but the rest of me was filled with such a helium-dizzy light-ness I thought for sure I would float away. It was the kind of hedonistic thrill only a good song, a four-beer buzz and a screaming mob of worshipful men can produce. I closed my eyes; it made it easier to concentrate on the elixir of their frantic voices mixed with the reds and greens of the neon lights. Somewhere along the way, Mick Jagger had morphed into Prince's "Erotic City," and I was letting my thigh muscles lead.

I don't know if I heard his voice or sensed his presence or what, but just as the second chorus of "Erotic City" started up, my eyes flew open and I found myself staring directly down at Coop. I had just unzipped my dress all the way, and the screaming had reached a fever-pitch when it slipped off my shoulders, revealing my white balconet bra with matching panties, garter belt, and lace-top stockings. Okay, yes, it was a very good lingerie day; four beers aside, I'd never have gotten that naked in my fraying-elastic period-undies. Plus, I'd waxed. That was about all I had to feel grateful for as I stood there, eyes locked with Coop, boots planted in a wide stance, my face going from sultry to horrified, my hips freezing mid-swivel.

And then, thank God, Portia finally made it past the rat-faced hippie and the room went black.

We escaped in the ensuing chaos. I was glad I'd folded my clothes neatly and placed them on the bar; they were easy enough to locate, even in the dark. Still, there was plenty of yelling and confusion, spilled drinks and big, sweaty bodies to navigate.

Back in the Subaru, Joni kept popping her head through the sunroof, yelling, "Ice, ice, baby!" at the top of her lungs. Nobody had managed to locate her discarded shirt, so she was wearing only jeans and her black lacy bra. I tried to pull her back inside the car each time, but it was no use. In the front seat, Portia and Miranda were laughing nonstop, Portia kept saying, "I kneed him the balls!" as she gasped for air, hysterical.

"Well, ladies," Ohm said. "There's a party at my cousin's if you want to get serious about this bachelorette business."

Portia squealed her approval. Miranda said, "Sure, why not?" Joni said, "Ice, ice, baby," which appeared to be an affirmative. Dannika just shrugged. She'd apparently managed to find her clothing, because she was dressed again, but her white blouse now had a large footprint on it and a couple of the buttons were missing.

I was barely listening. Coop's face, blank with astonishment, was etched into my brain and my heart was pounding like I'd just run a four-minute mile. I'd left without saying a word to him. Even if I could have gotten to him in the midst of all the chaos, what would I have said?

"That okay with you, Holly Golightly?" Ohm asked.

"Roger that," I said.

Ohm's cousin lives in an astounding house on the bluffs, a sleek, contemporary, big-windowed place with bamboo floors and modern Danish furniture. There were huge abstract paintings on the walls, glass coffee tables, plush suede couches and two big, fluffy cats who slinked through the sea of legs with haughty disinterest. The living room was packed with people, most of them in their twenties, though I spotted at least three grey ponytails. The air was thick with marijuana smoke and reggae poured from the stereo. Kids in ratty layers played hacky sack out on the porch. Beyond their silhouettes, past the deck railing, the sea stretched out under the moon, her voluptuous swells silver as mercury.

I was happy enough to lose myself in the loud mayhem of the party. Of course, I didn't know anyone and at that moment I didn't have enough mental vacancy for small talk with strangers, so I kept moving through the jungle of red plastic cups, smoke and anonymous limbs, hoping that I looked convincingly purposeful. I don't think anyone was sober or interested enough to care. As for me, my buzz was starting to wear off, but my head was still back at the Tip Top, replaying those last moments. I could feel the zipper vibrating slightly under my fingers as I slid it all the way down my body. Prince's quirky rhythm was directing my hips. There was the sound of a piercing wolf whistle and a unanimous roar as I let my dress fall away. Coop's face was a snapshot I couldn't get rid of and still I couldn't quite decode what I saw there. Was that laughter at the corners of his eyes or anger? Did his slightly parted lips signify shock, amusement or disgust?

I went to the kitchen and got myself a glass of water. The drinking portion of the evening was over, as far as I was concerned. You know me—beer number five would send me off on some terrifying trajectory and I wasn't ready to launch that rocket. At the sink, I ran into Joni, who was finally wearing something other than her black lacy bra. She had on a pink fluffy mohair sweater and in place of her hiking boots someone had dressed her in a pair of turquoise Uggs that looked at least three sizes too big.

"Nice outfit," I said. "Where'd you get it?"

"Melissa." The three syllables gave her a bit of trouble.

"Who's Melissa?"

"Ohm's…cuz," she said, leaning against me.

"You look good," I lied.

She looked down at herself. "I look like shit, but who cares?" The exuberance she'd displayed on the way here seemed to be replaced now with a sullen fatalism.

"How are you feeling?" I grabbed another plastic cup and filled it from the tap. "Do you want some water?"

"Water?" She made a disgusted face, as if I'd just offered her a cup of horse piss. "My last night of freedom, and you want me to hydate?" She was dropping crucial consonants.

"You're getting married, not going to Sing Sing," I said.

She just let out a world-weary guffaw and started rummaging through the cupboards until she located a half-full bottle of Jack Daniel's and a shot glass.

I winced. "You sure you want to hit that? I could make you a cocktail." My plan was to make her a very weak Jack and Coke, but she saw right through it.

"Forget it," she slurred. "You just want me to be respecable."

"Not at all," I said, "I want you to be your wild, woolly self."

"I'm not wooly." Suddenly her face fell. "Oh, shit, I didn't shave. Was I woolly?"

I put an arm around her shoulder. "Not at all. It's just an expression."

She looked at me, then, and her caramel eyes filled with tears. "Am I a loser?"

"No, Joni," I told her, sincere. "Why would you even ask that?"

"I just—you know..." She ran a hand over her face, forehead to chin, and blinked like a sleepy child. "I thought I was, like, ready for this shit."

"For marriage?"

She nodded sadly and the tears spilled over her bottom lashes, cascading down her cheeks. "I wrote a poem about it. And now look. Get me drunk, I'm just a slutty little stripper. Don't even have nineteen-year-old tits anymore." She went to unscrew the bottle of Jack, but she had some trouble with it.

I took the bottle from her and unscrewed the top. "I don't think those guys had any complaints about your tits." I poured her a very stingy shot.

She downed it and held her glass out to me again. "Were you...?" She didn't finish her sentence, but somehow I sensed what she wanted to know.

"Surprised?"

"Yeah." She jiggled her glass at me impatiently.

I hit her again. "I was impressed."

We both laughed, remembering the scene at the Tip Top. I wasn't sure if she knew about Dannika and me making our debut. I decided not to mention it. Maybe if enough people were too drunk to remember, it would cease to exist. Unfortunately, the one witness I really cared about had looked dead sober.

"When I lived in North Beach I had seven different wigs. I wasn't Joni, I was Bella."

"I love wigs," I said.

"Wigs are the pinna..." she looked confused, but pressed on "...the tip-top of human evolution." She held out her shot glass again for a refill.

"Are you sure you want more?" I asked, hesitating.

"Just pour," she said, "or I'll get someone else to do it."

I did as I was told.

She drank half of it, sighed, and furrowed her brow at the remaining amber liquid like it contained a message she could barely discern. "I just don't know where my edge went. I used to be streety. Now I'm all soft." She curled her lip in disgust, then tossed back the other half of her shot and looked at me pleadingly. "Phil wants a kid. That's like the last straw. My friend in Santa Barbara had a kid and she looks like she got run over by a truck."

"Come on," I said. "It's not that bad, is it?"

"I won't dance on a bar with stretch marks, I'll tell you that."

Before tonight, I would have said, *who wants to dance on a bar?* but after trying it myself, I could see why she missed it. It gave you a taste of power that could easily be addictive. A cliché popped into my mind that seemed to fit. "Maybe you should just go with the flow."

"Great," she said, "that's how I got here—wasted, in a pink sweater and turquoise Uggs, waiting to get knocked up by a bald anarchist. Fuck this, man." She slammed the shot glass down so hard on the counter that a few people looked at us disapprovingly. "Fill me up," she said.

"Joni, seriously, I think you've had enough."

"Give me the sdupid bottle," she snarled.

"Really." I held the bottle away from her while she tried to grab it. "I'm only saying this because I'm your friend."

She squinted at me. "If you're my friend, you'll give me the damn bottle."

Just then I heard a laugh that stopped my heart. It was a sound that reached down into the murky depths of my childhood and stirred until my insides were opaque with half-forgotten memories. It distracted me, and my grip on the bottle must have loosened, because when Joni lunged for it and grabbed hold it came away in her hands too easily and she fell backward. The laugher turned around in time to catch her in his sturdy arms and prop her back up.

I found myself face-to-face with my father.

"Gwen," he said, his mouth flaring into a confused little grin, "my God, what are you doing here?"

"Hi." My hands shot out from my sides in an embarrassed little *ta-dah*.

"Got it!" Joni declared as she stumbled away from us, gripping the bottle of Jack. I knew it was irresponsible to let her walk away like that, but there was a whirring sound in my head now and my father's face was suddenly so big and so real, close enough to touch, I felt clammy and a little nauseous.

"This is such a surprise, Gwenny." My father took two steps toward me. I knew he was going to hug me, so I braced myself, but I wasn't prepared for the surge of angst and longing that washed over me when he pulled me into his arms. He smelled of wool and marijuana and traces of the cold night fog. Probably the same could be said for ninety percent of the people in that room, but what my father did with those scents was altogether unique.

When he pulled away, we looked at each other for a long moment. He'd aged some in the four years since I'd seen him last, but he still looked good. It seems funny you've never met him, Marla, but I guess by the time you moved to Sebastopol he was already heavy into researching his third book—traveling a lot, that sort of thing—and then, after awhile, I was so mad at him, I no longer felt that sheen of pride when I introduced him to people, so what was the point? Tonight, though, facing him for the first time in ages,

I could sense again the charisma that used to make me so proud to be his daughter. He's handsome, but only in an offhand way; there's nothing fastidious or vain about him. People are always mistaking him for Michael Douglas; he's got the same stocky, wrestler's build, the same steely blue-grey eyes. He's the sort of man who smiles sparingly, but when he does, he makes you feel like you're basking in the warm light of an unexpected second sun.

"So, wow," he said, "look at you. You look great."

I nodded, chewing on my lip. "Thanks. So do you." I was annoyed to discover there were tears stinging at the back of my eyes.

"What are you doing here, anyway?" He clapped his hand on my shoulder like we were old football buddies.

I cleared my throat. "Bachelorette party. Friend's getting married tomorrow."

He looked confused. "This is a bachelorette party?"

"No, I just— I mean, we ended up here."

I felt a hand on my arm and turned to see Dannika smiling so hard it looked painful. "Who's your friend, Gwen?" She cut her eyes at my father quickly, then resumed beaming at me.

"Um," I hesitated, "this is my dad, actually."

Her lips formed a tight little O of surprise. "Really? What a coincidence, running into him here!" She turned to him. "And do you go by *Dad?*"

He stuck his hand out. "Martin Matson. Nice to meet you."

"Dannika Winters," she purred.

There was a sick, poisonous feeling taking shape in the pit of my stomach. I tried hard to keep my face completely blank, though. "Dannika drove us up here from L.A."

She laughed. "Just a glorified taxi! Actually, I'm really close friends with her boyfriend, Coop. You know Coop, right?"

Dad shoved his hands into his pockets. "No, I haven't met him."

Dannika's pretty forehead wrinkled in confusion for a moment, then smoothed out to its usual flawlessness. "Oh, right, well they haven't been dating for very long. But you should meet him! In fact, you should come to Joni and Phil's wedding tomorrow."

I wanted to shove her across the room. I pictured myself suddenly acquiring bionic powers and pushing her so hard she'd shatter the sliding glass door on contact. "Well," I said, "he's probably busy."

"Actually, I was—"

"Hey." A slender brunette in a fisherman knit sweater materialized beside Dad and slipped an arm around his waist. She had pretty green eyes that sparkled now with possessive interest. "Glad to see you're making friends."

"Kelly." Dad kissed her forehead and nodded at me. "This is my daughter, Gwen."

Her eyes widened and her lips parted in astonishment. "You're kidding!" She wasn't as young as the girl he was dating when I visited him four years ago. That one was twenty-seven, tops. Kelly was probably a well-preserved thirty-eight; at least she had the grace to wrinkle a little when she smiled. She was definitely my father's type—dark hair, creamy Irish skin—but she was missing the cosmetic perfection of his former girlfriends, that doll-like vacancy I'd always found unnerving.

"Nice to meet you," I said.

Before I knew what was happening, she'd pulled me into a hug. She smelled of eucalyptus or tea-tree oil—something hippie-ish and vaguely medicinal. "Your dad's told me so much about you."

I glanced at him, surprised, and I was suddenly aware of my cheeks burning.

"And this is Donnika," Dad said.

"*Dan*nika," she corrected him, her eyes flashing.

I choked down a nervous giggle.

"I was just telling them, I think we're all going to the same wedding tomorrow." Dad looked at Kelly. "Aren't your friends named Joni and Phil?"

Before she could finish, a heart-stopping scream ripped its way through the ambient party noise.

Joni.

"Excuse me," I said, and made my way in the direction of the scream, which had come from down the hall somewhere. Dannika was right behind me. When we got to the hallway, the bodies thinned out, though a few curious rubbernecking types were, like us, trying to locate the source of the trouble. We stood there a moment listening, waiting for another outburst. In just a few seconds we were rewarded: a low, tormented sob erupted just to our left, behind a closed door.

I knocked loudly. "Joni? Is that you in there?"

More sobs. Behind me, Dannika said, "Try the door."

I did. It was locked. "Joni?" I said, pressing my mouth close to the door. "It's me, Gwen. Please let me in."

A couple of kids stood behind us, looking on with interest. One had a blue Mohawk; the other wore a ski cap and his septum was pierced with a thick silver ring, which looked slightly damp with snot.

"Do you mind?" Dannika said.

"We're just looking for the john." The kid in the ski cap employed a defensive whine, his eyes locked on the gap created by Dannika's missing button.

"Well, go find another one. This one's taken," she sneered.

They shuffled off, mumbling insults at us.

"Joni," I called, trying a sterner tone this time. "I'm serious. Let me in right now." When she didn't answer, I whipped a bobby pin out of my purse and fiddled with the lock until it opened. I was surprised that I could still pull this off; I used to do it all the time when I lost my keys, but ever since you suggested stashing a spare in the aloe, I've been out of practice.

"Cool," Dannika said.

Joni was sitting on the toilet, her face in her hands. All around her on the white tiled floor were clumps of her dull brown hair. Somehow, removed from her person and disembodied like that, the dreads looked sinister. She, on the other hand, looked like Sinéad O'Connor. She'd shaved her head right down to a startling stubble. Once you got past the concentration camp associations, it was easy to see that her skull was perfectly shaped. As she looked up at me, her brown-sugar eyes were bigger and more striking than ever.

"Holy shit," Dannika said.

"Whad I do?" Joni whimpered.

I stepped around the little piles of hair and ran my hand over her stippled scalp. "I love it," I said. "It's a great look for you."

For a moment she looked hopeful. "Really?"

"Really," I said. "What inspired you?"

Joni leaned over and seized the bottle of Jack sitting on the edge of the bathtub, still partly full; she took a half-hearted swig, followed by a shudder. "I was standing in front of the mirror going, 'My hair…my *hair*.' I wanted it all off. You know? Like I just didn't *want* it anymore. Next thing I knew I had a shaver in my hand—instant baldie!"

Dannika shook her head, still staring at Joni in disbelief. "Damn."

Though it rather disgusted me, I started picking up the severed dreadlocks scattered across the floor and sticking to the bathmats. I glanced at Dannika. "Let's just clean up a little. Then we'll find the twins and get her home."

There was a soft knock on the bathroom door, and I heard my father say, "Gwen? Is everything okay in there?"

This was too surreal. If someone would have told me two days ago that I'd find myself gathering up dreads while my father hovered nearby, offering assistance, I would have laughed. "It's fine, Dad."

Of course, Joni chose this moment to be loudly and explosively sick in the bathtub. Dad pushed the door open and stepped inside. "Why don't I help?"

Kelly appeared behind my father, then Ohm, who said, "Jesus Christ, Joni." I shot him a look and he shut up. The five of us worked together to clean up the bathroom, trying not to retch. Then my father wiped the vomit from her mouth with his own handkerchief and carried Joni out to the twins' Subaru. He didn't offer commentary, which I appreciated. Every now and then our eyes would catch and I'd feel again the bewilderment of seeing him here, under these strange circumstances, after four years of chilling silence.

Once we'd rounded up the twins and everyone except me was packed into the Subaru, Dad pulled me aside and said, "Is it okay with you if I go tomorrow?" When I just looked at him blankly, he added, "To your friends' wedding?"

"Oh," I said, "yeah, of course."

He stared over my shoulder and clenched, then unclenched his jaw. "I won't go if you don't want me there."

I hesitated. I could hear waves crashing in the distance, and the fog felt good against my face—damp and cool. It was enough of a pause that he filled it in with, "Right. That's what I figured. I'll just tell Kelly I can't make it."

"No! You should come. Really."

His gray-blue eyes searched my face. There were so many moments like this in our history. I could feel the tower of them teetering inside me, stacked on top of each other like playing cards, until it was hard to tell one from the other. There he was, asking me to forgive him in his own oblique way. And there I was, not knowing how to answer.

"Seriously," I said. "It's fine. See you tomorrow." I walked away.

When I got in the car, Ohm said, "You got a thing for older men?"

"He's my father," I said in a flat, tired voice. Then I covered my face with my hands and started to cry.

Back at FUBAR Ranch, Coop was trying to keep Phil from burning down the house. As per tradition, the groom had imbibed more than his usual quota of beer. Coop had spent the evening babysitting, then had tucked him into bed, but was nervous about the cigarettes on the nightstand. Evidently, Phil's sort of famous for smoking while unconscious, especially when he's got a good buzz on. Coop tried to confiscate the smokes, but Phil got so belligerent, he finally gave up. Ten minutes later, Coop smelled something burning, and found Phil snoring while his smoldering cigarette engraved a ragged black hole in the quilt.

After the twins dropped us off, Dannika and I dragged Joni into the house and slowly made our way toward the spiral staircase. I spotted Coop at the top of the stairs, shaking his head.

"Holy shit," he said. "Look at baldy."

It was hard work carrying Joni's dead weight; Coop hurried down to meet us and scooped her up into his arms. He carried her to the top of the stairs, then propped her up against the wall and exhaled heavily.

Gingerly touching her bald head, he said, "Things got out of hand, I guess."

"You guessed right," I whispered.

"Long story, huh?" He looked at Dannika, then me. We both nodded. "Wow. You girls sure know how to party." I'd never seen him look so worn-out. There were dark circles under his eyes and his hair looked lank, but he offered a tired grin, anyway.

"Joni's drunk," Dannika told him, "and Gwen's depressed."

I wasn't depressed, exactly—just emotionally drained. I felt wrung out, depleted, empty.

Coop put his hand on my shoulder. "You didn't look too depressed at the Tip Top." His tone was difficult to decipher; then I saw the sparkle in his eyes and I knew he was teasing me.

Dannika said, "You've got to be kidding. You were there?"

"I just caught the tail end, so to speak."

"Did you see me?" Understandably, she was horrified.

He laughed. "What—you girls took turns? I guess I missed you."

"Joni started it." Dannika sounded about six. "Then Gwen got her bright idea and dragged me into it." There was no mistaking the mean edge to her voice. Another wave of exhaustion hit me. Joni mumbled something in her inebriated delirium about Uggs.

I was too shaky from crying all the way home to trust my voice, so I whispered, "Let's get Joni to bed."

"I don't think she should sleep with Phil. He's liable to cremate them. I can't get him to stop smoking." Coop explained briefly about his failed attempts to confiscate Phil's pack of American Spirits.

"So what do you suggest?" My eyelids were so heavy, I could hardly see straight.

"Why don't you go ahead and sleep with Joni in our room? I'll keep an eye on ole smokey." He raked a hand through his hair and it stood up in the wake of his fingers.

"Roger that." I was disappointed, of course. This was night two of our romantic weekend away, and so far I'd shared a bed with nearly everyone except Coop.

"Where's my proud beauty?" Phil stumbled out of the door at the end of the hallway and walked a crooked line toward us. He was wearing a loud paisley bathrobe over striped boxers and a white T-shirt. "Joni? Baby? Is that you?"

I held my breath. Phil didn't strike me as the sort of guy who'd get hung up on a haircut, but his bride was looking pretty rough at the moment and I was afraid he might be shocked at the sight of her. He nudged Coop out of the way and gently lifted Joni's chin with one finger. "Baby," he said, "you're bald."

Her eyes fluttered open and when she saw his face inches from hers she mumbled, "Do you hate it?"

He bent down and kissed her sweetly. "How could I hate it, cutie? You look just like me."

She smiled a woozy smile and they kissed again. I was just about to go, "Ahhh," when Joni threw up all over Phil's T-shirt. Coop, Dannika and I all backed away in disgust, but Phil barely moved. "That's my girl," he said, wiping her mouth with the sleeve of his bathrobe. "That's my party girl."

Phil protested a bit when he realized Joni wouldn't be sleeping in their bed, but Coop convinced him it was bad luck to sleep with the bride the night before the wedding. I finally got Joni tucked in with a bucket beside her in case she had another accident. Heading for the bathroom to brush my teeth, I spotted Dannika in the same filmy green camisole she'd worn to bed last night; tonight she paired it with miniature tap pants that showed off the full length of her radiant, razor-ad legs. She was standing very close to Coop, speaking in whispers. I ducked back into the guest-room and watched them through the crack in the door. Coop was in boxers and a T-shirt, nodding at whatever she said. A slow, queasy feeling came over me. I closed the door again, careful not to make a sound.

As I crossed the room, stepping through moonlight, I was so cold and depleted all I could think about was burying myself under that thick down comforter. I crawled into bed beside Joni and waited for sleep. When it didn't come, I decided to write you a quick note and now here I am, many pages later, amazed at everything that's gone down in a mere eight hours and perplexed at my own willingness to record it. I mean these are the sort of bacchanal nights you're supposed to be too smashed to recall, let alone document.

I guess I just needed to tell someone, and I'm finding the blank page is the most forgiving of confidantes.

Yours truly,
Gwen

11:20 a.m.

Dear Marla,

Well, here it is, the wedding day. Unfortunately, most of the occupants of FUBAR Ranch are hardly fit to munch dry toast, let alone participate in a grand rite of passage. The whole stag night concept, along with its scrawny kid sister, the bachelorette party, is starting to seem like a very sadistic tradition. It's a wonder anyone gets married at all with such hangovers.

The bride woke with a groan. She opened one eye and I handed her two Advil and a glass of water. She glanced around the room, blinking in bleary confusion, then gobbled the pills I offered and gulped downed the water like she'd barely survived a trek through the desert.

I'd had a hard night myself, and I was running on the fumes of free-floating anxiety. I'd slept fitfully and more than once found myself thrashing about, fighting the sheets, glazed in sweat. My eyes had popped open at 5:00 a.m. and had refused to shut again no matter what I did. Now I was bone tired but trying to rise above it, determined to be of service. One look at the bald girl with the puffy eyes made it clear: she needed me. If ever makeover magic was required, now was the time.

You know better than anyone how I get when I've got a project before me; a neglected face in need of serious transformation helps me focus like nothing else. Of course, I'm not a professional with makeup. Costuming is my bag and I don't believe in being a generalist. Still, the long hours I've spent backstage tending to torn hems and mussed wigs has taught me more about blush, eyeliner and lipstick than most people will learn in a lifetime. I was always fascinated by the art of disguise, even back in high school, and as long as some porky ingenue hadn't busted a zipper, you'd find me backstage with the hair and makeup people learning to hide a zit, apply a mustache, tease a beehive or (my favorite) create Audrey Hepburn lashes that won't streak no matter how tragic things get onstage. To me, makeup is magic. It can make old people young, young people old, men into women and women into men. Today, my job is to make a hungover, depressed, bald bachelorette into a luminous bride.

I've got my work cut out for me.

I reached over to the nightstand and handed Joni a cup of black tea. She sat up straighter and took it from me. As she blew the steam from the surface and slurped experimentally, I studied her face. Her eyes would definitely be the feature to play up—they were absolutely beautiful, with a color that ranged from cinnamon to butter, depending on Joni's mood, what she was wearing and the light. She had a mouth that was worth emphasizing, as well. Her lips were just full enough to benefit from a generous blast of color and perhaps a subtle layer of gloss. Obviously, she was a nature girl and I'd have to respect that. This wasn't a Bel Air clubber I was dealing with, someone used to slathering her face with an inch of foundation. I'd have to proceed with caution, talk her through it, be gentle. But we needed to get some cucumbers on those pink, bloated eyes right away.

"I look like shit," Joni said. "Stop staring at me." Then she went to hide her face in her usual curtain of dreads, but her fingers touched bare scalp and her face went white. "Jesus. I really did that? I thought it was a nightmare."

"You gave yourself a bit of a trim," I said. "No biggie. It's sexy."

She held tight to her teacup with both hands and flashed me an incredulous look. "Sexy? You've got to be kidding. I must look like a chemo patient."

"You do not! Anyway, there are always wigs if you feel too naked. I know you like wigs—you told me."

She put her tea down on the nightstand. "Oh, my God," she said. "I danced at the Tip Top, didn't I? Why am I such a skank?"

"You're not," I said. "You're a complex woman with a past. It's mysterious. Gives you an edge."

"Yeah, well, razor blades have edges. So do butcher knives and sharks' teeth. Would you want to marry one?"

I smiled. "I'm guessing your complexity is one of the qualities Phil likes best."

This seemed to placate her momentarily. She picked up her cup again and took another sip.

"So, what's the plan today?" I asked. It was a dangerous question; I didn't want to shatter her momentary calm, but if I was electing myself chief beauty consultant, I'd have to know the schedule.

"Ceremony down at Big River at three, then back here for the after-party—reception—whatever. God, I feel like shit."

"Where's your dress?"

"It's in the closet." Her tone was listless as flat champagne. It didn't bode well.

I crossed the room, slid the closet door open, and pulled out the only dress hanging there that wasn't mine. I'd noticed it earlier, when I'd hung up my things, but hadn't suspected it was Joni's wedding dress. Inspecting it now, my heart sank. It was one of those shapeless, empire-waist cotton numbers so popular during the summer of love. The bodice was embroidered with small flowers in piñata hues. The rest of it cascaded in totally formless yards of white cotton. The sleeves were long and a little frayed at the cuffs. There was a small stain near the left seam, a dime-sized circle of red wine. I forced myself to maintain a neutral expression, but it was precisely the sort of vaguely ethnic, totally unflattering hippie-garb I hate most. This dress is the reason I won't even touch anything created after 1963.

"Oh, God," Joni said, "you hate it."

"I don't—I—it's—"

"Oh, come on," she said, "It's hideous and you know it."

I cringed. "It's not exactly my style, but I'm not the bride, here."

She hung her head and started to cry. I dropped the dress at the foot of the bed and sat beside her. Her tears deepened to sobs. I stroked her scalp lightly, mumbling sounds of comfort. When she was able to speak again, she wiped her tears with the back of her hands and said, "It's all wrong. This whole thing is FUBAR."

"What do you mean?"

She sniffed wetly and I dug in my bag until I found a handkerchief. She blew her nose twice, looking miserable. "It was my mom's wedding dress. She wanted me to wear it. I don't know why I agreed. It's totally cursed."

"But aren't your parents still together?"

She nodded, pulling at the handkerchief absently. "Yeah, and they don't hate each other or anything. Still, she makes me so sad. You'd never know it now, but she was this really amazing dancer when she was young. She toured with Merce Cunningham for years." She looked out the window, her expression dreamy and faraway. "Then she fell for Dad and they bought this place, had me. She lost all her edges, got old. Now she's doughy and soft and doesn't dance or anything. The closest she gets to art these days is knitting tea cozies at Christmas." She looked at me, her eyes shining with tears. "I don't want to do that. But look at me. I've already gotten lazy. When I met Phil, what's the first thing I did? Moved to Santa Barbara and stopped dancing. Not that what I was doing was art, exactly, but it was something…." She gazed at the dress, rumpled at the foot of the bed. "I guess history repeats itself."

"It doesn't have to." I grabbed her hand and squeezed it harder than I meant to. The urgency in my own voice surprised me. "Why should it?"

She sighed. "I don't know why, but it does."

"Don't let it."

She shook her head. "Do I really have a choice?"

"Yes!" I could see from her face that she didn't believe me. I changed tack. "Do you love Phil?"

"Yeah, I do." The simple honesty of her answer gave me courage.

"So, isn't it your responsibility—for his sake, if not for

yours—to keep all those qualities alive that he fell in love with? I mean, you're complicated and edgy and sexy—you love art and you've got those dancer genes flying through your system. Who says you have to get soft, just because your mom did?"

She closed her eyes for a second and when she opened them again tears were spilling down her cheeks with fresh force. God, it was going to take a miracle to get the puffiness out if she kept on crying. "I don't know, Gwen...it's not that simple."

"We're not our parents," I said, squeezing her shoulders, looking her right in the eye. "Can you trust me on this?" I repeated it, more slowly this time, emphasizing each syllable. "We are not our parents."

Finally, she nodded, the tears started to let up. "Yeah," she said. "You're right. I've got to stop being such a total wimp about this."

"Good girl." I stood up, lifted the dress from the bed, put it back in the closet. "Now, I don't want to be bossy here, but in my opinion, a girl should wear something really, truly decadent on her wedding day. It should be something so beautiful, it makes her heart stop. I mean, just for a second. Don't you think?"

She looked at her lap. "Gwen, where am I going to find a dress now?"

"Don't worry about that. Just tell me: am I overstepping my bounds if I make it my mission to transform you into the most beautiful and glamorous bride this town has ever seen?"

She shrugged. "It's not bossy, it's just mission impossible."

"Darling," I said, "you underestimate me."

More later,

Gwen

4:33 p.m.

Dear Marla,

My God. What is it about a wedding that reduces everyone to weepy old women? Even Phil, who takes pride in his cynical, neo-punk persona, was crying like a girl during the ceremony. Okay, so I shed a few tears myself. Is that a crime? Not enough for extensive mascara damage, so don't worry yourself.

Joni's radiant. Some of it's the glow of love, some of it's champagne and some of it's the thorough exfoliation treatment I subjected her to this morning. Plus, her makeup is exquisite—I used just enough to give her the natural, satiny sheen of a woman filled with bliss.

At the moment I'm hidden away in a hammock on the hill with a glass of bubbly, which is nice. Everyone else is frolicking in the meadow, dancing to bluegrass or eating the amazing pan-Asian finger food provided by Joni's mom. The weather is divine—warm sun, cool shade. There are little mashed potato clouds that float by every now and then, but other than that the sky is one huge, silky swath of vivid blue. It's a day the gods whipped up in honor of love—not the somber devotion of old people, but the impulsive ardor of fools. Salty breezes play with your hair and the air smells of ocean, pine and redwoods.

How do you like the new notebook, by the way? That legal pad was way too awkward. Coop bought this in town today, after picking up the tuxes. When he handed it over, he said, "What exactly are you filling these things with, anyway?"

"My life story," I said. "Want to be in it?"

He grinned. "Depends. Am I the hero with huge pecs or the passing-fling dude?"

"Jury's still out," I said, "but you've got nice pecs, if that's the casting criteria."

You know what? Forget all this mamby-pamby he-loves-me-he-loves-me-not shit. Who cares what happened in Malibu? Dannika hasn't said one trustworthy thing since I met her. Why would I let her conniving little stories undermine the only relationship I've ever had worth saving? I'm just going to believe in Coop and love him and assume he's being honest until I've got reason—I mean *real* reason—to think otherwise. Damn the torpedoes, or however that goes. Seeing Joni and Phil today makes me want to be brave and stupendous; they make me want to love with the sort of abandon that can sink ships and scatter stars.

First things first, though: outfit update.

Quickly: I'm in my sunflower-yellow rayon faille strapless dress with a thin, rhinestone-studded belt, a fitted jacket with scalloped peplum, a rhinestone choker and matching teardrop earrings, an oval-brimmed hat made of genuine beaver-fur felt and, of course, as usual, my signature leopard-print kitten heels.

Phil and Coop are in classic tuxes with tails, at my insistence. I sent Coop all over town this morning looking for a place to rent them. I wasn't going to see my gorgeous bride standing next to a couple of guys in cheap corduroy blazers or velveteen or whatever it is boys put on when left to their own devices.

Okay, okay, Dannika's wearing a chiffon dress in pale orange with a plunging beaded bodice. The short, flowy, above-the knee style shows off her mile-long legs to great effect, but frankly the overall look is a little too Victoria's Secret for my taste.

Just so you can visualize the dramatis personae.

Joni's dress we'll get to in a minute.

Originally, the bride had no intention of hiding herself from the guests as they arrived. She'd planned on mingling with her friends, dressed in her shapeless nightgown-thing, drinking beer like it was any old day at the beach. That was one of many plans I had to alter today.

Luckily, Phil was able to scrounge up a big army tent; we pitched it near the dunes and I made it my on-site beauty headquarters. Joni thought it was silly to stay away from her guests, but I explained it was necessary if she was going to debut with any panache. I wanted everything to be perfect when she walked across the sand to join hands with Phil. I even had an old guy with a banjo work out a little ditty that sounded passably close to a here-comes-the-bride. I was going for gasps all around, with dabbing handkerchiefs from the women and choked-down emotions from the men. You know me: if I'm mystical about anything, it's the power of a truly glamorous entrance.

Remember when I prepared you for your first date with Jean-Paul? There was steaming and plucking, masks and lotions, an hour of experimentation to find just the right nail polish. Well, take that experience and ratchet up the intensity about twelve notches, you'll have a pretty accurate picture of our morning. Things were a little tense at times. Not only were we rushed, with inordinately high stakes, but I didn't have all of my tools, so a good deal had to be slapped together from the ingredients in Joni's kitchen: egg white pore-shrinkers, avocado masques, that sort of thing. In a way, this was just as well, since Joni's an organic girl at heart; no doubt some of my more chemical-edged products would have freaked her out, even though they're faster and more effective than nature's bounty.

The dress, though, was the real challenge. I considered lending her my elegant shirtwaist number with rhinestone buttons, but that seemed rather tacky since everyone had seen me in it just the day before. Even if we could overcome that, I knew the effect would be more chic than romantic, which just wouldn't do. I tore through Joni's closet in search of anything I might be able to work with, but it was wall-to-wall peasant-gear in there: torn jeans, aging cords, wool sweaters, frayed ponchos. She barely owned a single skirt, let alone a dress that could be transformed into a gown.

Finally, desperate but trying very hard not to show it, I asked about the grandmother whose riding gear I'd worn yesterday. Did she leave behind anything else? Joni thought about it a second, then told me if she had, it would probably be in her mother's attic. She explained how to get there, and as soon as I was out of view, I ran down that dirt road in the grandmother's boots until my lungs ached. When I arrived at the old Finnish farmhouse, Joni's mother greeted me with surprise. I told her why I was there and as soon as the words were out of my mouth I regretted my mistake.

"But Joni already has a wedding dress. Mine."

"Yeah, um, the thing is, there's a stain on it. Red wine.

We tried everything to get it out, but nothing worked." It wasn't a lie, exactly.

"Oh, that! I think that's from when I wore it, but who cares? No one will notice." She pushed some lank gray bangs out of her eyes and I tried to imagine her as a professional dancer. Her sagging breasts and bulging stomach were now encased in a cheap-looking sweatshirt with the logo of a roofing company splashed across the chest. Below that, ill-fitting polyester pants clung to her lumpy hips and thighs. I was in full-on makeover mode and I was already seeing what a little foundation and the right shade of matte lipstick could do for her washed-out, spider-vein riddled complexion.

"Mrs. Greenfield, I'll level with you. This is an important day and Joni deserves to look stunning." I took a deep breath and pressed on. "I'm sure your dress was gorgeous on you, but she should have something that reflects her personality. That's why I just want a few minutes in your attic."

She seemed a little taken aback by my earnest intensity, but she let me in. "Are you sure you want to bother?" she asked uneasily. "I mean, a dress is a dress, right?"

I had to struggle to maintain my composure. *A dress is a dress?* Where do people pick up such misguided ideas?

"The right dress," I said, "is nothing short of a miracle."

She gave me a funny look, but finally pointed me up the stairs. She apologized about not being able to help, saying she had a lot of cooking to do, but I assured her it was no problem. You know from tagging along at flea markets and estate sales that I prefer to paw through other people's junk alone. I was afraid I might have hurt her feelings, but I figured a slightly miffed mother was a small price to pay for Joni's resurrected beauty.

It took ten minutes of weeding through cluttered milk crates and decrepit rattan chairs before I found the steamer trunk. As soon as I saw it, I knew its potential, and my heart started fluttering inside me like a wild bird in a cage. A tiny brass padlock kept the lid firmly locked, but a little work with my bobby pin and voilá, the treasure chest was laid bare.

It was Granny's stuff, all right. I recognized the same subdued, understated taste responsible for the glorious riding boots I had on. Breathing in the heady scent of silks, chiffons and furs growing old together, I carefully unfolded one item after another. There were mink stoles and satin gloves, rayon dresses and wool blazers. It was clear this trunk was reserved for only the most cherished items in her wardrobe—the elite distillations of a lifetime spent loving quality clothes. Going through them was strangely intimate and as I removed each piece I refolded it and set it aside with the reverence of an archaeologist uncovering ancient jewels.

The last item in the trunk was a simple ivory silk dress. It was knee-length, sleeveless, with a fitted waistline and a subtle A-line flare. I loved the bateau neck and the tiny seed pearls embroidered along the waist and at the hem. It was Joni all over—or rather, the Joni I imagined, freed of her natty dreads and her Mexican ponchos. I held the silk to my face and inhaled deeply, thanking the attic gods for this rare find.

Hours later, when Joni emerged from that musty old canvas tent, I gasped along with everyone else, even though I'd left her side just minutes ago. She was beautiful. The naked curve of her scalp seemed to heighten the striking perfection of her face: she was all cheekbones, eyes, teeth and lips. The silk luster of the dress along with the buffed-to-perfection shine of her skin made her look lit from within. Walking across the sand in her bare feet, the afternoon sun pooling in the hollows of her clavicles, she was luminous.

Looking at her serene smile, no one would ever believe the conversation we'd had five minutes earlier:

JONI
I can't do this—God—what am I doing?
ME
Listen, babe: We're not our parents. You got that?
JONI
I refuse to get fat.
ME
Nobody wants you getting fat.

JONI

Shit! Just go out there and tell them I can't do this.

ME

Okay, one more time: We're not our parents. We're free. Now take a deep breath.

JONI

I can't breathe.

ME

In and out. There you go.

JONI

What if he doesn't really love me? He might not even know it. Boys never know what they feel.

ME

Joni, you came home drunk last night after table-dancing at a dive bar and puked all over him. You know what he said? "That's my girl." Are you telling me this guy doesn't love you?

JONI

No. You're right. I'm just being wimpy.

ME

Then let's do this.

JONI

Okay, okay, okay…I'm ready.

ME

Good girl.

JONI

Shit!

As she joined Phil under a driftwood arbor, she didn't look the slightest bit stressed or unsure. I was so relieved. Ever since last night, when her panic had manifested itself in none-too-subtle ways, I'd been gambling on my gut instinct. I sincerely trusted that she wanted to spend her life with Phil. If I didn't believe that—deeply, instinctively—there's no way I would have busted my butt making her glow.

The ceremony was gorgeous, if a little counterculture. Big River was more inspiring than any church could hope to be; it was an expansive, dramatic beach framed by the Navarro River on one side and steep, weather-beaten cliffs on the other. Instead of a preacher, Joni and Phil opted to be married by an elegant old woman sporting a halo of frizzy grey hair, flowing purple robes and a delicate orchid lei. Coop stood beside Phil as the best man, looking dapper and sexy as hell, even if his tux was just slightly on the small side. Joni's bridesmaids were Portia and Miranda. They wore matching green silk dresses that, paired with their fiery hair, brought to mind mermaids. Joni read a beautiful poem she'd written. I don't remember the whole thing, but there was one part that stuck in my head:

In love, we cannot make mistakes
we can only make beauty
fragile, deadly flowers
strewn about like confetti.

When they kissed, the crowd cheered wildly. Someone

threw a felt fedora into the air. The banjo player picked a few lines of something fast and jubilant that sounded suspiciously like "Ice, Ice, Baby." A couple of seagulls careened overhead in wide, giddy circles. Beside me, Dannika swiped at a tear with the back of her hand. I passed her my handkerchief and she blew her nose in it, hard, then handed it back. *Thanks.*

"I'm never getting married," she said, "but it's still so goddamn beautiful."

I nodded in agreement—with the beautiful part, not the never-getting-married bit. I found a patch of my handkerchief that wasn't defiled by her snot and dabbed at a few tears of my own.

Soon, the crowd started to disburse. Joni and Phil were mobbed by well-wishers. Coop made his way toward me, hugged me so hard I lifted a few inches off the sand. He just held me like that for a long moment, my toes dangling above the earth, while seagulls screeched and the ocean roared. I wanted to stay there forever, smelling his smells, wrapped tightly in his arms.

When he put me down at last, I said, "What was that for?"

"For everything," he said. "You're a genius. You know that, right?"

"A genius, really?"

"Obviously. Who else could take this ragtag bunch and whip us into shape like you did?"

"Gwen." I turned, and there was my dad holding hands

with Kelly. "We're going to head over to the house. You want a ride?"

"Oh, um, no, we'll probably help clean up here, first." Everything had been so frantic this morning, I'd completely forgotten to tell Coop about my father. "By the way, Dad, this is Coop, my boyfriend."

Coop looked from me to him and back again in surprise. My father took advantage of his confusion and gave him a squinty once-over. His bushy eyebrows furrowed in a look of paternal concern. He must have approved at least a little, because he stuck his big, rough hand out and Coop shook it firmly. It was all so man-to-man, I wanted to laugh, but I remembered in time to complete the introduction.

"This is my father, Martin, and his…" I hesitated for half a second.

"Fiancée," Kelly said, buttoning her coat.

"Fiancée," I repeated, a little hoarsely. "Kelly."

My father and I exchanged a look. Mine said, *You? Getting married?* His said, *What can I say? I'm in love.*

"Great to meet you," Coop enthused. "Wow. I had no idea." It was a little vague, what Coop had no idea about— that I had a father or that he was here or that he was marrying this cat-eyed brunette. It was probably better to leave it ambiguous.

"Well, I guess we'll see you there." Dad nodded at us,

flashed a crooked grin, and they ambled down the beach, along the river's edge toward the parking lot.

Coop stared after them. "Did you mention your dad would be here?"

"I just ran into him last night."

"What are they doing here?"

"I guess Kelly's friends with Joni's parents." I shrugged. It was a weird coincidence, that was for sure.

He looked at me. "Don't you sort of…dislike your father?"

In our three-month courtship, I'd only divulged minimal data: my parents divorced years ago, I was mad at my father, we weren't on speaking terms. "Well, it's a little more complicated than that."

His gaze went soft and he ran his thumb over my eyebrow. "Promise you'll tell me the whole story sometime?"

I just nodded.

Because, you see, I do want to tell him. I want to tell him about the time I trapped a monarch butterfly in a Mason jar, sealed it tight, and cried when it went still. I want to tell him about the day I almost jumped off the high dive, but instead climbed back down with hot pee running down my thighs. I want to tell him about the years when my dad and I were close, after the divorce but before I got mad at him—when he'd call me from a commune in Berkeley, a village of yurts in Arcata, a straw-bale hut in Ashland, and we'd tell each other secrets. I want to tell him everything about the girl I was before I met him and I want to hear everything about him, too.

All in all, things look promising (knock on wood).

Bubbly with Love,

Gwen

6:00 p.m.

Marla,

Okay, *chica,* get yourself another cappuccino, because what I'm about to tell you requires fortification.

When you get this letter, you'll disown me. I'm a disaster at love; my heart is a tiny, shriveled-up pea. The hard ones, you know? Like those wasabi kind we used to get at Trader Joe's.

Maybe it's the only-child thing. I never learned to share. I covet. I hoard. I can't afford a decent therapist.

Then again, she really is a bitch.

There I was, floating along on my pink cloud of champagne and pure, sugary optimism. My inner soundtrack was blaring "Some Enchanted Evening" and I just knew that Coop and I were destined for sixty years of sweet, monogamous bliss. I was already moving into our chic, *trés* retro apartment, arranging the furniture (his red leather chair would look divine next to my cream silk couch, incidentally) and naming our children (Audrey and Clark, of course).

That's when I walked into the kitchen.

And saw them.

With their arms around each other.

Embracing.

"I love you, Coop," the viper murmured against his shoulder.

"Love you, too, kid. I'll always be here for you."

I watched this touching tableau, paralyzed by horror. They stood in profile near the sink; her cheek was pressed against his lapel, eyes closed. He was looking out the window. She must have sensed me, because her eyes popped open. But she didn't move. She just stayed there in his arms, her glacial stare taunting me.

"How much more of this do you expect me to take?" My words were like knives slicing through the air.

"Gwen." He loosened his hold on her, but he didn't jump back like a man caught at something. He just eased himself away, turned to me with a nonchalance that was grotesquely out of sync with the toxic sludge bubbling up from my gut. "Something wrong, kitten?"

"Something wrong, kitten?" I barely recognized my voice; each syllable sounded hollow and cold. "I walk in on—on this—and you stand there like everything's cool?"

Dannika, the treacherous cow, actually pursed her lips together to keep from laughing. It took every ounce of control not to go for the eyes.

Coop took a step toward me, but I backed away. He frowned. "Maybe it looked sort of—I don't know, suspect—but there's nothing going on here that I'm ashamed of."

"Friends hug sometimes," Dannika informed me, like she was addressing a cranky toddler. "It happens."

"You've done nothing but provoke me all weekend!"

She widened her eyes. "Provoke you?"

"*Please!* I've tried to be a good sport, but for Christ's sake, you're a miserable bitch and you're after my boyfriend."

She offered me a saccharine, condescending smile. "I'm sorry you feel that way."

"Come on, Dannika, that smile is even faker than your tits!"

Coop put a hand up. "Whoa, let's cool down, Gwen."

"I'm not going to *cool down,* okay? Jesus, Coop, you expect me to just hang back while you cuddle up with this harpy?"

He ran a hand through his hair. "Look, I don't know what you thought you saw—it was just a hug."

"Oh yeah? And what about Malibu?"

He stared at me blankly. "What about Malibu?"

Dannika shook her head. "She won't let go of this fixation. I tried to tell her we've always been friends."

I whirled on her. "Liar!"

"Am I missing something here?" Coop was looking from her to me and back again.

"Dannika claims you had a really hot week in Malibu—from her account, it was *sizzling*."

Coop turned to her. "What's she talking about?"

Dannika shrugged. "No idea."

"Did you tell her that?"

"The girl's delusional."

I lunged toward her. "Say that again, you—"

"Gwen!" Coop angled between us, holding me back. "Look, Danni and I are just friends—I swear to you."

"Oh yeah? Try telling her that!"

Dannika addressed her fingernails. "This is what I was talking about…."

Coop just shook his head.

"What?" My temples throbbed and I was sweating under my dress. A fat woman in a flowered muumuu opened the back door and peeked into the kitchen; seeing us, she backed out again. "*What* were you talking about?"

Dannika looked at Coop. "You really want to spend your life with a woman who can't handle a hug?"

He shot her a look of warning. "She's upset, Danni. Back off."

"Oh, so now I'm reduced to the third person?" I was getting dangerously close to screeching.

Dannika didn't even spare me a glance. "Give it some thought." She picked up her champagne flute, swiveled away from us, and slipped out the door. I wanted to tackle her, wrestle her to the floor, lock my fingers around her size two neck until she begged for mercy in ragged gasps.

But I restrained myself. Already, I was getting that low, sick feeling—the nauseating remorse that settles in after you lose it. I was reminded of that torturous climb back down the high dive ladder, stinking of pee.

Coop exhaled. "You really don't trust me, do you?"

"She's a two-faced, lying—"

He gripped my shoulder. "Forget her for second. I'm talking about you and me."

"Coop, there is no you and me when she's in the picture."

He took a step back. "Well, she is in the picture. I'm sorry, but she's my friend."

"You always put her first!" I sounded like a child. *Stop,* I told myself. But I couldn't.

"I can't just amputate big parts of myself to suit you. It wouldn't work."

"You have to choose." Even as I was saying it, I knew it was stupid. Unreasonable. But I wasn't in control anymore. "Who matters more to you, Coop? Me or her?"

"Gwen, don't do this."

"I asked you a question."

His eyes darkened; they went from a mossy, muddy hazel to an opaque green I'd never seen before. "I heard you."

"Well?"

"You both matter. A lot. In very different ways."

"Separate but equal, huh?" My voice had an ugly edge.

"Gwen." Our eyes locked and then I saw his face go from frustrated to resigned. "If I have to give up my friends for you, then you're not the girl I thought you were."

Exit angry, gorgeous man.

I stood there, my mouth dry, my cheeks burning. *What just happened?* My heart was still pounding so fast and hard, I could feel it throbbing in my tongue.

I burst out the door. "Coop! Wait."

He was already lost in the river of guests. I froze, then, and felt a hundred eyes on me. The back deck had become my stage. I looked frantically from the hushed crowd assembled to the large, open kitchen window. They must have heard everything. No wonder they were studying me like I was an insect they couldn't quite identify. A couple of teenage girls giggled; two old, wrinkled ladies shook their heads knowingly. Joni made a sympathetic face.

The woman in the flowered muumuu said, "Jesus, girl, don't just stand there. Stop him!"

I ran from their probing stares, pushed through bodies in search of Coop, but when I got to the meadow, someone stepped in front of me and we collided.

"Gwen!" My father was taking a sip from a highball when

I plowed into his side. He used a cocktail napkin to dab at the spot on his pale, button-down shirt. He looked more amused than angry. "In a hurry?"

"I—yeah, but…" Coop was out of sight, now. I was drunk on a potent cocktail of adrenaline, rage, remorse and panic. I couldn't think straight. "Goddammit," I said to no one in particular.

"What's wrong?" He put a hand on my arm. His thick fingers squeezed my bicep, prompting a whole new storm of emotion.

I turned to face him. "You want to know what's wrong, Dad?" My tone elicited looks, and a couple holding hands near us backed away slightly. "I'll tell you what's wrong: nine years old, middle of the night, standing on a stranger's porch while my mother screams at the guy inside to leave his little slut alone and get his ass home to his wife and daughter. Sound familiar? Oh, but I guess you think there's nothing wrong with that, huh? That's just natural, right? Anarchists don't believe in monogamy. Well, you know what? Your little experimentation in free love probably just cost me the only guy worth having."

Okay, so the connection was tenuous, but I wasn't capable of solid logic with my heart hammering in my mouth.

"Gwen, honey, let's not do this here."

Kelly was headed for us with a flute of champagne in one hand, a plate of food in the other; I could see Dad glancing at her nervously.

"Great!" I barked. "Your selfishness made me a jealous, insecure mess and you want me to keep it down so your little girlfriend won't hear? That is just like you, Dad. That's just you all over."

I ran from him, then. I didn't know where I was going, I just sprinted as fast as my kitten heels would take me, away from the concerned faces, the craning necks, the tables of food and the bluegrass band and the kids spinning themselves drunk in the garden. The air was cool now, getting colder, and my strapless dress with the matching scallop-edged jacket provided paltry defense against the evening breezes, but I didn't care. I left the dirt road and plunged into the forest, even though the uneven ground forced me to take off my shoes. When I was finally far enough away from everyone to feel invisible, I leaned against an oak tree and sobbed for a good five minutes. The trunk was huge and solid, the branches a sinuous network above me. The moss under my fingers was thick and spongy. Touching it reminded me of playing with my father's beard when I was little. I hadn't thought of that in years.

"Hey."

I turned around and there was Joni, looking like a woodland nymph in the dappled sunlight. "Hey yourself," I sniffled.

She came closer. Her small hand reached out and brushed a strand of hair from my eyes. I could smell the lavender water I'd forced her to soak in; she'd said she hated perfume, but

I'd convinced her she should be fragrant for her wedding night.

"What is it?" Her big doe eyes found mine and I started to cry. "Shhh…" she tried to hug me.

"No!" I pulled away. "I don't want to get makeup on your dress."

"Okay, okay," she said. "Just tell me what's going on."

I sniffed and she pulled the handkerchief from my breast pocket, started mopping up the inevitable globs of mascara and even wiped my nose, as if I were a child.

"I made a scene. Well, two scenes actually. In the last ten minutes."

She looked impressed. "I only caught one—well, part of one."

I laughed, but the sound got sidetracked somewhere in my throat and came out as a strangled little sob. "I'm such a moron."

"No, you're not," she said. "What happened?"

"Things got out of hand. Dannika sucks. *Eugh*—I could kill her." I shook my head. "I should have just trusted him. Why did I say he had to choose? It's so childish."

Joni lowered her chin. "Gwen, you're going to have back up a little."

So I told her everything: The hug, the catfight, the ultimatum. It was all so junior high and dramatic; I couldn't believe the things I'd said. You know me. I like my drama onstage. Even then, I worry that all the fainting and fighting and thrashing about will wrinkle my perfectly pressed costumes.

When I got to the part about yelling at my dad, I felt even more sheepish. I mean, Jesus, this was a pretty random occasion to unpack all my baggage. Was it really fair to blow up like that when all he'd done was sleep with some chick twenty years ago? It wasn't even like he was sneaking around. Maybe it was my mom I should be mad at. She's the one who dragged me to his girlfriend's house.

Joni was wide-eyed, suitably awed by my stupidity, I guess. I felt bad about that. This was her day and here we were, gnashing our teeth at each other when we should be clinking glasses. I apologized, but she waved a dismissive hand at me.

"This is amazing, Gwen. I mean, how long have you been waiting to confront your father?"

"What do you mean?"

"You finally told him how much he hurt you. That's like a serious breakthrough."

I hung my head. "Then why do I feel like a spoiled brat who's just acted out at someone else's birthday party?"

She laughed. "Every wedding needs a scandal! Otherwise nobody will remember it."

I touched a finger to her nose. "You'll remember it."

Her smile was radiant. "You're right," she said. "I'll always remember it. And none of it would have happened without you."

"That's not true."

"It is! You were like my Lamaze coach, man. I was ready to just throw the towel in, and you totally talked me down. Seriously. Thank you."

I shrugged. "It wasn't a big deal."

"It was. But I won't argue because I know you're stubborn as shit." She tilted her head in the direction of the house. "You ready to go back?"

I sighed, felt for my notebook inside my clutch. "I think I'm going to take a few minutes, try to gather myself. Is my makeup a mess?"

"Not at all. Might want a new coat of lipstick, though."

Look at that; half a day of beauty coaching and the girl's an expert.

I couldn't go back to the guests yet. No amount of lipstick was going to camouflage my acute shame. I'd let the green-eyed demon possess me and I felt dirty inside, coated with the thick grime of my own inadequacy.

Joni lingered a moment, standing in the cool dark of the forest. Evening shadows were starting to gather and they pooled on the elegant curve of her naked scalp, turning it vaguely blue. "Listen," she said, "I'm going to tell you something you told me, okay?"

I grinned, knowing what was coming.

"We are not our parents." She enunciated each word slowly and deliberately. "Should I say it again?"

"No," I whispered. "I got it."

"Good," she said. "Don't take too long, okay? We're going to cut the cake soon."

I nodded. "Thanks."

She grinned. "Just returning the favor."

When she was gone, I dug out my notebook, and I've been curled up here on the forest floor ever since. With my luck, I'll get pine sap on my rayon; just one more humiliating detail added to an ego-destroying day. I was hoping I'd gain a little perspective if I confessed my sins. I don't know, though. I'm afraid reviewing the whole fiasco's only made me more embarrassed. I mean Dannika had it coming—she's satanic and must be destroyed—but Coop doesn't need my petty threats. What if he forced me to choose between you and him? I'd definitely ditch him. (Well, okay, first I'd get in some searing-hot, torturous breakup sex, *then* I'd ditch him.)

Got to sign off. Apparently, I've got a rigorous schedule of groveling ahead.

Your stupid, stupid friend,
Gwen

Midnight

Dear Marla,

When I finally came out of the woods, the guests were almost all sitting down. Someone had laid out ten huge picnic blankets in the meadow, each in a different brilliant jewel tone. It was a very beautiful scene. The bar was slammed, cheeks were flushed, eyes were bright and everyone was chowing down on the main course: meat kabobs for the carnivores, tofu for the herbivores, fluffy couscous and garlicky green beans for all. Towheaded kids zoomed about, toddlers trailed behind on chubby legs, babies cried. Iridescent dragonflies competed with gnats for airspace. I was so emotional and sleep-deprived at that point, I got misty-eyed just standing there.

Joni saw me lingering at the edge of the meadow and came over. "Are you okay?" She looked worried.

"It's just so…human…and g-good," I stammered, waving expansively at the meadow, knowing I wasn't making much sense.

Joni took it in stride. "I know," she said. "It is, isn't it? Listen, I think maybe you need a drink."

"Please," I agreed.

We went to the bar, a couple of long folding tables where Ohm was filling up flutes of champagne and pouring mean vodka tonics for a gaggle of nubile, starry-eyed girls. They were vying for his attention, but he just smiled benignly at all of them, refusing to play favorites. I could see him tugging rather obviously at his "wedding" ring, but the girls just went on giggling. *Isn't that just like us?* I thought. *We're irresistibly drawn to the ones who are bound to break our hearts.*

When Ohm caught sight of Joni and me, he finished pouring and cried out, "Here she is—the Goddess of Monogamy and her demigoddess Gwen."

The girls looked behind them and, seeing as they could hardly pick a fight with the bride, reluctantly moved on.

"What, I'm only a demigoddess?" I pouted as Ohm handed me the most beautiful flute of golden liquid I'd ever seen.

"Don't be a brat," he said. "You know it's bad luck to upstage the bride."

"It's not possible," I told him, smiling at Joni. "She's un-upstageable."

Glasses in hand, we turned around and surveyed the seating arrangement. Coop was nowhere in sight, neither was Dannika. I'll admit, that made my heart catch for a fraction of a second, but I caught myself just in time.

No more psycho jealousy.

After all, that's what had gotten me into this mess in the first place. Not that Dannika hadn't done what she could to fan the fires, but I couldn't blame it all on her. I'd been suspicious and nosey from the very beginning, with a long history of bailing on men just because they showed a glimmer of interest in the female gender at large. It was a tragic character flaw, and if I ever wanted to make it past the three-month mark with anyone, I'd have to get a grip. I didn't know if things were salvageable with Coop, but I hoped they might be. He was the first guy I really wanted to change for, and if he dumped me, I might just backslide to my old, psycho-jealous self.

"Gwen? Gwen?"

"Huh?"

Joni's brow furrowed as she studied my face. "You were really spaced out, there. Are you sure you're okay? Do you want to go lie down or something?"

"No, girl, are you crazy? This is your nuptial feast. I wouldn't miss it."

"I don't see Coop," she said, a little apologetic. "Want to come sit with Phil and me?"

"Sure. I'd be honored."

We got our plates of food, then made our way through the meadow until we reached the sapphire-blue blanket where Phil was kicking back, drinking a bottle of Corona. I didn't get a good look at the guy he was talking to until we were halfway there and it was too late to turn around. It was my father. He and Phil were obviously locked in some sort of heated discussion. I decided to bite the bullet and took my seat next to Joni, uneasy but figuring it was best to get this over with.

My father's eyes slid over Joni and landed on my face. "Hey," he said. "How's it going?" There was something so vulnerable in the lines around his eyes and the curve of his chapped lips. He looked sad and sorry and hopeful all at once. I guess it was lack of food, lack of sleep, the first flush of a champagne buzz, but in that moment I felt nothing but an overwhelming empathy. He tried. He was human. I mean, yes, he screwed up and he wasn't a model parent, but I knew right then that he loved me. The longer I went on hating him, refusing to take his calls, the longer I denied myself the pleasures of a father.

"It's going okay," I said. "You?"

He sort of tilted his head back and forth. "I've been better," he said, "but I've also been worse."

"Hey, Gwen." Phil tapped a cigarette from his pack. "I

just met your old man, here. You never mentioned you're the descendant of an anarchist."

"Yeah," I said. "Well, I am."

My father and I exchanged a look. His said, *I never meant to hurt you.* Mine said, *I'll get over it.*

"He's the bomb, man." Phil was excited, and possibly a little drunk. He lit his cigarette and said to Joni, "He wrote *No Priests or Politicians* and *The Anarchist's Guide to the Twenty-first Century*. It's like a dream come true, having this guy at my wedding."

Dad glanced around shyly. "Glad I could oblige."

Kelly came over with a paper plate in one hand and sat down next to Dad, popped a shrimp into his mouth. When she saw me she smiled. "Hi, Gwen. Great food, huh? You look lovely, by the way."

I'm always amazed at how quickly the social fabric mends its little tears. When I was a teenager, I used to resent it—the way you could throw a tantrum and as soon as it was over, everyone would stoically pretend it hadn't happened. That sort of thing used to give me the creeps. At the moment, though, looking into Kelly's pretty green eyes, I was grateful for the elasticity of it all; I was free to be a freak now and then, if necessary, and the world would revert to the status quo soon enough.

"Thanks," I said. "So do you."

"You know, your dad and I were just talking about having you visit sometime soon. Especially since you've got friends here already."

I smiled at Joni, then at Kelly and Dad. "Yeah," I said. "That would be cool."

We made small talk for the rest of the meal. I kept an eye out for Coop, but he was nowhere in sight. I told myself to eat, but I couldn't get much down, even though it was completely delicious. Something inside me just wouldn't relax. I craved Coop, ached for him in my bones. It was torture.

As the sun was just starting to slide behind the trees and Joni's dad was lighting the tiki torches, I heard glasses bring tapped for a toast. The cake had already been cut, and people were starting to transition from champagne to coffee. Joni's mom stood first. She appropriated one of the mikes from the band, who had stopped playing long enough to eat. She looked nervous, like she wanted to get it over with. She told a funny story about Joni as a baby and wrapped it up with some tender praise for Phil. It was short but sweet. Then one person after another took the mike, most of them spouting clichés about lasting happiness, how Joni and Phil were so perfect for each other and would never be apart. A thick-necked guy in a flannel shirt made a reference to the "Army of table dancers," that descended on the Tip Top last night. Joni and I both covered our faces and everyone roared with laughter. Evidently, our performance had been witnessed by at least a few of the guests assembled and talked about by the rest.

I stood up, thinking I'd get myself one last glass of champagne. As I crossed the meadow, I saw Coop standing at the bar. Ohm was pouring him a drink and he was laughing at something. I paused, trying to get my bearings, wondering if I should go over there, when all of a sudden someone was shoving a mike into my hand. I guess I must have lingered near the woman who was speaking for too long and she thought I was waiting my turn. As soon as I had the mike, several drunk guys who were splayed out in the tall grass near the trees let loose with catcalls and, "Take it off, baby!" Now I had everyone's attention. I swallowed hard and stared down at the mike.

You know I hate public speaking—I mean *loathe* it with a vengeance. In high school, I used to hide in the bathroom when it was time to give oral reports. And here I was, in front of two hundred people, at least a handful of whom had seen me strip down to my underwear in a seedy bar the night before. I could feel my face blooming pink and hot; my fingers tingled; my mouth went dry. I was about to thrust the mike at someone—anyone—when I happened to look up and catch Coop's eye. That's when I realized that this was my chance. I could tell him, in front of witnesses, through an amplifier, how I felt. Maybe, if I said it just right, he'd forgive me.

"So…" My own voice rang in my ears, sounding impossibly loud and detached. I felt dizzy, light-headed, my palms so sweaty I feared the large, clumsy microphone would slip right through my grip and land in the grass. I was entirely capable of fainting, right then, and it occurred to me in some distant control center of my brain that falling to the ground unconscious would almost certainly excuse me from the task at hand. Then I heard my old refrain amplified inside my skull: *What Would Jackie Do?* The answer was plain, so I grabbed hold of the mike with both hands and stood up a little taller. One of the derelicts at the edge of the forest called out, "Show us your panties, baby!" I saw Joni's grandparents frowning at each other quizzically.

"Actually, sir?" I looked pointedly at the guy in the baseball cap who'd just called out. "I think you're confused. The tradition is a garter toss, not a pantie toss, but since you're so eager to participate, I'm sure the bride will oblige you shortly." Everyone laughed and some clapped. The guy tipped his baseball cap slightly as if to say, "Touché." I took courage from this and plowed ahead. "I'm not sure what can be added to the toasts already made. Obviously, we're all very happy for Joni and Phil—happy enough to get good and drunk on their future." More laughs. I glanced at Coop, but his eyes unnerved me, so I fixed my stare on the huge blond beehive of Phil's aunt.

"Unfortunately, the future isn't all that easy to navigate. We'd like to send them off into the sunset, certain their love will last, except we all know life gets complicated. There'll be dentist bills and taxes, midlife crises and temptation. The divorce rate is catastrophically high, single parenthood even higher and all of this is compounded by the rising cost of living, inflated real estate, endemic dissatisfaction with the workplace, a lack of socialized medicine…." People were starting to frown and raise their eyebrows. Only my father was beaming proudly. I had to get back on track. "Not to mention a general lack of commitment to purchasing quality lingerie." That got a lot of laughs—relieved guffaws, mostly. As long as I stuck with panties, they seemed to like me. "Joni, I want you to remember, no matter how hard times get, your underwear drawer should be stocked with only the best." She gave me the thumbs-up sign and everyone cheered.

I knew it was time to wind down—nobody likes a mike hog—but I still hadn't said what I needed to say. "My point is…" I looked at my father. He was smiling uneasily now. I think he was afraid I'd back off from my political stance and get mushy. "My point is that many of us grew up with less than perfect childhoods, and—frankly—we're terrified of marriage. But, as a very wise woman recently reminded me," I looked at Joni, "We're not our parents. They tried and, okay, maybe their lives weren't always perfect, but the great thing is, they had the courage to make their own mistakes. Now it's our turn to go out and make ours." I looked at Coop. His eyes were fastened on my face, and for a moment it was just us there in that meadow; everyone else blurred and faded out. "I've made plenty of mistakes already. But the worst one I can imagine is being too scared to give love a chance, especially when you've found the man who makes the risk worth it."

I raised my glass, which was empty, but oh well. "To Joni and Phil," I said. "May they love each other forever and damn the statistics to hell." Everyone drank and cheered and clapped. I nodded in thanks and handed the mike to a fat man in suspenders sporting the ubiquitous long gray ponytail.

I was emboldened by the apparent success of my toast as I crossed the meadow and headed toward Coop. The fat guy started rambling on about Phil's heroic actions at an Earth First! protest. By the time I ambled up to the bar, a debilitating shyness seized me.

"Hi," Coop said when I reached him. "That was really…"

"What?" I said. "Really what?"

"Great!" He smiled. "Seriously. I was…" He shrugged hopelessly, as if words failed him.

"Oh my God, what?" I covered my face with my hands.

He peeled them away gently. "I was very moved," he said. "And no, I'm not being sarcastic."

"I didn't see you earlier…?"

He nodded. "I was trying to get my head on straight."

"Oh, you mean after I bit it off?" I looked at my shoes. "I was totally out of line, Coop. I'm mortified."

"You're human," he said. "I probably didn't handle things all that great, myself."

I peeked up at him. "You're not mad?"

He chuckled and smoothed my hair with the palm of his hand. "Kitten. Come on. How could I stay mad at you?"

I couldn't resist another moment. I threw myself into his arms. He pinned me against his chest in a strong, solid hug. My head filled with his smell and everything disappeared: the meadow, the fat man rambling into the mike about Redwood Summer, the screaming children, the whining mosquitoes. All I knew was the safe, sublime warmth of his body against mine.

When he released me at last, we both started to speak simultaneously. I said, "Coop, I'm sorry," and he said, "I shouldn't have—"

"You go," I said.

"No, you," he insisted.

I decided it was now or never. He'd already seen evidence of my pettiest, least attractive side, so there was no reason to hold anything back. "I'm psychotically jealous, okay? I've broken up with every guy I ever dated—none of my relationships last more than three months—because I freak out. I can't trust people. My father screwed around and I got caught in the middle and I guess it scarred me. I'm emotionally warped. Damaged goods. And that's why I've been such a complete idiot this weekend."

Coop nodded solemnly. "I see."

I waited for him to continue. When he didn't, I said, "I see? Is that all you're going to say?"

He said, "You didn't act like an idiot this weekend."

"I didn't?"

He grinned. "Well, you were under duress."

"You can say that again."

He brushed his fingers across my cheek lightly. "Dannika's not my type. You are. You're an original. Who else would table dance at the Tip Top one night, and give a heartwarming speech about marriage less than twenty-four hours later?"

I punched his arm. "I was the undercover rescue effort, I'll have you know."

"Yeah, well, you had agent provocateur underwear, anyway."

I shrugged. "How was I supposed to know I'd be so good at it?"

He bent down and put his mouth to mine, tentative at first, asking questions. As I leaned against him, parting my lips, he kissed me more deeply, until we were both a little drunk.

"How touching."

The kiss ended abruptly at the sound of Dannika's voice. We both turned and there she was, her hair amber in the flickering light of the tiki torches. The outside world came zooming back into focus; all I wanted was to crawl back inside Coop's kiss, let it eclipse the wedding guests and the picnic blankets and the sneering goddess before me.

"Hey, Dannika." I decided to make a stab at peacemaking. I had the guy; I could afford to be generous. "I'm sorry I got so heavy with you earlier."

She raised an eyebrow. "Looks like your little tantrum got results."

Coop stepped forward. "You think that's funny? I don't think that's funny."

"Apparently, you're not *thinking* at all," she said.

Around us, I noticed that the guests were starting to turn in our direction. The rambling guy in suspenders had finally surrendered the mike, but nobody else was toasting. In fact, they were shushing each other, honing in on our little spectacle-in-progress.

"Danni, why does everything have to be a test with you?" Coop paid no attention to their stares. "The minute I get close to someone, you have to butt in, see if I'm still your friend."

"That is *so* not true," she cried. "She's just manipulating you."

"Oh, yeah?" His eyes were dark again, that pure mallard green. "And what do you call what *you're* doing?"

Her hand flew to her chest and she scoffed, indignant. "I'm your friend!"

"Then act like one." He slung an arm around my shoulder, pulled me close. "I love Gwen, okay? If you really care about me, you'll treat her with respect."

Her jaw dropped. "What are you *saying*?"

"I'm not letting this one go—and I won't let you interfere. I've let you have your way for years, Danni, but this time I'm putting my foot down."

The verb *to swoon* comes to mind. He looked so incredibly attractive, standing there defending me, defending *us.* I wanted to gloat, to cry out *nah-nah-nah-nah-nah,* to do a giddy spin, my hands in the air.

But then I turned to Dannika, and my cockiness faded. Our eyes locked; chills of recognition bloomed along my spine. We were exactly alike. We both loved him and feared each other.

"It's okay." My words were filled with a tenderness that surprised me. "I know how you feel."

"You don't."

"I do. Trust me." I took a step toward her. "You don't have to lose him."

Her bottom lip started to quiver and she looked around furtively, like a cornered animal. "I just wanted…" Her voice trailed off.

"I know. But he needs both of us. So let's not fight."

"I can't—" Her voice broke. "I don't—"

"You don't have to say anything." I seized her hand, squeezed her fingers in mine. "We'll work it out, okay? We will."

She emitted a small, strangled sound—part sob, part giggle—and nodded.

I heard clapping nearby and turned to see Ohm, still manning the bar. He was watching me, his eyebrows arched in a look that was half touched, half amused. Then a few others joined in and it kept growing, until there were four hundred hands applauding and cheering our maudlin little moment. What the hell? In the last twenty-four hours I'd stripped down to my go-go boots, starred in two impromptu scenes as the spoiled, possessive brat. For once, I was playing a role I could embrace: a girl confident enough to wear her kitten heels with class.

I turned to the crowd assembled in the dusky twilight and took a bow.

I'd like to think it's exactly what Jackie would have done.

Later that night, after a fight broke out between a red-headed Rasta and the three-hundred pound woman in the flowered muumuu, things got a little crazy. Phil tossed the garter (mine, actually, I'd lent it to Joni—but I didn't mind); Joni pitched the bouquet (the girl's got a mean arm—it nearly knocked the wind out of me when I caught it). The fog rolled in, thick and opaque as cotton batting, and still we danced under the stars we couldn't see. We faked our way through some loose, sloppy steps that were part elementary school square dancing, part salsa until the bluegrass band grew palsied with exhaustion. Then Ohm abandoned the bar to DJ, and we danced to all the terrible top-forty shit from our miserable teenage years; we even did the Macarena, though I pray to God there's no footage to prove it.

"I can't believe Phil's actually dancing to 'Fields of Gold.' He must be wasted." Coop was holding me close, the entire length of his body pressed against mine, and I was having a little trouble following the thread of conversation. I'd only had two glasses of champagne all afternoon, but I was drunk on his proximity.

"Why?" It was a sleepy mumble directed at his shoulder.

"According to him, Sting is the Antichrist. Anything that's not linked historically to The Kinks or the Ramones, he'd rather die than listen to. Let alone dance to."

I turned my head a little and shuffled us around so I could still press my cheek against his chest while checking out the bride and groom. Phil was dipping Joni as she giggled like a child. "Guess it must be love."

"Yeah," Coop said. "Either that or he's pussy-whipped."

I smiled up at him. "Is there a difference?"

He considered this. "For a man? Probably not."

Before Dad took off, he came over and pulled me into a warm, lingering embrace—our second now in four years. "Don't be a stranger," he said into my ear.

I smiled. "Me? Would I do that?"

He just chuckled and shook Coop's hand. "Great meeting you, Coop. Take care of this little scamp, okay?"

"Yes, sir." He mock-saluted. "Good meeting you, too."

Then Kelly hugged us both, saying to me, "I can't believe we finally got to meet."

"Sorry it took so long," I said, stealing a sideways glance at Dad.

He cleared his throat. "Yeah, well, we've been out of touch." He pinned me with his eyes, and I remembered why he was such a good coach, back in the day. It was that face.

It could terrify, entertain or inspire. It was probably what made him such a good womanizer, too. "But we're going to change that, aren't we, Gwen?"

"Yeah." My voice was tight and small with emotion. When I felt my throat relax enough to let words through again, I added, "We're going to try."

"When are you getting married?" Coop asked Kelly.

"We haven't nailed a date yet," she said, "but we'll let you know when we do."

The third and final look between Dad and I went like this:

Me: *I like her; don't mess it up.*

Him: *I'll give it my best shot.*

After they'd gone, Coop just stared at me. We were still dancing; I could feel his eyes boring into the top of my skull.

"What?" I asked when he didn't look away.

"You are a woman of many surprises, Gwen Matson."

I grinned in what I hoped was a delicious, come-hither way. "Speaking of surprises, let's go upstairs."

"Why?" He turned his head and squinted at me suspiciously. "What is it now?"

I traced a finger down his tie. "You think my underwear was good last night? You should see it tonight."

His eyes glazed slightly. "Not another word," he said. "Let's go."

Okay, you lascivious little bodice-ripper junkie; one last sex scene for you and then it's off to beddie-bye for both of us. It's after one, Coop's snoring beside me, and I've been writing so long my hand's turning into a hideously gnarled claw, but I know you won't forgive me unless I finish it off with a little smut.

There was a good deal of kissing on the spiral staircase. I was giddy with the smell and feel of him. We hadn't had sex since Thursday, which was only the night before last, but it seemed impossibly long ago. The weekend had become epic in its scope. I guess when you battle a blond nemesis, marry off a bald stripper and reunite with not one but both of your emotionally damaged parental units, time warps a bit. I led him up the curving spire with my lips and tongue, teasing him every step of the way. When we were almost to the landing, he got impatient and slipped past me to the top step, his hands fondling my breasts with hot, drunk fingers. We stumbled, bumping teeth. My foot missed the next step and I staggered again. As my waist pressed against the iron banister I felt how easy it would be to tumble backward over the railing and plunge through the center of that corkscrew stairway. Falling. I understood for the first time why they call it that, falling in love. It was this vertigo they were talking about, this crazy elevator drop in your stomach. Losing control. It was the very thing I'd fought against since that night on the porch in Sebastopol, watching my mother disintegrate as she screamed at a stranger's door. But losing control was good now. It was better than good; it was frightening and delicious.

Coop dragged me into the guest room and locked the door. He started pawing at the buttons on my little jacket, but I slapped his hands, pulled him over to the bed and pushed him backward. He sat up, looking surprised. He tried to catch hold of my waist but I evaded him.

"What are you up to now, little vixen?" His voice was hoarse and his eyes narrowed to slits.

"Private show for the best man," I said. "Bride's orders." Then I lit the candles Joni had given me, ran to the closet and put on her best wig, one she wore as Bella; it was straight, dark red, and it fell all the way to the middle of my back. I felt very naughty in it, like someone you shouldn't trust with your boyfriend for five minutes.

"Wow," Coop mumbled when I came out. "Who're you now?"

"Who do you want me to be?"

He shook his head. "I just want you naked."

"All in good time, Mr. Cooper."

He wore a bleary, endearing look of fascination as I took off my gloves very slowly, biting each finger and tugging with my teeth. When the gloves were off, I started on the jacket. By the time I worked my way down to the last button and the scalloped peplum fell open, he was propped up against the pillows, enjoying the show. I peeled it off and turned my back on him. It took every ounce of control to let it fall on the floor. It was the right effect—the essential baring of shoulder blades in candlelight, all that red hair—

and I couldn't ruin it by reaching for a hanger or even folding it neatly, but still it was torture. A girl like me just doesn't drop her rayon faille on the floor. If that's not evidence of love, I don't know what is.

Now I was down to the strapless sheath. First I unbuckled the rhinestone belt and let it drop to the rug. Then, very slowly, I unzipped the dress and it, too, tumbled to a limp circle at my feet. Coop sucked in his breath as I stepped out of it, my kitten heels still on. I was wearing a strapless, black satin corset, circa 1957. The coiled boning and underwire bustier weren't exactly built for comfort, but the aesthetics were unbeatable. Long, slim garters attached to sheer black silk stockings, also vintage. But the leopard-print panties were my pièce de résistance.

"You know I'm a sucker for anything leopard," he said, his voice ragged.

"Which is convenient," I said, "since it's my signature look."

I walked toward him slowly, my hips swaying. Unhooking one stocking from the garter, I raised my leg onto the bed and unrolled. God, to think that women today opt for cotton briefs and sports bras—it's astounding, what they miss out on. Even I was mesmerized by the effect of that sheer, shimmery silk in the candlelight, revealing one inch of creamy white thigh at a time.

As I was working on the second stocking, Coop crept forward and ran his tongue over the subtle indentation of my inner thigh. A wave of dizziness hit me, but I steadied myself against the bedpost and pressed him gently back against the mattress with my foot. The show wasn't over yet. I was barely halfway through the lingerie act. I wanted him good and hungry.

The corset itself had at least thirty hook-and-eye closures, mercifully placed down the front. I took my time with them, until Coop's face was veering beyond pleasure into pain. I undid the last two and let it drop quietly. Then, locking eyes with him, I slid my panties over my hips and thighs until it was just a wisp of leopard-print fabric on the floor, the final dot on the exclamation mark of discarded clothing strewn across the rug. Lastly, I stepped out of my signature kitten heels.

We got rid of Coop's suit with considerably less fanfare.

When we were finally naked together on the bed, I felt myself melting into him, edges dissolving. Outside, the night wind tossed through the pines, whispering softly. A bullfrog's plaintive song found its way through the open window. Coop's mouth was hot enough to scorch. When he was inside me at last, I had to bury my face in a pillow to keep from screaming.

Enough! My God, you're a cannibal, devouring my exploits whole. If this thing gets lost in the mail, I'm going to kill you.

Yours truly,

Gwen

(a.k.a. The Little Sex Kitten That Could)

2:30 a.m.

Right, just one final note. I'm dead tired, but I have to fill you in on the postscript of the evening or I won't be able to sleep. At risk of sounding like a made-for-TV movie, I have to say, we *are* all human.

Even the size-two blondes.

I was lying there in the dark, listening to Coop's snores and the crickets and the wind in the trees. Every now and then, I could hear Joni erupt in giggles down the hall and sometimes Phil would pipe in with an animal noise, like maybe they were playing an X-rated version of "Old McDonald Had a Farm." They don't leave for Costa Rica until Tuesday, so they're enjoying their wedding night in their own four-poster bed. It made me happy to hear their laughter. I felt, for the first time all weekend—maybe the first time in my life—that human beings might have a shot at lasting love. The odds are far from perfect, but they're better than nothing.

Champagne and postcoital bliss had rendered my body all rubbery, as if my bones had turned gelatinous inside me. I was exhausted and deeply relaxed, but still the river of sleep didn't carry me off to dreamland. I had a sour taste in my mouth and I was incredibly thirsty. I lay there and fantasized about a cold glass of water and a good, frothy encounter with my toothbrush. Also, I had to pee. Tired or no, I realized I'd never sleep until I got up and took care of business.

I peed first, brushed my teeth, then tiptoed down the staircase and made my way past several bodies crashed out on the couch and curled in sleeping bags on the rugs. In the kitchen, someone had left the pantry bulb on, so there was just enough light to see by. I selected a thick, hand-blown, lapis-rimmed glass from the cupboards and filled it from the tap. I gulped down half of it and was just refilling when I heard a little sniffle behind me.

There was Dannika, wearing too-big flannel pajamas and floppy wool socks. Her eyes were puffy and rimmed in red. She looked miserable.

"You're awake." My voice was hoarse.

"Yeah." She leaned against the counter. "I just can't seem to sleep."

"Maybe Joni's got something you can take," I suggested.

She shrugged. An awkward pause fell over us. I was trying to decide if it would be weird to just take my water and head back upstairs. I was hardly in the mood for more Dannika-style combat after all that delicious sex. Sure, we'd had our touching little moment out in the meadow, but I wondered now if anything had really changed. For Coop's sake, I was determined not to put him in the middle anymore, but I also wasn't optimistic about the chances of friendship between me and this temperamental diva. Maybe we could just politely deny one another's existence for the rest of our lives.

"Well, good night," I said, heading toward the stairs. Awkward or no, I was tired and didn't have the energy to initiate more peace talks.

"Wait."

I turned, and was surprised to see there were tears in her eyes. "What's wrong?"

She leaned against the counter. "Can we talk?"

"Um, okay." We'd made some progress today—I was pretty sure of that—and I didn't want to be the one to take a step back. I glanced at the sleeping forms in the living room. "You want to go out on the deck?"

She nodded. "Yeah, hold on a sec." She ran to the front closet and came back with two enormous down parkas and a pair of fuzzy slippers. "Here," she said, handing one of the parkas and the slippers to me. "It's cold out."

I'm not saying it was time for matching friendship rings, but I have to admit I was caught off guard. It was the first affable gesture between us that wasn't riddled with ulterior motives, and I felt the weight of hating her slip from my shoulders just slightly. Maybe she wasn't Satan, after all.

We wrapped ourselves in the parkas and I put the slippers on. They must have been Joni's because they fit perfectly. Stepping out onto the deck, the night smelled of fog and overripe apples. We leaned against the railing side by side. A dog barked in the distance.

"I know we haven't exactly hit it off this weekend," she began. "But I—well, I just wanted you to know…" She stopped.

"What?"

She laughed. "I've never done this before. It feels really weird." She inhaled deeply, exhaled, then said, "I'm sorry. That's all."

I just stood there, mulling this over. "Okay…"

She turned to me and said in a rush, "I was totally out of line. I thought you two were wrong for each other and that made it okay to interfere. Sometimes you have to hurt people for their own good. And okay, yes, I love him." She glanced at the window upstairs where he was sleeping. "I've always loved Coop. But the truth is, there was no Malibu. There's never been anything between us except the most amazing friendship—which he'd have every right to give up on now that he's seen what a bitch I can be." She raised her shoulders half an inch in a tiny, little-girl shrug. "Except he doesn't. That's the thing about Coop. He never gives up on me."

I looked at her. The tiny diamond in her nose sparkled in the moonlight. Her blond hair glowed, unearthly and luminous as usual. I had to ask the question that was forcing its way from my brain to my mouth. "Are you *in* love with him?"

She sighed. "No, probably not. I mean, I don't want to *marry* him or anything. All I know is he's the only person who ever stood by me, no matter how bitchy or moody I get. That's something, you know?"

"Yeah," I said. "That is something."

A gentle breeze sloshed through the pines, rustled through the last leaves on the apple trees, their silhouettes gnarled and twisted.

"I should have been nicer to you," she said.

"I guess we were both kind of threatened, huh?"

She said, "Women never like me."

"You're gorgeous," I told her, "and talented, successful. That's hard for us mortals to handle."

"I put people off with all my insecurities."

I scoffed. "How could you be insecure?"

"How? Easy. I'm ugly and fat and people hate me."

My voice pitched upward in disbelief. "You're ugly? You've got to be insane."

"Yeah, that, too. My shrink thinks I should take Zoloft but meds freak me out."

I laughed; I couldn't help it. "Dannika, if you're fishing for compliments…."

She furrowed her brow. "Gwen, why do you think I get plastic surgery and do drugs and have an incessant need to be the center of attention? Because I feel *good* about myself?"

She had a point. "But you're beautiful."

We locked eyes for a moment. "No," she said, "you're beautiful."

This was too much. "Come on. I'm five foot one and I've been carting around fifteen extra pounds since puberty."

"Please!"

"And," I said, "*I'm* the one who's insecure. I was terrified to go on this trip because I didn't want Coop to know what a jealous fiend I am. I've never had a relationship that lasted more than three months because I'm so skittish I always freak out and bolt at the slightest sign of trouble. Ask anyone."

She squinted at me, suspicious. "Really?"

"Would I lie about this?"

"But you seem so confident…"

"Ha!" I was on a roll, now. "When you showed up on my doorstep Thursday morning I thought I'd shrivel up and blow away, you looked so gorgeous and skinny and… blond!"

She looked down. "I'm not skinny. I gained seven pounds when Coop told me he was in love with you."

I nearly choked. "Seriously?"

"Yes, seriously. I still have five to lose. I'm going on a weeklong juice fast starting tomorrow."

"When did he tell you that?"

She looked puzzled. "What?"

"That he was in love with me?" I whispered.

She rolled her eyes. "The day after he met you at the Laundromat. I binged on Hostess cupcakes that night. The point is, you win, I lose, and I'm going to have to get over it. I'm not happy, I don't expect us to be friends, but I'm going to do my best to be cool from now on." She put a hand on mine. "And just for the record, I'm rethinking my position. You two might be good together, after all." Her grip tightened. "But if you ever hurt him in any way, I'll hunt you down and slit your throat."

I took a small step back. "Understood."

"Good," she said. "I'm glad we had this talk."

So now here I am, propped up in bed beside my snoring man. He told her he loved me the day after we met. Amazing. Do we ever know what's really going on just under the surface of our own lives? Are we all so caught up in our wretched phobias that we ignore obvious truths until they kick us in the teeth?

She's still trying to lose five pounds? Jesus, she must have been a size *zero*.

I wonder if I should try yoga?

12:10 p.m.

Dear Marla,

Oh my God, you're going die when you read this.

It's too crazy!

Just let me catch my breath, here. I have to tell it right, without giving anything away before I've worked up to it.

WE'RE ENGAGED!

Oh God, I suck. I have to cross that out later. And this, obviously. But maybe I shouldn't. You might have a heart attack when you get to the end if I'd don't prepare you along the way.

Right, as always, let's start at the beginning. We decided to stay Sunday night. We all had dinner in Mendocino, cute café, beautiful evening, blah, blah, blah.

I'm sorry, I just can't pace myself, here. I have to get to the good part right away. Besides, I'm almost out of pages in the fourth journal and I refuse to start another one.

So, where was I? Oh yes, dinner. When we were finished eating, Phil and Coop spouted some bullshit about running down the street for groceries. It was a little suspicious, but Joni and Dannika seemed fine with it and I was too happy to make a fuss. Exit, boys. Joni, Dannika and I sat sipping our decaf coffee. Ohm wandered in. He ordered a coffee too, we gossiped, I convinced him to move to L.A. I know, this is totally the CliffsNotes, but *come on,* I don't have all day.

No, seriously, a brief summary of the conversation with Ohm.

"So, were you serious when you said I should move to L.A.?"

I reached across the table and grabbed his hand, spilling his coffee a little on accident. "Sorry. Yes, yes, yes! Are you thinking about it?"

Joni rolled her eyes. "I can't believe you're poaching him," she whined.

"Come on! He would love it there and you know it," I said.

Ohm looked at Joni. "There'd be a significantly enlarged dating pool."

"Exactly," I said, "and career opportunities galore. I know everyone in theatre down there. I even know some people in film."

He looked excited. "Really? You could hook me up?"

"Absolutely. If you don't get cast right away, you could work for me part-time. I even know a very nice Prada model with excellent bone structure who's looking for a roommate."

His eyes widened. "Male or female?"

"Very male. Jock. Can you believe that? I swear to God his name is Jock."

Joni slumped lower in her seat. "Tragic."

"I think it's a great idea," Dannika said.

We all just looked at her. Was this possible? Was she seriously endorsing something I wanted? The tension between us was somewhat diffused, but I was still on code-yellow alert. Now that we both knew what the other was capable of, all I wanted to do was get through the rest of the trip without going any deeper than "please pass the salt."

"You do?" I asked uneasily.

"I do—really—why are you all looking at me like that?"

Joni ignored her question and went back to whining. "It's not right," she told me. "You've unleashed my latent interest in fashion and now you're going to whisk away my only fashionable friend."

Ohm was still studying Dannika. "Why do you think I should move?"

She smiled sweetly. She really was a pretty girl. Somehow, though, sitting there in the evening light, with her hair scraped back into a ponytail and a Giants cap on her head, she just didn't look as threatening as she did that fateful Thursday morning on my doorstep. I decided my insecurities lent her an otherworldly radiance she doesn't normally possess.

"Because, like you said, you'll meet more guys—lots of guys." She wiggled her eyebrows suggestively. "And you'll become a movie star, which is obviously your calling."

Ohm nodded solemnly and sipped his coffee. "This girl's a prophet."

"And you'll have Gwen here to take care of you." Our eyes met. She looked both wistful and sincere when she added, "I think she'd be a great friend."

"Oh, s*uperb!*" Joni practically screeched. "What am I, chopped liver?"

So that's how we decided Ohm belongs in L.A. I'm supposed to call Jock as soon as we get home. If things go smoothly, he might move down as soon as October. Marla, you are *so* going to dig this guy. He's like us, only better.

But shit, see? I'm nearly to the last page and I still haven't gotten to the really good part. Okay, so I already spilled the beans about the engagement, but as everyone knows, it's not about what you do, it's how you do it. And Coop came through in spades on that score.

We'd been lingering for a good half hour over our coffee, and the boys still hadn't returned. When I noticed it was almost eight, I said, "Where the hell are they?"

I could've sworn the three of them exchanged cagey glances, but I told myself I was just being paranoid. I was determined not to go off half-cocked anymore. Gone was the old Gwen of unfounded suspicions; the new Gwen paradigm was *innocent until proven guilty*. Not the most original mantra, I realize, but us levelheaded, fair, trusting girls don't need flashy bumper-sticker sayings to live by. We revel in the scientific method, avoid logical fallacies and insist on justice in all sectors. Just because Dannika, Joni and Ohm *looked* like sixth graders who'd just been caught smoking in the john, that didn't mean they actually *were*.

"Um, why don't we go for a walk? See if we can find them?" Joni suggested. "There's a little market right up the street. Maybe they went there."

"Yeah," Ohm said. "I think I saw them headed that way."

Half an hour later we'd looked for them in every store, café and bar in Mendocino, including a knitting shop offering night classes and a Christian bookstore that was open late. They'd simply disappeared.

As we stood on Main Street, squinting this way and that, Joni looked at her watch and said, "Well, it's eight twenty…." She glanced at Dannika, then Ohm, avoiding my eyes. "Maybe they walked out to the bluffs."

"This is so weird," I said. "Why would they just take off?"

Dannika shrugged. "They probably had guy stuff to talk about."

"You think?" The whole situation was bizarre in my opinion, but since everyone else took it in stride, I didn't want to be difficult. Together we made our way past a Chevron station into the parking lot of a quaint little church with a lovely blue door and a tall, pointed steeple. We stopped to look at it there in the gathering dusk, Ohm going on about the time he made out with the sheriff's son in the pews, but I was restless and kept looking around for Coop. I'd started to worry that something bad had happened to him. I knew it was sort of silly, but I kept visualizing him bound in the trunk of a drug lord's speeding Mercedes with duct tape over his mouth. What a drug lord would want with Coop, I had no idea, but I'd nearly convinced myself I was having a psychic moment, not a paranoid one.

"Huh," Joni said, looking at her watch again. "It's eight-thirty."

"Where are they?" I whipped my head this way and that impatiently.

"Let's try the bluffs," she repeated. "Come on, this way."

Joni led us down a path that connected the church parking lot with dramatic cliffs overlooking the sea. It was a small, somewhat rugged trail that meandered through pale, wheaty grasses and overgrown blackberry bushes. Once again, my kitten heels were being subjected to an inordinate amount of dirt.

"They're not out here." I'd just gotten a splatter of mud on my wool gabardine slacks and I was feeling snappish. "This is ridiculous."

"No, really, I think they are," Ohm said. "I think I saw them heading this way."

"When?" I asked.

"Um—before I saw you in the café," he supplied.

"I thought you said they were headed for the store."

"Well, yeah, but they said they were coming out here afterward."

"Come on," Dannika called from farther down the trail. "There's an amazing swell!"

"Jesus Christ," I mumbled, but they were all so insistent I trailed after them, stepping gingerly around the mud puddles.

When we got to the edge of the bluffs, we had a panoramic view of the ocean and it was stunning, I'll tell you. The sun had gone down and the sky was a deep, moody blue. The feathery clouds were stained flamingo-pink. The water reminded me of Coop's eyes. It rose into huge, majestic waves that hurled against the rocks in foamy surges. Unfortunately, I was way too obsessed with the image of Coop in a drug lord's trunk to really appreciate it. I kept fidgeting, looking back toward town, hoping to see my man somewhere, anywhere, alive and well.

Then I noticed that everyone else was beaming down at the beach, looking positively misty-eyed. What the hell? I looked down, following their gaze, and saw a miniaturized Phil leaning over something white in the sand. What was he doing? About ten yards down the beach from him, also messing with something white, was Coop. Coop! He wasn't in a drug lord's trunk! I was so relieved, I started jumping up and down, waving, but Joni and Dannika both grabbed my arms, saying, "No, wait. Don't move. Just watch."

All at once the beach caught fire. They were lighting something. As the flames took shape, I read the words spelled out in orange, glowing light: *Marry Me Gwen*.

My hands flew to my mouth. I think I screamed. I saw Coop's miniaturized form twist toward me, his face upturned. A huge wave crashed against the sand behind him, extinguishing some of the flames. Now it said *lllarry llle, Gwen*, but I didn't care. My heart was doing somersaults inside me.

"So, do you know your answer?" Joni asked, her eyes hopeful and maybe a little scared.

"Yes!" I laughed. "Yes."

She hugged me hard and then there were other arms around me, until the four of us were tangled in a crazy swirl of elbows and laughter. When we pulled apart, Joni took my hands in hers and said, "Here's the code: No is arms straight up, Yes is arms straight out. You got it?"

"Yeah. I've got it."

I stood on the edge of the cliff, a hundred feet or so above the beach. Everyone held their breath. Coop was watching me; the little stick figure on the beach was motionless. The orange words flickered and danced in the dusk.

"Wait a sec." I looked over my shoulder at Joni. "Which is which again?"

"Yes is out!"

"Right," I laughed.

And then I flung my arms straight out and jumped up and down and screamed at the top of my lungs, so loudly that I swear he could hear me even over the crashing surf, "Yes, yes, yes, you crazy man!"

I answered him just in time, too, because right then the cops showed up.

Don't worry, they didn't get arrested. They got a written warning. Even the cop had to admit it was pretty damn romantic. Can you believe that? I'm so thrilled to finally have a story I can tell my grandchildren that isn't X-rated or riddled with foul language.

And the ring! My God, the ring. You're going to die when you see it. Seriously—you'll faint. Even a confirmed slob like you will appreciate the white-hot force of this rock.

He gave it to me just after the cops let him go. We rushed down to the beach as soon as we could, giggling and tripping over ourselves as we ran down the long staircase that led from the bluffs to the beach. By the time we got there the officers had finished writing up their warning and were walking away.

Coop turned to me with a bashful grin, hands shoved into his pockets like a naughty boy caught playing with matches. After a few slaps on the back from Joni and Ohm, a quick hug from Dannika, the four of them wandered off, obviously trying to give us privacy.

He didn't say a word. I, too, found my voice wouldn't cooperate when I opened my mouth. Silently, he pulled one hand from his pocket and held it out before me in a fist. Slowly—Jesus, it seemed to take forever—he stretched out his fingers, and there, cradled in a miniature abalone shell in the center of his palm was the most beautiful ring I'd ever seen. At first glance I knew it was totally me: a late deco antique setting in platinum gold, just ornate enough to catch the eye yet still maintain an understated elegance. The European-cut diamond was flanked by two tapered baguettes on either side, and even in the twilight its sparkle took my breath away.

"Coop! My God, it's gorgeous," I whispered.

He slid it onto my finger and I saw that his hand shook slightly. "You really like it? It took me a month to find the right one. You're no easy girl to shop for, you know that?"

A month! That meant he'd been planning this almost half the time we'd been dating. "It's perfect," I said, looking from him to the ring and back again. "I'm going to wear it forever."

You know better than anyone, if I commit on the spot to any accessory with that kind of verve, it's got to be pretty damn spectacular. Remember when we shopped for sunglasses last spring? It took me two weeks to find just the right cat-eye frames with the original green lenses and the gold Lurex inlay. Believe me, though, this is one piece I didn't have to think twice about; it's going to stay on my finger until they put me in the cold hard ground.

Here we are, Marla, the final page. And here I am, tucked between two surfboards once again, cruising down Highway 1 under a perfect sky. I've got the Pacific on my right, my man riding shotgun and my blond nemesis-turned-tentative ally at the wheel. You know what they say; keep your friends close, but keep the blondes closer.

I suppose you might take it as a bad sign, me still stuck in the back, but this time I really did insist. I've decided this is the only way to travel. Back here, I can keep an eye on things. I can watch the arrhythmic swish of Coop's hair as the wind tosses it this way and that. I can study the gorgeous gleam of my engagement ring without anyone thinking I'm obsessed. Most importantly—not that I think this way anymore—if Dannika tries anything, I'll be the first one to notice.

And besides, the backseat's pretty fantastic. It's not just a storage zone for dogs and luggage and children. It's the queen's seat, the starlet's spot, the place you put people too regal for the windshield's glare. It's the helm of power. All you have to do is claim it, and it's yours.

Love always,
Gwen

I closed the last notebook and looked around. The café was nearly deserted. I spooned the final dregs of cappuccino foam from the bottom of the cup. My third. When I noticed the time on the brass clock above the bar, I couldn't believe it. I'd been sitting in that place for seven hours. Forget bodice-rippers, man. I'd no idea Gwen's life was so readable.

Then again, anyone who wears a blue fox stole while crushed between two surfboards should never be underestimated.

I ran my hand over the final notebook, the glossy one that said Mendocino Coast. Gwen was full of surprises. Who knew she was so riddled with self-doubt? I'd always thought of her as supremely self-assured. She wore her wacky ensembles with such pure, regal confidence, she made it seem like the rest of us were the freaks. There we were, bumbling through life in blue jeans and hoodies, getting caught in traffic, spilling our coffee as we shifted gears; meanwhile, she glided over the sidewalks of L.A., her kitten heels taking her wherever she needed to go. If someone had told me yesterday that Gwen was insecure, I would have laughed. Sure, there was her little problem with chronic psychotic jealousy, but I'd always assumed that was more a nervous aversion to commitment, not deep-seated self-doubt.

As I tucked all four notebooks back into my bag, I saw a pretty brunette walk in the door. She was wearing a bright blue trapeze coat I just knew Gwen would love. She sat down at a table near the window and ordered a glass of wine. She had dark, shining eyes and perfect burgundy lipstick. After a few minutes, a petite blonde in jeans joined her. They kissed on the cheek and the blonde ordered a coffee. Pretty soon their table exploded into bright, girlish giggles, and the old man sitting at the bar scowled over his spectacles.

I knew I should get back; no doubt Jean-Paul and his parents were wondering where I was by now. Still, I sat there and watched the two women, fascinated by the intimacy of their little world. The brunette bent her head toward the blonde in a conspiratorial way. The blonde widened her eyes, and I saw her feet under the table tapping against the marble floor in excitement. They were sharing secrets. Stealing glances at them, I missed Gwen so much I could feel my throat growing thick and I had to swallow.

How many of their secrets did they share? I wondered.

Did they only reveal the gossipy bits, the tabloid fluff of their lives? Which parts did they leave out—which confessions were too dusty and dull for an afternoon rendezvous in September? I'd known Gwen twelve years. I thought I knew everything about her. Yet right there in my bag I had several hundred pages of scrawled evidence to the contrary. She was full of shadowy corners and locked closets. Even she was only beginning to investigate the quiet mystery of her own interior.

I stood, slipping the strap of my bag over my shoulder. Thanks to Gwen, I was wearing very stylishly cut slacks with a purse that matched the cherry-red suede of my ballet flats. As I made my way to the door, I mumbled *"merci"* to the waiter and he nodded, his face solemn. The girls near the window glanced at me. I smiled and they smiled back. *Take care of each other,* I told them silently. *Watch each other's backs.*

Out on the street, the air was crisp and smelled faintly of singed garlic. I walked up Rue Mouffetard toward Jean-Paul's childhood home. A gray-haired man lit a cigarette as he pushed a stroller. A teenager flew past me on an electric blue moped, splashing my shoes a little as she tore through a puddle. I saw it all, but my mind was fastened on Gwen. I thought of her pillbox hats and her pearls, her sneaky smile and her leopard-print kitten heels. I couldn't wait to get home and see her engagement ring.

Just before I reached the house, a light rain started. I stepped under an awning and watched it fall. It had been hot that morning, and the sun-warmed pavement smelled delicious as it turned wet. I closed my eyes and thought, *I'm happy for you, Gwen. I really am.* Then I dashed the last ten yards to the house, knowing Gwen would scold me when she saw what I had done to the cherry-red shoes.

A Rachel Benjamin Mystery

Jennifer Sturman

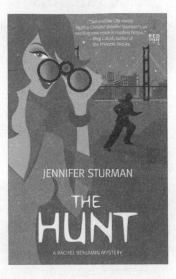

Rachel Benjamin's weekend of meeting her future in-laws turns out to be quite challenging when she discovers her friend Hilary is missing. As someone orchestrates an elaborate scavenger hunt across San Francisco, dangling Hilary as the prize, Rachel must track down her friend while proving to her future in-laws and her fiancé how normal she really is!

The Hunt

"Sex and the City meets Agatha Christie!"
—Meg Cabot, author of *The Princess Diaries*

*Available wherever trade
paperback books are sold!*

RED DRESS INK ™